Stones of Power

Mira Singer

authorHOUSE®

AuthorHouse™
1663 Liberty Drive
Bloomington, IN 47403
www.authorhouse.com
Phone: 1-800-839-8640

First published by AuthorHouse 6/29/2009

ISBN: 978-1-4389-4753-2 (e)
ISBN: 978-1-4389-4752-5 (sc)

Library of Congress Control Number: 2009904311

Printed in the United States of America
Bloomington, Indiana

This book is printed on acid-free paper.

Dedication

To my friends
You guys are magic

Acknowledgements

First off, I'd like to thank and acknowledge Esther Binstock. Without her this book would not exist as it does today. She has been a wonderful help in many ways, making suggestions and helping me develop the plot while at the same time correcting typos and grammatical errors every time she read through the story (including laughing at me for continuously writing that my characters would "meat" each other). It was she who made the suggestion that I use letters to end the book, as well as many other useful things, like developing several background stories (including that of Lisha's mother, which I'm not going to tell you. Mua ha ha.) If it weren't for her help, a lot of the scenes would make no sense or simply go too quickly. All in all I think that Esther is the person besides me who has contributed most to this story.

Thank you also to my friend Shoshi Musher who took time out of her busy work-filled schedule to tear my story apart. Practically demanding it from me and running through the entire book with a metaphorical pen, this story would not be the same without her (as it might be lacking several essential things, like chapter breaks). Also, thanks especially for your help on the Emra storyline. I hope I've made it—how did you put it? Gushing blood? Thank you so much!

Thank you to all of my wonderful beta-testers who read through a draft of the story and made comments/suggestions. Thank you to Karlo Haddad, Wendy Humphreys, Julia Vrtilek, and Esther Binstock, who read through the first finished draft, which was no mean feat as it was very long, and made lots of very helpful comments. Thank you to Leora Spitzer, Martha Minow, Joe Singer, and Shoshi Musher who read through the nearly last draft and helped me pull everything into place. I would also like to thank the rest of my friends for, well, being my friends and inspiring me to write and for laughing at my jokes. Two of my oldest friends and one newer one especially I would like to mention, and they are Phia Hausner, Jess Nahigian, and Ranya Gale. Thank you guys so much for just being there. To everyone else, you know who you are, so thank you all. Thanks to my parents, of course, who read through the story and helped me out when spell-check failed me (traitor!) and didn't embarrass me too much in the process.

Special thanks goes to Julia Vrtilek for taking the picture that became the background of the cover. Without even knowing it she captured the exact image I had in my mind, which is pretty cool.

One of the most helpful things in the writing, well more the editing, of *Stones of Power* is spell-check. I'm not the best at spelling and I make a lot of typos (meat vs. meet) and spell check has never lost hope in me and has forever been a dear companion (even if it does sometimes make idiotic suggestions or fails to find the right word at all). Through thick and thin spell-check has been there for me. I will never forget you, *sniff*.

Oh, and the thesaurus too. Can't forget you.

I would also like to thank all my correspondents from Authorhouse. These people include Lisa Metcalf, who helped me through the process of publishing and was always so nice and excited for me, Ida Walker, who edited the final draft and caught the remaining mistakes that slipped through the other rounds of editing and painstakingly fixed all of my backwards apostrophes, and Sara Kelly, my Design Consultant, who was extremely helpful and replied to all my emails incredibly quickly.

A thanks goes as well to Tamora Pierce, Eva Ibbotson, J. K. Rowling, and all the other writers who have inspired me and who continue to inspire me.

Last, but certainly not least, I would like to give a big thank-you and a hug to anyone who is reading and/or has read *Stones of Power* (yes, I'm talking to *you*). Without you, none of this would matter quite as much. Thank you, thank you, thank you, especially to those of you who do not know me personally. It means a lot that you're willing to give a 16-year-old author a chance.

Without further ado, I give you *Stones of Power*!

Well, what are you waiting for? Start reading!!!

Mira Singer

Characters

In order of appearance (sort of)

Troupe in England:

<u>Leader</u>: **Jasper**: (m) Black-haired with pale skin, insecure, loyal to his friends. Grand ideas. Family was English upper class. **Jordan**'s brother.

Lisha *lee*-shah\\: (f) Peg leg. Captain of a ship. Perceptive. Seems to know everyone. Family from the Caribbean. Can swim like a fish.

Kiara \\key-*ar*-ah\\: (f) Skin the color of cocoa. Cynical. Troubled past. Lived on the streets for a long time.

Emra: (f) Country girl. Lived on a farm. Long hair the color and texture of dried cornstalks. Power: can turn into a corn snake.

Kit: (f) Cockney-speaking street urchin. Knack for telling stories. Newest addition to the troupe.

Troupe in France:

<u>Leader</u>: **Tristan:** French: \tree-*stah*\ or English: *tris*-ten\: (f) French. Tall, dresses like a boy.

Minuette: (f) French performer. Hair the color of butter. Special connection with **Jasper**.

Jordan: (m) English. Black hair. Tall, quiet. **Jasper**'s brother.

Lali: *lah*-lee\ (f) English. Cockney accent. Nose ring. Power: can make people tell the truth.

Halie: French: \ah-*lee*\ or English: *hay*-lee\: (f) French. Quiet, shy. Power: can see and show things happening in the past, present, and sometimes flashes of the future. Name means "heroine."

Troupe in Ireland:

<u>Leader</u>: **Fala:** (f) Raven-haired. Quiet, calm. Power: can talk with birds (especially black-colored birds—crows, ravens, etc.) and can turn into a bird. Dark family history. Name means "crow."

Nat: (m) Assistant troupe leader. Power: sensing and manipulating plants and their growth. Gets seasick. Slightly greenish hair.

Kadin-Lave: *kade*-in lave\ (m) Irish. Good fighter. Power: can change the temperature of things. Has a temper that can quite literally flare up at times. Kadin means "fighter," and Lave means "lava."

Leandra: (f) Stubborn, persistent. Long mane of wild hair. Power: can change into any wildcat. Name means "brave as a lion."

Mica: *mee*-kah\ (m) Youngest. Quietly wise. Thinks a lot. **Genna**'s younger brother.

Genna: (f) Artist with a photographic memory. **Mica**'s older sister. Protective.

Kaida: \ki-dah\ ("i" pronounced like "eye") (m) Catlike. Cynical, resentful, talkative, proud, likes people.

Primary crew of the *Compass Rose*:

<u>Captain</u>: **Lisha:** (f) See above.

First Mate: **Jasmine:** (f) Lisha's old friend. Troubled by something. Cinnamon colored skin, almond eyes, musical voice.

Ship Surgeon: **Isaac:** (m) Awkward, clumsy, kind. Wears glasses.

Boatswain \bow-sun\: **Oliver:** (m) Annoying and insubordinate. Dull, black hair and a flat face.

Cabin Boy: **Quito** *key*-tow\: (m) Creepy and nearly invisible. Name means "filth."

Cook: **Hilda:** (f) Very curly orange hair. Wears a kerchief. Quietly resentful. Power: Can control people with her singing voice. Name means "sweet melody."

Others:

Mr. Loxlyheart: (m) The greedy, evil entrepreneur. Slick, gray hair, blue eyes.

Mr. Bumbleweed: (m) "Evil minion comic relief" number 1. Short, fat, bothered by people doing bad things.

Mr. Tweeble: (m) "Evil minion comic relief" number 2. Scrawny. Light, messy hair. On the surface, he doesn't seem too bright.

Mr. Thornton: (m) "Evil minion" number 3. Haunted by his past.

Desdemona: (f) The creepy, evil witch. Catlike. Haughty and self-centered. Eyes in a permanent half-lidded glare, black hair, and sharp features. Tattered gown. Name means "of the devil."

Aradia: \ah-*rah*-dee-ah\ (f) The powerful, evil witch with the porcelain-perfect complexion. Deceptively kind appearance. Power: can bend shadows. Name means "goddess of witches."

Xylon: *zi*-lon\ ("i" pronounced like "eye") (m) The wise hermit. Gray beard and eyes. Name means "from/lives in the forest."

Cameron: (f) The crooked-nosed Mason. Name means "bent nose."

Laramie: \lah-*rah*-mee\ (f) Desdemona's missing sister. Name means "tears of love."

British Isles 1801

Prologue

A cloaked figure hurried down the decrepit London street in the dead of night, trying hard to conceal its face. Shouts followed behind as the men chased it down an alleyway toward a dead end. The figure looked around frantically, realized it was trapped, and attempted to dash back up the alley. It met the mob straight on and stepped back slowly, hiding its face in the folds of cloth. Its head jerked around, searching for a way out, as the men surrounded it. Finding none, the shadow looked around desperately one more time before crumpling to the ground, hooded head down.

The mob began to move closer, and one man stepped forward, reaching out a hand to grab the figure's shoulder. But just as his hand brushed the cloth, it fell to the ground, an empty cloak. He cried out in shock, and his eyes widened with surprise. He stooped, picked up the cloak, then threw it back down and looked around in confusion. The other men called out, and a few went up to help the man search the alley. But their hunt was in vain; they would not find the person they sought. The man who had reached out to grab the hooded silhouette faced the crowd and announced the result. But even while he spoke, proclaiming the apparition gone, a small, inconspicuous snake emerged from the cloth and slipped quietly into the shadows. No one noticed, as the man speaking held everyone's gaze. The snake slithered down the alley and into the cobbled street, slipping from shadow to shadow as it made its way through the city. It turned onto one last street and found its way into a darkened stairwell that led down to a supposedly deserted building. It curled around the banister and disappeared down the stairs.

In an abandoned toyshop rotting with age, three people were sitting hushed, waiting for a sound they all knew well. Two of them were playing chess in the flickering candlelight, while the other watched edgily, glancing up every few minutes. There was tension in the air. They all pretended to be busy and concerned with nothing other than the chess game, but really they were all watching the brown dress hanging on the clothesline in a corner. Then there was a noise, an odd sliding sound that moved from the stairway that led to the street to the dark corner with the hanging dress. The sliding sound stopped, and a girl emerged from the shadows and pulled on the dress. A sigh went around the room.

"Well done, Emra," said a pale boy with elegant black hair, whose name was Jasper, as he looked up from the chess game. "I'm glad you could make it. You had us all worried for a little while there." The girl, Emra, had light, straw-colored hair and a freckled, childlike face, which at this moment was split with an almost wicked grin, as if she were very proud of herself. Which, of course, she was. She appeared to be no more then ten, though her real age was probably older. Still grinning broadly, she extricated herself from the clothes hanger and went to join the group.

"Sorry to keep you waiting. I had a bit of trouble getting here," said Emra.

"We guessed that," said one of the others, a gruff-voiced girl named Kiara, whose skin was the color of coffee beans. She had a bandana tied around her braided, thick, black hair and wore a dirty dress that had once been white. "So ... you did get it, didn't you?"

"Of course she did! She wouldn't look so pleased if she hadn't!" said the other chess player proudly. From Lisha's clothing, it was apparent that she was a seafarer. Strands of her hair had fallen out of its loose bun, tangling in a pair of large hoop earrings. She wore a loose, thin, cotton shirt with large baggy sleeves and brown pants. Over the shirt she wore an old leather vest tied up with strings.

Lisha motioned to the empty stool beside her, and Emra sat down, the picture of an excited little child. Which was not entirely inaccurate. With a dramatic flourish, she produced a smooth, light gray stone slightly smaller and flatter than an apple and unremarkable except for the strange sign carved into its surface.

"That's it?" asked Kiara skeptically.

"What did you expect? The Hope Diamond?" asked Lisha, playing with one of her hoop earrings. She grabbed the stone and ran her fingers along the carving. "Curious. The carvings on most of the Stoens I've seen are more difficult to make out, but this one is as clear to read as the sign over the toyshop."

"Maybe for one who knows how to read this sort of thing," said Kiara, snatching it away and turning it over to see the other side. "Which one do you think it is?"

"Who cares?" asked Emra. "Does it really matter?"

"It does if the Hunters are looking for it," said Jasper. He was taller than Emra and Kiara, and his clothes were slightly nicer than those worn by the others. His eyes were serious and focused, those of a leader. "They probably know which one it is, and if so, they know something we don't know. Which, as you know, is bad."

"Yes, we know," said Kiara.

"We can figure out which Stoen it is later," said Emra. "The more pressing question is: where are we going to keep it?"

"That cupboard above the sink has a lock on it," said Lisha. "We could keep it there."

"Maybe. Emra, what did you do with your Stoen?" asked Jasper.

"I keep it in a pouch near my bed."

"That'll never do. You should move it to the cupboard with this new one. We can keep all the Stoens that we come across there."

"Works for me," said Kiara, standing up.

"Good," said Jasper, standing up too. "Now everyone, to bed." Emra and Lisha also stood. It was clear to see that there was something wrong with Lisha's left leg. The problem was that she didn't have one. Her leg ended at the knee, where a peg leg had been attached to it.

Lisha had a striking appearance, and not just because of her peg leg and seafarer's clothing. She was the tallest of the four by far and conducted herself with self-assurance and poise. Unlike the others, who dressed to blend in, Lisha always stuck out in a crowd.

They pushed back their seats and walked off toward their rooms. The girls shared a room, and Jasper had one to himself. They each had a hammock to sleep on and some sort of small table on which they could put the few things they owned.

"Night all," said Jasper as they all climbed into bed and blew out their candles. At night, without the candlelight, the toyshop was black as coal.

❦

"Help! Help! Thief! Help!" A dirty young girl rushed down the street with two men chasing after her. She careened through the marketplace, ducking under carts and weaving through strangers as she went. The men tried to follow, but she was too small and fast, and they kept banging into the obstacles she had avoided. At last, they were out of the marketplace and had no trouble catching up with the girl. They cornered her in a back street near an old toyshop. The first man raised his arm to strike the girl. As she raised her arms to protect herself, an odd rock slipped from her hand, unnoticed by any of them. Just as the man was about to strike her, a hand caught his arm. Someone walked up behind the girl and, after surreptitiously picking up the stone and putting it into her pocket, put her hands on the girl's shoulders. Two more girls walked up and stood on either side of the other man.

"And just what do you think you're doing?" asked a voice. The man turned around.

"I'm punishing this thief. She stole from my cart," he said.

"Did she now?" asked Jasper. He had a confident air about him, which made him seem somehow older. "Well then, little girl, what did you steal?" he asked, leaning his head toward the girl.

"I din't steal nothing!" said the girl truthfully, frustrated that no one ever seemed to believe her. "I's just lookin' et this here rock," she said, looking confusedly at her empty hands, "an' 'e sees me an' says ''ey!' an' I'us scared so I run. An' 'e caught me and 'as gonna hit me ifn't you were 'ere wot to stop 'im."

"Now see here," said Jasper to the men, squaring his shoulders. "This young lady is not a thief! She wasn't going to steal anything! So why don't you let her go?"

"But I need that stone back," said the man.

"Musta' dropped it when you was a'chasin' me. I ain't got it now," she said. The man glanced back at the marketplace, and his face fell as he realized there was no way he could find a dropped stone in the crowd.

"Oh very well," said the man grudgingly, lowering his hand. "Let's go, Bill." And with that, the men walked away. The girl turned as if to run away too.

"And where might you be off to?" asked Jasper, pulling her back.

"Um ...," said the girl, stalling. She had sweet blue eyes and long, tangled brown hair caked with dust and grime. Her dress was so dirty it was difficult to tell what color it had been originally.

"Where do you live?" asked the boy more kindly.

For a moment she didn't answer, and then she said glumly, "Nowhere, really."

"No, no. That won't do," said Jasper. He thought for a moment before saying, "Why don't you stay with us for the night? After all, you do deserve our thanks." The girl was smart enough not to ask for what.

"I guess so. After I's askin' me mum if it's all right that is."

"Certainly. We're staying here, in this old toyshop. It may look run-down from out here, but it's nice and cozy on the inside."

"Me mum won't mind if I's stayin' jus' one night without askin'. Any longer, an' I'd 'ave to tell 'er where I was."

"Well great!" exclaimed Lisha eagerly, her hands still on the younger girl's shoulder as she led her inside. "There's an extra hammock in our room that we can set up for you. By the way, what's your name?"

"Kit. Kit Taylor."

"Kit? Kit?" Kit looked up from her musings as a voice called her from downstairs. After being given a quick tour, she had been left to wander. The toyshop had been a combined shop and house. There were two stories, not including the cellar where the workshop and storerooms had been. The ground floor consisted of the shop front, with store closets for more toys and the family kitchen in the back. The shop front was in the condition the previous owner had left it. There were a few scattered toys on the dusty shelves that hadn't been valuable enough to be stolen.

Kit had gone to explore the top floor, which held the old, unused bedrooms. She was just looking over some sad-looking broken dolls when Emra appeared at the top of the stairs.

"There you are! I've been looking all over for you. Come, it's time for dinner."

Kit got up from the floor, not bothering to wipe the dust from her dress. She followed the bouncy girl back down to the kitchen on the ground floor. When Kit came into the room, the other people were already seated and engaged in an argument of some kind. Lisha was balanced precariously on her chair, tipping it back onto two legs so she could lean against the wall, her hands clasped behind her head. Her right foot was propped against the edge of the table, while her peg leg hovered near the ground for balance. Jasper sat to her left, back straight, leaning forward over the table to glare across at Kiara. Kiara glared back just as fiercely, arms crossed stubbornly across her chest. So engaged were they that they didn't notice Emra and Kit enter.

"We got the Stoen, so why did we have to take her in?" asked Kiara.

"For Heaven's sake, Kiara, that man was going to pound her!" said Jasper.

"Yes, but that doesn't explain your idea of inviting her to *live* with us!" said Kiara.

"She has nowhere else to go; the poor thing is living on the streets!"

"A lot of people are living on the streets! We can't just go around taking in every urchin who turns up on our doorstep, can we?" said Kiara emphatically.

"She's got a point," said Lisha, rocking her chair slightly. "But I stand with Jasper on this one. I've got a good feeling about her. We *should* ask her to stay."

"Weren't you lot listening? I told you, there's something funny about her. I mean, why do you think she was so quick to trust us?" asked Kiara.

"Ahem," said Lisha, nodding her head sideways toward Kit and Emra. Jasper sat back and Kiara uncrossed her arms. Lisha let the chair fall back to the floor with a thud, taking her foot off the table.

"Why, Kit," said Jasper awkwardly, "Sorry, didn't see you. Um, how did you like the tour? Find anything interesting upstairs? You were gone for quite awhile." Kit scowled slightly in Kiara's direction. Jasper's smile faded.

"Won't you join us?" asked Lisha, glaring at Jasper, who looked away, and at Kiara, who glared back. Lisha pulled up two stools so Emra and Kit could sit down. Jasper spoke.

"Um, Kit ... we've been talking, and we've decided to offer you the option of staying with us. You see, we've got rather a special mission, and I think we could use your help. Besides, I'm sure we'd all like you to stay," he said.

"Who's 'we'?" grumbled Kiara.

"Emra's with us, which means we have a majority. You're overruled!" he hissed back.

Jasper turned back to Kit, looking rather sheepish. "Ahem. Anyway, as I was saying, our job can be rather dangerous, but I imagine you've seen a lot of that, living the way you do. And we can offer you food and lodging, and we'll try and protect you from anything bad out there. So then, what do you say, Kit?"

"I don't wont to be a bother," she said cautiously.

"Not at all," piped up Lisha, encouragingly. "We'd be happy to have you."

Kit looked between them, uncertainly. She glanced once at Kiara's face, but upon seeing her expression, looked promptly away and avoided looking at her again. In the faces of the others, she saw warmth and encouragement. She remembered how they had saved her from the merchants. Even Kiara had helped then. Settling her resolve, Kit took a breath.

"Woll, it can't be much worse than living on the streets. I think I'll stay," she said decisively. "At least, for a little while."

Jasper beamed triumphantly and Emra whooped, jumping up and down. Lisha smiled warmly, and Kiara sank a little lower in her chair.

"That is, after I's asked me mum."

"Of course, naturally," said Jasper. "Well, I think it's about time for a formal introduction. Kit, this is Lisha," said Jasper. Lisha waved. "Kiara," Kiara looked up at Kit and gave a quick smile before looking back down, "Emra," Emra grinned, "and I'm Jasper. Welcome to our humble abode," said Jasper, which got a laugh from Emra.

"All right, all right. Let's get on with it," said Kiara. Jasper looked disgruntled.

"Erm, right. Anyway," he said, speaking to Kit, "I think it's time to explain what exactly our job is. It may be a bit confusing at first, but you've earned it. Tell me, Kit, do you believe in magic?"

"You mean like witches and stuff?"

"Not exactly. You see, Kit, all people in the world have a certain magical power within them. Long ago, these powers were sealed away so no one could use them. We're not exactly sure how this happened, only that it was a long time ago, so long that most people have forgotten the powers exist. We do know, however, that people have these powers. There are, you see, special stones that can allow people to use their power. They are called Stoens," said Jasper.

Kit noted that he pronounced the word "Stoen" as having two syllables: Stow-en. Jasper got up, unlocked a cupboard and took out a dark, smooth stone that Kit recognized as the one she'd been falsely accused of stealing. He sat and held out the stone for Kit to see.

"There are many different kinds of Stoens, just as there are many different kinds of powers," continued Jasper. "No two powers are exactly the same, like no two people are exactly the same, but the powers all fall under certain categories. If a person holds the Stoen that corresponds to the kind of power they have, the power will be unlocked and the person will be able to use their power from then on," said Jasper. Kit picked up the stone and turned it over in her hands.

"So this rock I'us supposed t' 'ave stolen is won o' these Stoen things?" asked Kit.

"Yes, that's right," answered Jasper. Kit's eyes grew wide.

"I never knew. Imagine tha'; ev'ryone's got magic, an' no one knows it!" Suddenly realizing, Kit looked around at the others, wide-eyed. "'Ave you lot all got powers then?"

They looked around at each other.

"Er, no," said Jasper. "That is, we have powers, but they're still locked away. All except Emra, that is. The rest of us haven't found the right Stoen for us yet."

"Personally, I'm not sure I'd want to," said Kiara, provoking a surprised reaction from the others. "I mean, it's a bit of a gamble, isn't it? You have to learn to control the power. Suppose your power was setting things on fire. Well, without training and practice, you might end up setting something on fire by accident! Besides, I've done fine so far without a power."

"Me too, actually," said Lisha. "Although it would be nice to know, of course, it isn't really essential to us."

Jasper turned to Kit.

"You see, Kit, the point of us knowing about the powers isn't simply to find a Stoen so we can unlock ours," explained Jasper. "Most people who unlock their powers do so by accident. Those of us who know the secret have a much more important mission. The mission is the reason so few people know about the powers anymore."

"Wha' is this mission? 'Ow come no one knows about it?" Kit asked.

"It's one of the best kept secrets in history," replied Jasper.

"Why does it 'ave t' be a secret?" she asked. Jasper looked around at the others uncertainly.

"Um, well, there is this legend that if someone were to collect all of the Stoens in the world, or at least a great many of them, they would be able to unleash unlimited power. The Ultimate Power. With this power, the wielder would be able to do anything. Anything they can imagine they would be able to make real with only the slightest effort of will. They would have absolute power over anything they wished. That's where we come in. We are Protectors. We make sure that no one gets that Ultimate Power. Some people would use this power for evil, and even if they tried to use it for good, it's just too dangerous for someone to have that much power.

"We are not the only Protectors," Jasper continued. "There are troupes of us all over the world, because there are Stoens all over the world. We are all united in our cause: to stop anybody from acquiring the Ultimate Power. At the moment, there are several people we know about who are trying to gain that Ultimate Power. One is named Mr. Loxlyheart. He hates disorganization, likes things to be neat and orderly, with himself in control. Several years ago, he started rounding up homeless children off the streets and forcing them to work in his factories. The conditions there are terrible, and no one's done anything to stop him. If he gets the chance, Lord knows what he would do. Right now, his power is limited. But if he were to get the Ultimate Power ... no one would be able to stop him. Then there's Desdemona." Jasper paused for a moment and frowned. "We don't know very much about her. All we know for sure is that she's stealing Stoens. The strange thing is that none of the people she's stealing from try to stop her, and afterwards they can't seem to remember why. It's all very odd. But the most dangerous by far is Aradia. She is already very, very powerful and has manipulated an army's worth of people to her service. She is cunning and forceful, and she gets whatever she wants. Hate is her middle name. She loathes everything concerning light, happiness, or laughter. She has been called the black goddess of witches, and—"

"Oh, for crying out loud! Does someone *pay* you to advertise Aradia's power?" interrupted Kiara. She turned to Kit. "Honestly, I don't know where Jasper gets this stuff. He thinks we're in one of those fantasy novels he used to read, and we've got some sort of grand purpose, when mostly we're just trying to stay alive. The Drifters pumped our heads full of glory and responsibility and then they just disappeared and left us to fend for ourselves," said Kiara bitterly.

"Who're th' Drifters?" asked Kit.

"They're the ones who organize this whole thing," jumped in Jasper, who seemed to have regained his steam. "They're the ones who found all of us and told us about Stoens."

Kit rubbed her eyes, tired. Emra patted her shoulder, mistaking exhaustion for confusion.

"There, there. I know it's a lot to take in. Besides, it's late. We should be getting to bed." Emra rose and started toward the door.

"Wait," said Lisha. "One last thing." Turning to Kit, she said: "Now, you might be thinking that this absolute power could be a good thing, that the Ultimate Power could be used for good. But absolute power corrupts absolutely. Remember that, Kit: absolute power corrupts absolutely." *Absolute power corrupts absolutely,* thought Kit as she drifted off to sleep that night. *Absolute power...*

❦

Kit woke up, not quite sure where she was. She looked around and saw the sleeping forms of Emra, Kiara, and Lisha. Then it all came flooding back. Stoens, powers, *absolute power...*

"Wake up, it's morning! Time to get up." Jasper's voice rang through the shop. "Come on, come on, no reason to be lying around all day." The three girls stirred, yawned, and sat up.

"Oh, Jasper, look what you've done!" said Lisha, looking at her pocket watch.

"What have I done?" asked Jasper, taken aback.

"You've gone and woke us up half an hour earlier than yesterday. You could've let us sleep s'more," said Lisha jokingly, lying back down.

"Get up, will you! For Pete's sake, Lisha, get up!" said Jasper, trying to push Lisha out of bed. Emra jumped down and came over to Kit.

"Well, look who's awake," she said, kneeling down so her face was level with Kit's. She was wearing a sort of nightdress, which had seen better days. "Let's go get some breakfast while we wait for Jasper to give up on Lisha. Sometimes I think she'd get up on her own if she didn't enjoy making Jasper annoyed," said Emra thoughtfully. Kit and Kiara (who were both wearing their clothes from the day before) got up. The three of them walked into the kitchen, where Kiara and Emra busied themselves with getting breakfast ready. They had some stale bread, which they toasted over a little stove, and today Lisha had stolen a small basket of eggs from the market. Kit's eyes went wide when she saw the eggs. Emra smiled at her.

"For the occasion," she explained, inclining her head to Kit. "We don't get to entertain company very often."

After a moment, Lisha came stumbling into the room, pulling on her vest, laughing merrily. She was followed closely by a very annoyed Jasper. Lisha, too, had slept in her clothes, but had taken the vest off. It was apparent that, whatever these people were, they didn't have money to spare. But although they weren't wealthy, they usually had enough food. Lisha had a job that provided a helpful, if inconsistent, income. Anything else they needed they were usually able to steal.

Lisha sat at the table with Kit. Kit looked down and noticed her peg leg. Lisha saw her looking. Kit looked away.

"I's sorry," she mumbled quickly. "I din't notice."

"It's all right," said Lisha, patting Kit on the head.

"What's for breakfast, Emra? I'm starving!" said Jasper, changing the subject.

"Eggs and toast. How do you like your eggs, Kit?" inquired Emra cheerfully.

"I dunno. I 'ent had eggs fer a while now, us livin' on th' street an' all. I's forgets what they tastes like," said Kit.

"We'll make it scrambled, then," said Emra. "Later, you can go ask your mum if you can stay with us. That is, if you still want to," she amended. Kit looked at Kiara. She didn't want to stay if she wasn't wanted. Jasper saw her look.

"Kiara's all right," he assured unconcernedly. "She just needs a little time to get used to you." Kiara glared at him.

"Well, if you're sure it's no trouble," said Kit, trying not to seem too eager. It had been a long time since she'd had a roof over her head, and some of the things they had said the previous night about protecting the world from bad people had stuck a chord with her.

"Then it's settled. After breakfast, you and Lisha can go talk to your mum," said Jasper, putting his napkin on his lap and starting to eat. Jasper was the only one who seemed to have any table manners. Lisha speared her hard-boiled egg with a knife and ate it whole. Emra and Kiara just used their hands. This might have been because there weren't enough forks and knives to go around. Kit sure didn't get any utensils. With or without table manners, the food was soon gone, and Kit was on the way to see her family, Lisha trotting along beside her.

❧

Lisha walked alongside Kit as they made their way down the street. Beside the faint pat pat pat of Kit's feet, Lisha's steps, alternating between leather-booted foot and peg, kept a regular rhythm of **thunk** *tap*, **thunk** *tap*.

"So, where are we going?" asked Lisha, following her small companion.

"Um ... to the marketplace first," said Kit. "I know how to get home from there."

As they walked, Lisha watched the way Kit's eyes stayed to the ground. *She's clearly used to life on the streets*, thought Lisha.

Soon, the pair turned around a bend in the road and came out into an open market. The marketplace was a mess of people, customers and passersby filling the square, colorful stands and pushcarts, people shouting out their wares, haggling over prices, dirty children running around between people's legs, sunlight streaming down upon them all.

Lisha drew in a deep breath and let it out with an audible sigh, taking it all in.

"Mm, I love the smell of the market!" she said exuberantly, stretching her arms. "Even the bad smells, they all mix together to give you a full picture of the world." She shrugged. "And at least it's fresh air. It can get kind of musty in the toy shop. I swear, the air in there is the same as was there when the owners left it." She glanced down sideways at Kit. "D'you like the market, Kit?" she asked as they wove their way through the throngs of people.

"S'ok, I guess," said Kit, eyes still on the ground. Lisha made a contemplative sound.

"'Course, I prefer ocean air," said Lisha. "I love the sea. Did you know that when I'm not staying here in the toyshop, I'm the captain of a ship?"

At this, Kit forgot to be invisible and looked up, eyes wide.

"Really?" asked Kit with interest. Lisha smiled.

"Aye. I work for hire, mostly. When people want to go somewhere or need someone to transport goods overseas for them, they can come to me. 'Specially if they don't want to be found. They know I'm discreet. It's an irregular job, but it pays well." Lisha paused as they ducked between two carts and squeezed past to come out on the other side. "It's nice to come back to the shop at the end of a day," continued Lisha, "but I yearn to be back on the open ocean. I've been on land too long." She glanced down at Kit. "So Kit, tell me about yourself." Kit looked up, surprised.

"Wha' about myself?" she asked.

"Oh, let's see, how old are you?" posed Lisha as they walked along the edge of the square.

"Ten, I think," said Kit uncertainly.

"You think?" asked Lisha. Kit nodded.

"I'm not sure, 'xactly." A shout rang out from a far corner of the square, where a group of kids were playing catch with small pebbles. Kit looked up at Lisha.

"How old are you?" she asked.

"I'm fifteen," said Lisha. Kit's eyes widened.

"Really?"

Lisha smiled. "Aye." They passed a vender and a customer engaged in a heated argument about the quality and price of meat pies. While they were distracted, one of the children playing on the street snuck up and nicked a pie before scampering back to his friends.

"What else do you want to know?" asked Kit.

"Hm, lets see ... do you have a favorite animal?" asked Lisha.

Kit considered for a moment before answering. "Do dragons count?"

Lisha laughed. "Sure!" They walked on, Lisha following Kit through the square, and soon came through to the outside edge on the opposite side from where they had entered. Kit hesitated for a moment, looking at the streets leading away, and then chose one and walked purposefully down it, Lisha trotting along behind. Kit slowed, letting Lisha catch up.

"So tell me about your family, Kit," said Lisha, beside Kit once more. Kit walked on, looking at her feet thoughtfully.

"Woll, there's me and my mum, an' my sister, Charlene. She's still little. I dunno who my dad was. We 'ad a 'ouse, once, but I can't remember it too well. It was small, an' it was dark inside. We 'ad to leave; I dunno why. We beg most of the time now. Mum doesn't like stealing, so we don't if we can. Summone gave us a lute once. It's this thing with strings." Kit made strumming motions with her fingers. "Mum plays it an' I try 'n dance a li'le. They give us more now, but it's still not much." She stopped and looked up at Lisha. "Wha' abou' you?"

"My parents were merchants," said Lisha. "We lived in our ship, the *Compass Rose*, named after my mother, Rosemary. Father was the captain, and Mum navigated." Seeing Kit glance again at her peg leg, Lisha explained. "When I was younger, I had an accident," she said, tapping her knee just above where it connected to the wood. "I got in a fistfight with one of the boys. I climbed up onto the railing, thinking to either tackle him from above or climb away on one of the lines, but he grabbed onto me, and while we were struggling, I lost my balance and fell overboard. I would have been all right, except that when they were pulling me up, the rope broke and I fell back, right on the anchor, and it ripped through my leg," said Lisha calmly. Kit stared at her, a look of alarm on her face. Lisha readied herself for the tumult of questions that usually followed, but Kit said nothing about her leg.

"Didja really live on a ship?" asked Kit. The question surprised Lisha, and she smiled.

"Aye, I did. My parents didn't own a house on land. We'd take goods and sell them all over the place. It was magnificent." She closed her eyes, remembering. Those were the days. "Of course, there were some hard times, too," she recalled, "My good friend, Nat—"

"Kit! There y' are!" came a voice from the alleyway. A woman dressed in dirty, disheveled clothing strode forward and hugged Kit with one arm, a baby cradled in the other. Kit laughed as she hugged her mother and sister.

"And 'o's this?" asked Kit's mother, looking at Lisha.

"This is me new friend, Lisha," said Kit. Lisha smiled warmly.

Kit's mother stood up, balancing Charlene on one hip, and held out a hand to Lisha.

"'Ello, dear," she said. "I'm Kit's mum, Penel'pe."

"Pleased to meet you," said Lisha, taking Penelope's hand.

"I's jus wanna ask ifn't I could stay with Lisha an' th' others fer awhile," said Kit.

"Me and my friends would be more than happy to take care of Kit," said Lisha. "We'll feed her and give her a safe place to spend the night,"

"They's got food an' lodgin', " said Kit. "An' they invited me t' stay."

"*They?*" asked Penelope. "Wot *they?* O' else?"

"They's nice people, Mum!" said Kit. "They do good things, an' they say tha' I can 'elp!"

Penelope looked at Lisha critically, sizing her up. Lisha tried to appear as friendly as possible. Penelope looked back down at Kit. She knelt next to her daughter.

"So d'you trust 'em then, love?" she asked. Kit nodded.

"Yesterday, some men was a'chasin' me 'cause they'd thought I'd wot stolen sommun, which I didn't!" added Kit defensively, seeing her mother's sharp look. "They stopped 'em," she said. "They rescued me."

"'Izzat so?" Penelope considered, chewing on a fingernail. "Woll, it's up t' you, really, innit? I trust you. If you trust them, then tha's good 'nough fer me."

Kit's face lit up, and Lisha smiled happily. "So long's I know where she is," added Penelope. "Where will my Kit be sleeping?"

"We're staying in the toyshop on Windmill Street," said Lisha. They usually didn't tell people where they lived, just in case one of the Hunters heard, but Lisha felt that this was a special case.

"Aw right then, Kit? I want you to be a good girl and stay outa trouble. Also, I'd like you t' visit often. I'm gonna miss you," said Kit's mother, giving Kit a squeeze.

"I promise." Kit hugged her mother again and ran up to Lisha. Lisha felt glad that Kit could stay with them. She liked Kit and was sure she would have a better chance at a lot of things now that she didn't have to live on the street.

Lisha and Kit talked some more as they retraced their steps back to the toyshop. The day was warm and sunny, and the streets were filled with people. Before they knew it, they had reached the toyshop.

"Lisha and Kit are back! Jasper! They're back!" called Emra. Smiling, Lisha walked toward the shop with Kit. Emra was always so cheerful and easily pleased. Together, they went into the shop. Jasper was sitting at the kitchen table looking some at sort of map with a magnifying glass. He rolled up the paper when he saw Lisha.

"Why, Lisha, Kit. Nice to see you back. So Kit, what's the word?"

"I's stayin' wif you lot fer now," said Kit.

"Great!" he said, smiling. "Emra!" he called. When she appeared, he asked, "Could you help her get set up?" Emra nodded happily and motioned for Kit to follow her. Kit ran off after Emra. When they were out of sight, Lisha sat down at the table.

"What were you looking at?" asked Lisha.

"Just some papers. Nothing important," said Jasper casually. Lisha frowned at him.

"Oh, come off it, Jasper! You know you can't lie to me. Out with it, then."

"You'll see. We'll have a meeting after dinner. After dinner...," he said absentmindedly, standing up and walking out of the kitchen. Lisha saw his half-finished drink, took it, and chugged it down. She watched him leave and frowned darkly. If they started hiding things from each other, even for a little while, there could be trouble, leaving the Hunters a perfect time to strike.

❤

Kiara sat on the curb by the side of the road, thinking. She munched quietly on a stolen muffin. It had been an uneventful morning. She had made her rounds through the market and shops but no more Stoens had turned up.

Lisha should be back by now, thought Kiara. *I wonder if that urchin's still with her.* The urchin... *What's her name? Kit,* Kiara reminded herself, attempting not to be callous, even in her own mind. Kiara picked up a pebble and tossed it across the street, skipping it off the stones. She scowled. *Jasper's a fool for taking her in on such short notice, when we know almost nothing about her,* Kiara thought. *And not just for taking her in, but for telling her so much on the first night! That's not the way it's supposed to work! Protectors aren't supposed to reveal anything ... ever.*

Finding new Protectors and assigning them positions and troupes was the job of the Drifters. *It's been awhile since I've seen one of those,* thought Kiara suddenly. *I wonder why.* The Drifters were the mysterious group of people who, well, drifted around looking for children who had what it took to save the world (or at least, do their part). They were the ones who were supposed to do all the explaining and choosing. *Who's Jasper to say that Kit has what it takes?* Kiara reflected bitterly.

Kiara decided she had to step back and take another look at their young, new recruit. If Kit were on the Hunters' side, the other Protectors would never figure it out. They liked her too much. If anyone was going to turn a skeptical eye on Kit, it had to be Kiara.

She started with Kit's background. From what she knew, Kit had been living on the streets since who knows when, hadn't had an egg in years, but did have a mother who obviously cared about her. *Lucky...* Kiara shook her head to clear it. She might be a thief. In fact, it was very likely she was. She would never have survived so long if she weren't. Kit could have been lying when she said she was only looking at the Stoen she had dropped. She might have actually been intending to steal it all along. *Sharp eyes,* Kiara conceded, *to have seen the Stoen and decided it was valuable, not even knowing what it is. If indeed she was stealing it.*

And sure, Kit seemed honest enough, but Kiara hadn't known her long enough to be sure. The only thing left would be to see if Kit was the type who would blab. She could easily undermine the whole operation that way. If the Hunters found out where the Protectors were, they were done for. If the bow street runners found their hideaway, they were done for. If Kit told people what she had heard and who had been there, it could hurt Lisha's reputation, which would cut off their main source of income since Lisha's career depended on people trusting her. But, somehow, Kit didn't seem like one who would talk. Kiara was starting to see that this girl would have no reason to hurt them and more cause to try to be of assistance. As long as things stayed that way, they would be all right. But Kiara would be keeping an eye on Kit, just in case.

❦

After dinner that same day, Jasper held a meeting in the workroom of the shop. They were all seated around the same table on the mismatched chairs and stools.

"Good news. Today I've come across some important information. The word is the Hunters plan to break into the Tower of London two days from yesterday. Which, as you know, means tomorrow," said Jasper.

"But why would they want to do that? Everybody knows how incredibly strong the security on that place is! Anyone sneaking in would be asking to be caught," said Emra.

"They're sneaking in because they've figured out that one of the jewels, the Cullian II diamond, is one of the Stoens they've been looking for."

There were sharp intakes of breath.

"The Cullian II diamond? The one in the Imperial State Crown? But that's the second-largest diamond in the world!" exclaimed Lisha.

"Are you sure you got it right?" asked Emra.

Jasper nodded.

"Positive."

Kiara shook her head in disbelief.

"The Cullian? The Cullian II diamond is a *Stoen*?"

"I's sorry," cut in Kit, "but I don't get it. O's trying to break in? An' o're these Hunters ev'ryone keeps takin' about?"

"Ah, those would be the Stoenhunters," said Jasper. "The Stoenhunters are the people set on getting the Ultimate Power I spoke of last night. They have no intention of even *trying* to use it for good. This lot, the ones trying to steal the Cullian, is led by Mr. Loxlyheart, who has convinced the rest of them that if he gets the Power, he will reward them all greatly. He's lying, of course, but they're too greedy to notice."

"We just call them 'Hunters' for short," said Emra. "We try to keep in the habit of not mentioning Stoens in public. Attracts too much attention."

Kit nodded, understanding.

"So what're we gonna do 'bout the 'unters stealin' this rock?" she asked.

"We're going to beat them to the punch. We're going to steal it first." Everyone in the room sat up a little straighter and leaned forward, suddenly alert.

"But 'ow are we gonna do that?" asked Kit. In answer, Jasper spread a poster on the table before them, as well as a couple sheets of paper. Lisha recognized the map as the one Jasper had been looking at earlier. It wasn't a map, exactly, but a blueprint of the Tower of London. Red dots showed where entrances would be guarded. The other sheets of paper pointed out a safe route to the gem, as well as a clear way out.

"This is what they're planning. Now, all we have to do is get there first. They'll go in, find the jewel gone, and while they're looking for the Stoen, we alert the constabulary of a break-in," said Jasper.

"Kill two birds with one stone, eh?" said Kiara. "We get the Stoen and, at the same time, get some of the Hunters out of the picture."

"Exactly," said Jasper. "Emra will do the actual stealing, as always. Kiara and Kit will cover her back. Lisha will watch for them to get out and warn me if anything goes wrong. I'll watch from the outside and alert a constable of a break-in as soon as I see the Hunters sneak in. Any questions?" Nobody said anything, but there were many questions flying through people's heads. Kiara wondered why Jasper trusted Kit to help and how she'd gotten stuck with her. Kit and Lisha shared the feeling that this was too easy, but they kept their mouths shut. Emra wondered if she'd be able to swallow this Stoen like she usually did (it was easy as a snake), because this one was so much sharper and it would do no one any good if she choked. Jasper, oblivious to all of this, simply said, "Good. Then get some rest. We've got an exciting day coming."

The hooded figure dashed down the deserted street at twilight. It turned a corner down an alley and came into view of Ye Olde Cheshire Cheese tavern. The figure paused for a moment at the threshold and then slowly stepped inside. Once indoors, it looked around quickly and upon seeing what it had been looking for, skulked over to a table where two people sat, masked by shadow. As the figure sat down, one of the others pushed a cup of coffee forward. The figure picked it up and started to drink. Jasper would not approve if she drank something stronger. She set the cup down and looked at the other two people there. In the darkness, she could never be quite sure if it was them or not. Her foot felt around until it found the wooden leg.

"Just checking," said Emra. Lisha grinned in the darkness.

"Glad you could make it. Both of you."

"We always do," said Kiara. She, Emra, and Lisha raised their glasses.

"A toast to our friendship," said Lisha grandly. "May it last longer than the night." They all drank. "A toast to our lives. May they not end tomorrow." They drank again. "And finally a toast to our mission. May it all work out in the end." They drained their cups. As they set their glasses down, several people came and occupied the table next to theirs. "It's good to be back here. How long has it been?" asked Lisha.

"Too long," said Emra.

"You two! We were here last week to wish Emra good luck," said Kiara.

"That's nothing. We used to come here every night," said Emra dreamily.

"That's right," said Lisha. "I remember when I found you two wandering the streets that first night and brought you here. Can that really have only been a few months ago? It seems like we've been coming here forever."

"I remember that," said Emra. "After the farm burned down, I fled to London, where I ran into Kiara—"

"And started shadowing me everywhere. I thought I'd never get rid of you!" said Kiara, feigning anger. The other two laughed.

"Can you believe after all our hard work we've still only got three Stoens?" asked Emra.

"It took us awhile to locate that one you got last week, and pure luck that Kit dropped hers," said Lisha. "The others we were able to find were all safe enough where they were."

"Mine had been lying under the floorboard of the barn for ages before I stumbled on it and came up able to turn into a snake," said Emra. The three of them sat in silence for a while before Lisha said, "Well, we should turn in. Jasper will be missing us soon."

They stood quietly and walked to the door. Emra and Kiara walked out into the night and disappeared, already on their way back to the toyshop. Just as Lisha was about to leave as well, she caught a phrase that made her stop.

"...Jasper an' the other Protectors. Fools'll never know what hit 'em!" The man who had said it was sitting at the table just behind where Lisha and the other two had been, conveniently hidden in shadow. The man was at a table with three others, all of them huge with even bigger muscles. They were talking more loudly than they should have been, due mostly to the fact that they had obviously had too much to drink. Otherwise, Lisha would never have heard them. She crept closer in the darkness.

"... sending the false map and all. I'll bet you anything they fell for it. Think they're gonna trap *us*, the fools. I can't wait to see their faces when they realize that the joke's on them!" The men started laughing uproariously. *Fake map and plans?* thought Lisha. *Oh no! The plan to steal from the Crown Jewels! I knew it was too good to be true!*

"An' more 'n that," said another man, one with an angular frame and a scar across his cheek, "he even pointed them to the wrong jewel! After they go and steal the Cullion II, we sneak in and take the real treasure!" They laughed. "See, the Cullion's a diamond, right, the second-most valuable in the world," he said between laughs. "So, who'd guess that right above it, on the very same crown, is a Stoen! With what a name, too: the Black Prince's Ruby! We follow after them, pry it out of the crown, and notify the constabulary about the break-in! They'll find them with the Cullian, and with that to distract them, no one will notice the ruby's missing too! We'll get off scot-free, while those pesky orphans get carted off to the workhouse! Or if we're lucky, maybe even the gallows!" Lisha gasped, covering her mouth just in time. *I've got to warn the others!* she said to herself, turning to go.

"And where do you think you're going?" Lisha looked back at the table and saw that three of the men were missing. She felt her belt for her dagger but found it gone. Looking around the floor for the blade, she caught a slight glimmer out of the corner of her eye. Now she knew where her dagger was. It was pointing right between her eyes. Thinking fast, she swung her wooden leg up, knocking the dagger out of the man's hand. Lisha made a mad dash for the door, pushing chairs and people out of her way, but huge hands caught her arms and pulled her back. A cold sweat trickled down her face. The man hadn't needed her dagger after all. Now there was a pistol pressed against her temple. If Lisha tried to escape, she knew that he would pull the trigger. Some kind of rough cloth was being wrapped around her wrists, pinning them behind her back. The men pushed her outside, where the only light came from the moon and the streetlamps. If she tried to run away, they would kill her before she could make another move, for now there was another pistol pressed to the other side of her head and a large hand covering her mouth. Not that she'd have screamed; it'd be a really quick way to end up dead. The acrid smell of too much drink coming from the men made her feel weak and nauseated. But she knew that if she fainted, she might not wake up. Frantic thoughts raced through Lisha's head as she was led silently into the night.

Kiara's mind wandered as she swayed gently in her hammock, half asleep. She longed to sleep, to rest, but something was nagging at the back of her head. Finally it surfaced: Exactly where *had* Jasper gotten those plans?

Kiara sat up. Something was wrong. Something was very wrong. Startled by her own thoughts, Kiara looked around the room. In the darkness it was hard to make out anything clearly, so she lit a lantern. She got up and walked over to Emra's sleeping form, still and dreaming. Kit was also fast asleep. Emra walked over to Lisha's hammock and pulled back the covers. It was empty. Lisha hadn't come home with them. Kiara and Emra had left together and had taken different streets so as not to attract attention. Kiara realized she hadn't even seen Lisha leave the tavern. So where *was* she?

Lisha sat, bound and gagged, in a closet at the Hunters' headquarters. She listened to the Hunters discuss what to do with her. One man wanted to kill her. Another wanted to hold her for ransom. A third suggested making her tell them where she and her friends were staying. Yet another wanted to let her go but follow her to wherever she was hiding. One man suggested using her as a spy, but the rest thought that it'd be too easy for her to trick them. They argued in this manner for quite some time, defending and re-defending their ideas while trying to prove others to be foolish. Occasionally, there was a new idea, but often it was quickly rejected. Suddenly, everything stopped. Lisha edged forward and peeked through the keyhole. Julian E. Loxlyheart stood glaring at everyone and everything at once. He was tall and thin, with one gold tooth, shiny black shoes, and greasy gray hair. He leaned forward slightly, his hands clasped behind his back. His eerie blue eyes shifted from face to face. His eyes were a completely solid shade of baby blue. No other colors disrupted the blue of Mr. Loxlyheart's eyes. They were stunning eyes. But they looked out on the world with an empty, unblinking stare, which completely lacked kindness or any other emotion besides hunger. Or perhaps it was greed.

"What's this I hear you arguing about?" he asked softly.

"It's really nothin', Mr. Loxly'eart," said one of the men, a short, fat man with a wide, cheerful face. "Just a meaningless fight 'tween friends."

"We ent meant nothin' by it," said a scrawny man with unkempt tawny hair. Lisha's eyes widened. She recognized him! But from where? He seemed very familiar, but she couldn't place him. Who was he? "We's jus' wondren' wot t' do wif th'—"

"Shut up, you idiot!" said the first man, cuffing the other man on the head with one big hand. "Sorry, Mr. Loxly'eart, 'e don't know wot 'e's talkin' about. Been drinkin' too much, I reckon." Mr. Loxlyheart's eyes narrowed.

"Mr. Tweeble," said Mr. Loxlyheart, addressing the scrawny, fair-haired "idiot," "is there something I should know about? What is it you were arguing about?"

"Oh, nothin' much. We's jus' decidin' what t' do wif th' 'ostage," said Mr. Tweeble absentmindedly. Behind the locked door, Lisha caught the scent of alcohol. Mr. Loxlyheart's eyes widened, and he raised his thin eyebrows.

"Since when do we 'ave an 'ostage?" asked Mr. Bumbleweed, feigning innocence. Lisha frowned. *Why is he lying to the man he's working for? It's almost like he's trying to protect me!*

"Be quiet, Mr. Bumbleweed, you're in hot water as it is. Don't make things worse for yourself," said Mr. Loxlyheart calmly. "What was that, Mr. Tweeble? Did you say *hostage?*" Mr. Tweeble nodded languidly. Mr. Loxlyheart paused for a moment. "Mr. Thornton," he said commandingly, addressing a third man. Lisha heard a *thunk* as the man in question jumped. *Thornton ...,* thought Lisha. *Where have I heard that name before?*

"Yes, Mr. Loxlyheart?" said Mr. Thornton, nervously.

Lisha looked more closely at Mr. Thornton. Clearly, Mr. Thornton had once been handsome, but that was many years ago. There were deep circles below his bloodshot eyes and stubble on his gaunt face. He had a haunted look about him, his shoulders hunched, his clothes disheveled.

"Tell me, Mr. Thornton," said Mr. Loxlyheart. "Is this true?"

"Yes, sir," said Mr. Thornton hollowly. "It is."

Mr. Loxlyheart considered for a moment before saying, "Now, will someone please tell me how we acquired a hostage?" Everyone started talking at once. Quick as a flash, Mr. Loxlyheart pulled a cane from behind his back and slapped the nearest man across the face. The room went dead silent. "I asked for someone to explain how we acquired a hostage. I did not ask for a room full of *squawking turkeys!*" he said, starting out quietly but slowly getting louder until he was shouting. Back in the closet, Lisha resisted the urge to cover her ears. In a matter of seconds, Mr. Loxlyheart's voice could go from chilling to scorching. "Now, will someone please tell me how we acquired a hostage," said Mr. Loxlyheart, even softer than before.

"Wol, some of us were down at th' tavern earlier. We sat in diff'rent groups t' blend in, jus' like you told us. Some blokes got to drinkin' an' all, you know 'ow i' is, an' she over'erd this one group talking 'bout 'er an' th' others," said Mr. Bumbleweed, glancing to the side at the group of men Lisha saw in the tavern. "We can't 'ave 'er go warnin' the others about the trap now, can we?" he asked in a friendly manner. Mr. Loxlyheart glared. Mr. Bumbleweed cleared his throat and went on. "So we brought 'er back 'ere."

"Where is she now?" asked Mr. Loxlyheart.

"We've got 'er tied up in th' closet," said Mr. Bumbleweed. Lisha heard more than saw his approach. She backed away from the door as his footsteps drew nearer. Closer ... closer...

❧

"Jasper! Jasper! Emra! Kit! Wake up, you lot!" Kiara's sharp voice pierced the darkness. Kit, who had been sleeping soundly, sat straight up in her bed and looked around wildly for the fire. Alarmed by Kiara's piercing voice outlined and strengthened by fear, Emra flung off her blankets and jumped over to Kiara, fumbling with a lantern. They heard a *thunk* from the next room, and Jasper staggered in, bumping into things. He had been so startled he had set his hammock swinging in circles, which had dumped him on the floor. All of this happened in a matter of seconds.

"Where's the burglar? Where's the burglar?" asked Jasper, looking around wildly, squinting in the bright light from the lantern.

"Don't panic! Don't panic! There's no thief," said Kiara. "I just want you to take a second to look around. Do you see anything *missing*?" They all looked around confused, until Emra, comprehension crossing her face said, "Stars—Lisha!" The others looked around once more and saw that she was nowhere to be found.

"Lisha?" asked Jasper, confused. "*Lisha!* What do you think could have happened to her?" Emra put her hand to her mouth and looked at Kiara, who, raising her eyebrows, nodded. Jasper watched them looking at each other. Kit stared at Jasper watching Kiara and Emra look at each other. Jasper's eyes met Kiara's. "Correct me if I'm wrong, but I believe I have a pretty good idea what's happened." Emra stared at him. He knew about their trips to the tavern, but he never spoke about it. "You three weren't ... celebrating ... our finding those plans, were you?" Emra looked at her feet.

"Will some'ne please tell me wot's goin' on?" Everybody looked at Kit, then back at each other, and then at Kit again.

"No time to explain. To make a long story short, Lisha's gone and she didn't get ... lost," said Kiara, looking at Jasper. Kit understood. You could read it on every shadow on her face.

"So, I suppose we ain't gonna steal that Stoen..." Kit's sentence trailed off. Jasper looked at her. He'd completely forgotten the plan, and so had the others.

"We can't do anything about finding Lisha before tomorrow. I guess we'll have to do it without her and look for her later," said Emra. Kit looked at her, shocked.

"But why? What wif Lisha gone missin' an' all, ain't you lot a bit worried?" asked Kit.

"Kit's right. It's far too convenient. Lisha goes missing the night before we plan to steal a Stoen from the Crown Jewels," said Jasper.

"But then what are we supposed to do? We can't just pass up an opportunity like this. It's a double bargain," said Kiara.

"She's right and she's right. How can they both be right?" asked Jasper, turning to Emra.

"He's also right," said Emra. "We can't continue the mission as planned, because something fishy's up. But we can't *not* continue the plan. It may be our only chance!"

"Maybe there's a way we can do both," said Jasper. "Instead of stealing the jewel before the Hunters do, why not let them steal it for us—"

"—and then steal it from them!" said Emra, finishing his thought.

"Exactly. The Hunters take the jewel, we take it from them, and we turn them in to the constabulary."

"But what about the jewel?" asked Kiara. "When we turn them in, the constables will want evidence, which we can't give them. We'd be risking arrest ourselves!"

"Then we'll just have to say that we saw them sneaking in but weren't sure whether they'd taken anything," said Jasper uncomfortably.

"I dunno," said Kit. "It still seems mighty hasty if't you's a'askin' me."

"Oh, come on, Kit, you have to take risks once in a while," said Emra.

"Aw right then," said Kit. "But howsabout this: When we turn 'em in, why don't we just give 'em the Stoen? The constables, I mean. With the Hunters wot caught an' all, the guards'll no doubt increase security, so the Stoen should be safe where it is." Everybody looked at Kit.

"She's got a good point," said Emra. "Our job isn't to collect the Stoens. It's just to find them, determine if they're safe where they are, and if not, move them to a safer place. We'd just be risking ourselves unnecessarily if we tried to steal a jewel from the Tower of London." There was a silence as the Protectors considered their options.

"Well, I guess it makes sense," said Kiara grudgingly. "Anyway, we never had a chance of not getting caught, did we?" They shook their heads.

"So it's settled then," said Jasper. "Wonderful. Now everyone eat a good breakfast and prepare for tonight," said Jasper.

"Breakfast? But Jasper, it's the middle of the night," said Emra, rubbing her eyes.

"Not anymore it isn't," said Jasper. "We've been talking all night. It's morning! Plus, we need to get up bright and early." The other three looked at each other.

"I'll go get breakfast started," sighed Emra, breaking the awkward silence.

"None for me thanks. I'm going for a walk. I'll pick up something to eat on my way," said Kiara, standing up. *On her way where?* thought Kit, but she said nothing as she watched Kiara climb the stairs to the street.

Kiara hummed to herself as she walked down the bustling London street. She was on her way to the Tower of London so she could scout ahead for any dark spaces nearby she needed to watch out for. There could be Hunters hiding anywhere.

As she walked, her thoughts drifted back to Lisha. Where was she? What had happened after they left the tavern? Lisha could fight and protect herself. There was no reason for Kiara to worry. But she couldn't shake the nagging feeling that she might not see Lisha again. Alive, that is.

Stop it! Kiara mentally scolded herself. *You're overreacting. She's just fine. And won't she laugh when she finds out how worried you were. She'll say, "You were worried about me? Really, Kiara, you're not one to waste time worrying about things you shouldn't. 'Not come back?' How ridiculous! Why, here I am, and I'm perfectly fine."*

Perfectly fine, perfectly fine, perfectly fine ...

> *"What do you mean, she would have been perfectly fine? Rodger, are you suggesting it's the child's fault—what are you doing? Good God, man, what are you doing! Stop it! Stop it this instant! Rodger, you're scaring me, Rodger! Can you hear me! Put the child down, do you hear me? Put the child down."*

No. I will not remember. I refuse to remember. It probably never happened, anyway. It's just a figment of a bad dream. Kiara shook her head. What could have possibly triggered that memory? Forcefully, she pushed the thought to the back of her mind.

Kiara soon reached the marketplace. A delightful scent met her and drew her toward a food cart. Cinnamon buns. Kiara searched her pocket and came up short. When no one was looking, she grabbed one and slipped out of sight. She and Lisha used to split these. *Oh, I hope she's all right,* thought Kiara. *I hope she's all right.*

❦

Jasper reentered the kitchen where the remaining two Protectors were having their breakfast. They looked up as he entered.

"I just received word that some old friends of mine from France are in England. We'll be meeting them tomorrow by the docks so they can help us with the mission. They're Protectors, too," he added as an afterthought. Kit stared down at the table, still worrying. Emra looked up at him nervously.

"That's great!" she said, her tone not matching her expression.

I wonder what's gotten into her, Jasper wondered as he wandered from the room again. He took a deep breath. Yes, it would be good to see his old troupe again. Aside from his current Protectors troupe, his old friends were all he had left. Thinking of them brought back memories. And those brought back even older memories. A ship tossed in a storm. The warmth of an old townhouse. Packed into a tight space with his brother. Theater tickets. His mother's face that last time—

Jasper sat on his hammock, hard, the last image filling his mind until there was no room for anything else. Yes, that was the last time he'd seen her. Her dark hair and eyes as she blew out the candle. She'd told them everything would be all right. She'd even wished them sweet dreams. Then she was gone.

The next morning they'd heard. Their father had come in and woken them up, his face tearstained. *Mother's gone,* he had said. They didn't understand. They knew Father had been in trouble with the government. It had sounded serious, but what did that have to do with Mother?

Mother went and told them she was me. They even believed her at first, he'd said. *Where's Mother now?* Jasper and his brother had asked. *Is she coming back soon?* Their father looked at them then, and his eyes were enough. Even if he'd said yes, they wouldn't have believed him.

That's when they showed up. They thought Father had sent her on purpose, and they'd come to take him away. The boys were confused, but one thing they understood: workhouse. We're going to the workhouse.

When they'd got there, Father put up a fight. Said they could have him, but his kids weren't to grow up in the workhouse. There were blows, and blood, and a *Run!* And they ran.

Ran and ran until they could run no more. They'd stowed away on a ship headed for France. They'd stared out a porthole from down in the hold, wondering if they could see the gallows. Would they see their father hanging from it?

England disappeared before their eyes.

Lali, an English girl with a nose ring, had found them half-starved on the streets of France. Lali brought them to Tristan, the leader of a Protectors troupe. She'd introduced them to the Drifters, and the Drifters had allowed them to join her troupe. That was where he'd met Minuette.

Minuette, kind, gentle Minuette, had become his sun, moon, and stars. His breath quickened, and he could feel his heart pound at the thought of seeing her again. He hadn't wanted to leave her, leave any of them.

Lali, the frank little pirate with her nose ring and strange ability to make people tell the truth. She'd found them, given them a home and hope when they had none. She'd advocated for them and said they could still stay even if they weren't accepted into the troupe.

Tristan had fed them first and asked questions later. When she heard their story, she had agreed with Lali that the two brothers would simply have to stay. She was always welcoming, and before they knew it, they felt as if they had known her forever.

Then there was little Halie. Shy, strong Halie, mysterious and quiet. Knowing the future could be a burden, after all. She'd curtsied and greeted them in broken English and set about like a little maid or house fairy to make sure they were comfortable.

Jasper's brother, Jordan, who hid with him in the hold of the ship and shivered in the rain and the streets. Jordan who'd run with him away from the workhouse, and Father, and England. Jordan had been with him through it all. They held each other up, one more step, one more day, until things get better. All of Jasper's memories before France were usually in the plural. We did this or we did that.

Everyone had always said that Jordan looked like their father. Taller, rougher than little Jasper. Jasper looked like his mother. They'd been inseparable for so long, it had been hard to imagine leaving him. But the Drifters told him that they needed a new troupe back in London. He couldn't refuse. It was an order, a call to duty. He was scared and reluctant to leave his new friends, especially Minuette, to go somewhere far away. Especially London. He hadn't been back there since they'd escaped years before. But this was his chance, he told himself, his chance to lead, be a part of something bigger.

And so he'd made a new life.

"Look out!" said a voice from behind Jasper. He whirled around only to be strangled by the arms of a moving blob of color. When he was finally let free, Jasper saw that his assailant was a very pretty girl wearing a very pretty smile. She had pinned-back hair the color of butter and chocolate brown eyes shining with happiness. Slightly shorter than he was, she seemed to glow in the sunlight, beaming at Jasper. He felt his mouth open in wonder, unable to find words to express his joy. He smiled and hugged her again, his heartbeat quickening. *Minuette...*

"Jasper! Long time no see!" Jasper turned to see a familiar face.

"Tristan! Am I glad to see you! Halie and Lali! Where's Jordan?" asked Jasper, grasping Tristan's hand and then Lali's.

"Right here," said a voice from behind Jasper. Jasper turned, saw his brother, grinned, and caught him in an embrace. It was awhile before they let go of each other.

"Nice to see you again," said Jordan quietly. Jasper nodded.

"And," Jasper said, turning to the girl whose arms were still locked around him, "Minuette. I've missed you."

"Ahem," said Kiara. "I don't believe we've been introduced." Jasper pulled reluctantly away from Minuette's tight embrace.

"Right. Sorry, Kiara. These are some very old friends of mine. They're Protectors, too. Kiara, Emra, Kit," he said, gesturing to each of them, "meet my old troupe. Before I joined you lot, I used to be a part of theirs. Tristan here is the leader," he said, nodding to a tall girl wearing boy's clothing. If the English Protectors hadn't already been told previously that Tristan was a girl, they would have thought she was a boy. "This one's Lali," Jasper continued, nodding to the girl with the nose ring. "Halie," a small girl with long brown hair almost covering her face waved shyly. "My brother, Jordan," Jasper clapped his hand on the back of a boy who looked like a older, rougher version of Jasper, with black hair and a serious face. "And this," he said, "is Minuette." Tristan grasped Kiara's hand and shook it firmly.

"Pleasure to meet you, Kiara? Is that right?" Tristan was tall, with a firm grip and a friendly nature. Her hair was short like a boy's and dirty blond.

"Right. You're ... Tristan. Jasper told us you'd be coming. What brings you to England?" asked Kiara, rubbing her hand where Tristan had grabbed it. The visitors from France exchanged looks. Tristan began.

"We had a bit of a ... *qu'est qu'on dit* ... how does one say ... *un vol*? Eh ... a robbery, you might say. Someone, or something, broke in and stole all our Stoens. We have tracked the whatever-it-was back here, but we lost the trail after arriving in London. Awful messy city you have here. We heard tell of some fuss over a Stoen among the Crown Jewels," she said with a teasing grin, "and we came to see what the excitement was about. I knew Jasper was living near to here, and I thought it was time we came to visit," said Tristan, looking sideways at Jasper.

"How did you lot hear about the plans to steal the Stoen?" Jasper asked Tristan.

"Tristan 'as 'er ways," said Lali mysteriously, touching her temples. Lali had light hair and a tarnished nose ring. She wore a thin collared shirt that was missing several of its buttons.

"Quiet yourself," said Tristan jokingly, cuffing the girl lightly across the head. "We received word from a certain messenger."

Emra shrugged.

"Lisha thought they should know, so I sent the word around."

Kit remembered being told that all the Protector troupes had some means of communicating with each other on very short notice. Lisha was in charge of the communications for their troupe.

Emra looked at the ground. "And ... well, about Lisha," she added, not looking at anyone.

"What's up wif Lisha?" asked Lali. Apparently they all knew her.

"She disappeared, just last night, at the tavern on Fleet Street, I believe...?" said Jasper, glancing sideways at Kiara and Emra.

"That's right. The Cheshire Cheese. One moment she's right behind us, the next..." said Emra.

"Person'ly, I don't think they should go an' steal that Stoen thing 'til we know wot 'appened wif Lisha," said Kit. Everybody looked at her, startled, for up until that moment she had been very quiet.

"I must agree with you on this one," said Minuette. "It is too dangerous. It could be a trap." Jasper swallowed. Minuette was careful not to look at him.

"Halie, wot d' you think?" asked Lali. Everybody got quiet to hear the shy Protector's answer. Jasper remembered that Halie's power was being able to see events happening at other places at that moment, and sometimes flashes of the future. He wondered if she ever saw anything concerning him and Minuette. He looked back at Minuette. Jasper remembered being told that those with a strong connection could sometimes form a psychic bond. He stared hard at her, hoping to make it happen, but his mind stayed locked in his head. He almost didn't care. She looked even more beautiful than he had remembered. The light glinting off her hair, those creamy brown eyes—

"Jasper! Wake up! Are you deaf?"

"Huh? What?" asked Jasper.

"I asked you if you thought such a thing could happen, and you acted as if you couldn't hear me!" said Kiara.

"Sorry," he said, blushing. "What was it you were saying?" He'd been daydreaming about Minuette again. He couldn't help it. She was just so easy to daydream about.

"Halie was just saying that she saw one of the Hunters draw up a map and plans and leave it with a pickpocket with instructions to give it to you," said Kiara.

"What does that mean?" said Emra.

"It means," said Jasper, "that they have played quite a trick on us." Now Jasper could see it. It was a hoax. A trap. He ran his fingers through his hair in quiet distress. How could he have been so blind? The job of the Protectors was to protect the Stoens, but the job of the leader was to protect his troupe. Why hadn't he seen this coming? That was his job. *A jolly good leader I'm turning out to be*, he thought. A small voice reminded him that it wouldn't have mattered, since they were planning on letting the Hunters steal the jewel and then turning them in. But, he reminded himself, that wasn't even his idea. If it had been up to him, he probably would have had the Protectors steal the jewel themselves. He would have walked right into the trap.

"There they are!" said Lali. Everybody sat up and peered around their various hiding spots. They had been waiting for over an hour in complete silence across the street from the Tower of London, waiting for the Hunters to steal the Stoen.

A silhouette tiptoed in the shadows, looked around once, and disappeared as it passed beyond their sight.

"It's working," Jasper whispered. "Good thinking, Kit." Finally they were getting somewhere. After Halie's vision, the consensus had been to continue the plan as, well, planned, as the revised version posed little danger to the Protectors themselves. Quiet Halie had been set to the task of using her vision to try to find Lisha, and the rest waited patiently (or in some cases, not so patiently) for the outcome of events. Kit was being unusually sullen. She still thought that it was too risky to steal the Stoen until they knew exactly what had happened to Lisha. They didn't have any proof that there even was a "Stoen among the Crown Jewels," as Tristan had called it. Kit liked Lisha and was afraid for her. But it wasn't just Lisha she was afraid for. It was all her new friends, her new life as a Protector, fighting the eternally thirsty eye of greed. *Eternally thirsty eye of greed. That's a nice phrase you got there, Kit*, said Kit to herself. *You've got to remember that one.*

Just then, Kit saw the shadowy figure reappear. The Protectors all exchanged excited looks and began to discuss who should be the one to take it from the thief. After brief deliberation, the task of retrieving the Stoen fell to Emra. She walked behind a stone wall to transform and reemerged in snake form. Kit's eyes widened. At seeing her shocked expression, Tristan and

Lali laughed, but kindly. Emra, in snake form, slipped forward and slithered toward the silhouette, curving around its ankle. Kit held her breath involuntarily and stared unblinking as she watched the snake slither up the figure's leg and around its arm. Whoever it was jumped and slapped himself, trying to get at Emra, but the snake was too fast. The person made one last, desperate attempt to catch Emra—and succeeded. Kit gasped—or tried to. It was difficult, since she had been holding her breath for so long. The figure walked slowly, yet purposefully, toward the troupe of Protectors. Kit saw Jordan and Lali simultaneously reach for their daggers as Jasper wiped a nervous sweat from his face. They were just about to jump up as the figure came out of the shadows and into the light in front of them. He—no, *she,* pushed back a stand of hair from her face and said, "Calm down, you lot. Don't you recognize me?"

"Heavens above ... it's—"

"Lisha!" said Kit, jumping up to hug her. Lisha let go of Emra's tail, and she slithered behind the wall. Lisha hugged Kit back, as the others stared on in amazement. Kiara exhaled, deeply relieved to see her friend again, and smiled.

"What—how did you—" said Jasper, completely befuddled.

"A few of the Hunters caught me in the tavern and took me back to their headquarters. I overheard them talking about how they meant to trick us into stealing the wrong jewel and then getting us arrested while they made off with the real one. Turns out we were right—the Cullian's not a Stoen, but the Black

Prince's Ruby *is*. But anyway, after I was captured, it took forever for them to decide what to do with me. They finally settled on making me help steal the Stoen for them, cover them you might say, so that in case I was caught it wouldn't mater. The Hunters assumed that you'd have already stolen the wrong one and set off the guards, so they could enter unnoticed while the constables were after you. Anyhow, as you can tell, the lights weren't all on inside, and with a little reverse psychology, I got them to let me do the actual stealing," she said. Halie smiled. Jasper knew what she was thinking. She would be glad to know that the trap she uncovered had been avoided.

"You didn't actually steal it, did you?" asked Kiara incredulously.

"'Course not. Naturally, that was unnecessary as all I had to do was tell the guards the truth—that I'd been held hostage by a group of people that were planning a break-in—and set them off in the direction I'd come. I'm afraid they won't find them though; Loxlyheart's too clever. They had me all turned around before bringing me here. But it's a start. I handed them the plans and blueprints so they know I wasn't lying. Don't worry about me," she said, seeing their worried faces, "I've got certain friends, and half the people in London owe me a favor or two. The Hunters won't come after me, or any of us. And this way, we can make sure that the Stoen stays safe where it is."

As everyone congratulated Lisha on her success, Emra walked back out from behind the stone wall as if nothing unnatural had happened. Kit looked at her with a mixture of awe and fear. *She never looked at* me *like that,* thought Jasper, and then he mentally kicked himself for his jealousy. He shook his head, biting his lip to keep from showing his embarrassment.

The next thing he knew, Minuette was at his side. Jasper hadn't noticed drawing away from the group as the others questioned Lisha about everything she could remember and asked her to tell them the whole story again. Minuette, however, had.

"Jasper, is there something the matter?" she asked. She looked at him, worry filling her eyes. Jasper hated to see her like that. Quickly, he blinked a few times and looked back at her, trying to appear normal.

"No, there's—" Jasper couldn't lie to her, lie to those brown eyes. He looked away. "I'm just ... tired. I couldn't sleep last night." That was partially true. He had lain awake for many hours thinking of Minuette, and as soon as he really fell asleep, Kiara had come to wake him. Minuette didn't buy it, but she said nothing.

"This demands a celebration!" called Tristan. "Hey, Minuette! Jasper! You two coming with us for drinks?"

"We will meet you there," said Minuette. Jasper's insides gave a lurch, and his heart jumped up into his throat. Tristan shrugged and followed the rest of the group. Minuette sat down next to Jasper. He started to sweat and looked away. "What is wrong, Jasper? I know that look, what is the matter?" Japer looked back at Minuette. She looked so enchanting as she gently touched his hand that Jasper though he would melt. Their eyes met, and all other thoughts flew from his mind. For a moment, it was as if their two minds occupied the same space. Minuette saw herself through Jasper's eyes. Looking back at her own face, she felt his thoughts and perceptions of her: beautiful and incredibly kind. His memories of how she had cared for him and empathized with his sad tale. His admiration of her stubborn optimism, of her way of always seeing the silver lining, no matter how opaque the storm. She felt his shame at his perceived failure and his insecurity about his own leadership. Jasper was baffled as he became aware of how he looked to Minuette. He was suddenly looking at her looking at him, and to her, he was handsome and sweet. He was doing his best, and a brilliant job at that. Being a leader was difficult, and she saw great bravery and strength in Jasper, surviving and even thriving after he had faced so much. No one blamed him for the close call. He felt more than ever Minuette's kindness and her intense desire to help him, to comfort him … and something else. Their eyes closed as their lips met, and they felt they would never be alone again.

❧

The clock struck six as Emra watched the hour hand move on the clock tower. She tapped her foot anxiously and sighed in impatience. Where *were* Jasper and Minuette? Had they been captured by Hunters, just like Lisha had been? Emra felt panic threaten to surge through her at the idea. *It would make sense*, she thought, *although* … if she let herself think about it, she could think of a much more likely scenario. Based on the way Jasper and Minuette had been looking at each other,

Emra had a pretty good idea what was keeping them. She felt a terrible sinking sensation as despair settled on her like a physical weight. She leaned forward and stared down blankly at the counter, hands pressed against neck for support. She shook her head, trying to drive away the thought, and with it, the pain she felt whenever she thought of *him* with Minuette.

To distract herself, she tried to listen to the others' conversation. They had arrived at the tavern, sat down, and proceeded to augment the general hubbub with their roars of laughter. Lisha and Tristan alternated telling stories and jokes to the rest of the Protectors, punctuated often by dry comments from Lali and Kiara.

"So then he said, 'Curse the idiots who built this hunk o' wood. Another wave like that, an' we'll be swimmin' wif the fishies!'" said Lisha, imitating a gravely voice. All the others started to laugh. Emra laughed with them, burying her worries and trying to look cheerful. "And then do you know what that old salamander does? He trips over his own beard and falls into the fishing nets!" They all laughed again. They were having such a good time that no one but Emra noticed Jasper and Minuette enter the tavern, hand in hand, and sit down with the other Protectors at the counter, emanating an air of contentment. Emra's first emotion was a flood of relief that they hadn't been captured by Mr. Loxlyheart's men. But when she saw their linked hands and glowing expressions, she was overcome by a sudden feeling of defeat. She was extremely glad that her first fear had not come true, but wished that she had also been wrong about the second. Jasper ordered drinks for Minuette and himself and paid the bartender. Emra watched them, downhearted, as if from a great distance, noting acutely the way they looked at each other and the linked hands they thought no one could see. Finally, she couldn't take it anymore. She put on a sunny expression and took a deep breath.

"Jasper! Where have you been? We were starting to worry!" said Emra brightly, pretending to have just noticed them.

"Oh! Oh, we were just enjoying the nice weather," said Jasper. "Were people really worried about us? They don't seem too anxious to welcome us back."

"I was worried," said Emra quietly.

A few hours later, the thrill of victory was starting to wear off. Lisha looked out the window of the tavern.

"It's getting dark. You lot want to stay with us for the night? It's no trouble; we've got extra space," said Lisha to Tristan's troupe.

"No, *ça va*. Thanks, though," said Tristan.

"Lisha has got a point, though," said Jordan. "We don't want to be out too late. Better get a good night's sleep and avoid the nighttime mess I remember around here." Everyone got up and said their farewells. Tristan shook hands with all of the members of Jasper's troupe and started to yawn. Jasper and Minuette looked at each other once more. They hadn't let go of each other's hands the whole time they were in the tavern.

"Well, I guess I'll see you later then," said Jasper, looking at his feet.

"Yes," said Minuette, looking down also. "*Au revoir, mon chéri.*"

"*Á bientôt, ma chérie,*" said Jasper. They dropped hands and turned away from each other as they left the tavern. The two troupes headed in opposite directions, Jasper and Minuette glancing back for one last look at each other.

As soon as they had gone, a shape emerged from the shadows in the tavern. Dark eyes watched the two teams disappear. Pushing long black hair from her face, Desdemona muttered imprecations under her breath that would have made a sailor look at her strangely and back away. Her catlike eyes narrowed in annoyance. Bother. These children were proving to be quite a nuisance. Now she had to decide which team to follow. She tapped two slender fingers together indecisively. Her fingers were long and thin, with clawlike nails. She could follow Jasper's troupe. But they were inexperienced and did not pose much of a threat to her. Besides, Julian could take care of them on his own. Tristan, on the other hand...

Desdemona waited a moment longer and started after her chosen Protectors' troupe, her purple sash trailing in the wind behind her like a tail.

❦

It was night. Tristan and the others found shelter in an abandoned dock house. The Protectors crawled into their makeshift beds and blew out the last candle. Several of them stayed awake, exchanging words in the darkness. Minuette sat on the edge of the group, lost in her own happy thoughts. She lay back with her hand behind her head and held up a smudged locket. Clicking it open, Minuette gazed sleepily at the picture inside. The Jasper in the picture smiled at her. Minuette smiled back. From across the room, Jordan caught her eye. He nodded slightly and gave her a small smile. She nodded back gratefully, knowing from his look that he approved. Her connection with Jasper sometimes set her apart slightly from the others, but she didn't mind. They had each other, and that was all that mattered.

❦

Bang, bang, bang! Someone was pounding on the inside of a low cabinet in an abandoned toyshop, shaking the whole wall. *Bang, bang, bang!* Five bodies fell out of their hammocks, and five pairs of feet staggered groggily to the kitchen. Five pairs of hands reached for the knob to pull open the cabinet. Finally, the small door swung forward, and a girl with messily tied up, short, blond hair and a nose ring fell into the toyshop. The Protectors gaped at the sight. Lali lay on the floor, rubbing her head where she had banged it on the top of the cabinet doorframe as she fell into the room. Halie, most of her still in the secret passageway, was clinging onto her arm.

"Lali? Halie? What happened? What are you doing here?" asked Lisha, confused.

"It's th' Hunters wot done it! They'd near trashed the place when we two escaped! Halie 'ere told us there'd be trouble, but did we listen?" said Lali quickly. She was clearly of breath.

"Girls, calm down," said Jasper. "What happened? When? How? Why?"

Lali gulped air before replying.

"What? We were attacked. When? Jus' now, or as long ago as it took us t' get 'ere. How? I couldn't tell you. Why?" Lali looked around at everyone, pausing to catch her breath. "Them wot took our Stoens figured we was after them, and they came after us first. The Hunters've captured the rest of the troupe!"

The Protectors from the toyshop looked at each other with shock on their faces.

"Hunters ... tell us everything that happened," said Jasper urgently. "You left the tavern, and..."

"After we left you lot, we walked t' th' dock, you know, th' abandoned hideaway from the last London troupe. It's got a secret passageway from there to 'ere, you know, for escapes. An' a good thing to. Anyway, Halie 'ere suggested we should leave a guard to stay up and warn us if anyone should show up."

"Why all the extra security?" asked Jasper. "Leaving a guard in case anyone showed up?"

"Well, you see, after our Stoens got stolen, on our way 'ere, chasing whoever took 'em, we jus' got about five Stoens from a gem salesmen a' fisherman's point. We's jus' makin' sure that them wot took the rest don't come back for more, or if they do, that we're ready. We don't want the Stoens to end up back in somebody's pocket. 'Specially not Desdemona's."

"Desdemona? Wasn't she th' other one that Jasper wot mentioned?" asked Kit.

"That's right. What do you know about her?" asked Lisha.

"Not much," replied Lali, "but I'll tell you what I do know. She' s after th' Stoens, or the power she can get from them just like Aradia an' Mr. Loxly'eart. Desdemona 'as a strange effect on people, which is that they usually end up doing wot she wants. And it's very 'ard to keep tabs on her, 'cause no one seems to remember seein' 'er. That's pretty much all I know, 'cept for rumors," said Lali.

"Rumors?" asked Kiara.

"People say tha' she can kill with a look an' tha' she stole 'er powers from 'er sister, Laramie, before throwin' 'er into the sea." Eyes went wide at this. "And tha's not all!" continued Lali. "It isn't only us who've 'ad our Stoens stolen. It's been 'appening all over! Yesterday, we got a message from Fala saying that their Stoens 'ad been stolen, an' the day before we 'eard from Warrick!"

"Who're Warrick and Fala?" said Kit.

"Warrick is a leader of a Protector troupe out in Scotland, and Fala leads the troupe from Ireland," explained Lisha, worry lines between her eyebrows.

"What happened next?" asked Emra. "How did you escape? What happened to the others?"

Lali's face took on an odd expression.

"Woll, it's strange. Halie said we should leave a guard, like I said, so I stayed up wif a lantern. T' keep myself awake, I started countin' things, like th' floorboards, wha' I could see, th' stars. An' then I saw somethin' movin', one o' th' shadows, so I looked around t' see which one o' th' others it was what stirred, finding each one an' seeing where their shadow was. But y' se, there were five of us there, right? But I counted six shadows."

The others, all except Halie, gaped at her.

"Six shadows?" asked Jasper, aghast. "Are you sure?"

Lali nodded vigorously.

"The sixth one," she continued, "the one that didn't belong to no one, well, it was th' one wot was movin', an' when it saw me lookin', it—well, it waved." Jaws dropped. "Not like a greeting, mind, it was a wave like when your tryin' t' get sommun's attention. Well, it worked. I woke Halie an' pointed it out. As we were lookin', th' shadow started writing! She wrote—"

"It started writing?" repeated Kiara incredulously, just as Lisha said thoughtfully, "You're sure it was a 'she'?"

Lali nodded quickly.

"Yes an' yes. Now, let me finish!" The others hushed up. "Now," continued Lali, "It wrote: 'they're coming,' an' pointed to the door. It motioned us toward the secret passageway. She wanted us t' go out, so we went t' wake th' others. But jus' then ... it was strange, I'm not really sure what 'appened.

"Halie, can you show us?" asked Jasper. She nodded. Lisha left and came back a few minutes later with a tray filled with water. She brought it over to Halie. Halie closed her eyes. Her thick brown hair started to lift around her shoulders as if being blown by a gentle breeze. Halie raised her hands above the water.

Slowly, an image formed on the surface of the water. Jasper and Lisha leaned forward for a better look. In the tray of water, the Protectors could see the inside of a dock house. In the image, four of the Protectors were lying on the floor, apparently asleep, and Lali was sitting up by the window with a lantern glowing dimly. At first, everything was still, but soon they could see movement in the shadows. The Lali in the image looked around.

"That's when I was countin' the shadows," put in Lali, pointing down at the water. "See, there's Tristan's," she said, indicating the shadow that belonged to Tristan, "an' Jordan's ... there's Halie's an' mine, an' Minuette's ... an' then, look there."

Lisha furrowed her brow and Kiara stared down, not saying anything. Jasper cried, "What!" Kit's eyes went wide, and Emra gasped and put her hands over her mouth. There was an extra shadow! The silhouette of the woman on the wall waved her arms wildly. They watched as the Lali in the image got up and shook Halie awake. The two girls looked at the shadow woman, who started moving her hand as if writing. The words appeared, just as they had said, and the shadow motioned to the rug. The Lali and Halie in the image glanced, confused, between it and the shadow woman. Then, seeming to realize something, they went quickly to wake the others.

Suddenly, the image in the water seemed distorted somehow, the room in the image swirling before the observers' eyes. The shadows in the dock house started moving, joining together to form chains and shackles, which moved to bind the Protectors. They awoke with a start, screaming, and a huge struggle ensued with the Protectors pulling at their chains, trying desperately to get away. The chains formed as if out of thin air and reconnected with themselves when the ends met.

Lali had grabbed the lantern and was using it to fend off the shadows as Halie clutched to her desperately. The two of them huddled under the lamplight, the glow like a physical barrier that kept the shadows away. Lali glanced desperately at the door, but a second later, a wall formed out of shadows, blocking the way. The windows, too, were being filled with shadows, sealing the Protectors in. Lali kicked aside the rug the shadow woman had motioned at to reveal a trap door in the floor. Opening the hatch, she yelled something that sounded like "follow us!" Lali grabbed Halie and threw her down the trap door before jumping in after. The force of the landing knocked the door back down against the floor with a loud thud.

Meanwhile, the others were still trying to fight off the chains wrapping around them. Some of them went so far as to hurl the shadow chains against the wall. More chains were collecting all around them, chaining their hands to their sides, for they were not shadows now, but solid objects. Minuette cried out in pain as Tristan's chain struck her on the arm. She collapsed to the floor, chains wrapping around her.

"Minuette!" cried Jasper, watching her try to stop the bleeding with her blankets before the chains could secure her arms. Jasper's heart ached as he watched her, helpless.

After that, there was silence. The lull in activity didn't last long, however. Soon, the shadows blocking the door dispersed like smoke from a fire, and a woman floated through. Her light, reddish brown hair was done up on top of her head. Under a dark cloak she wore a torn black dress with red stones around the waist. Her face was pretty, with porcelain skin and hand-painted lips, yet her olive green eyes stared out emptily into space, as if not really seeing the room. She hovered several inches above the ground, with shadows swirling around her slippered feet.

"Aradia," Emra mouthed, watching, her eyes wide. Aradia was a shadow bender and could turn shadows into solid objects and control them to suit her needs. Aradia waved her hand, and a box was lifted to her by a stray shadow. She took it in her hands and opened it. She closed the lid and nodded to the two men beside her. She turned and floated out the door, lifting the Protectors along behind her. The last to go was Minuette, the gash in her arm still bleeding.

The image disappeared. Nobody moved. It was as if they had suddenly turned to stone. Jasper sat staring down at the now clear water for a long moment. Emra wondered if she should put a hand on his shoulder. Lisha and Kiara looked at him expectantly. His breathing was heavy. He was thinking hard. Finally he looked up.

"We have to do something. Aradia has to be stopped," he said forcefully. "They all do. Mr. Loxlyheart and Desdemona ... they're getting close to getting the power. We can't just sit here while they steal and kidnap, and—we have to rescue the others and stop the Stoenhunters once and for all. We need a plan of action." Everyone sat up straighter. "The Hunters must have somewhere they're keeping the prisoners and the Stoens. We need to know where to look. We'll have to talk to Xylon. But first, we need to know exactly how the Ultimate Power works. We need a Mason."

"Cameron lives relatively close," said Emra, "just up around the coast, in the Lake District."

"Good, we'll go to her. Then find Xylon, and we'll use his map to find where the Hunters've made their headquarters. We'll find them—and stop them. But we'll need help." He looked up. "Lisha, collect your crew and prepare the ship. Halie, get information from the other troupes. See how many are close by. Ask if they've still got any Stoens. Find out if they can meet us once we know where to go. Send word to Fala and Warrick and anyone else you can find. Keep it concise, though. Lisha can send word later with more details. Emra, Kit, Kiara, start packing." They all nodded. "In this century, please," said Jasper. Everyone scrambled off, except for Emra. She sat down next to Jasper. He was shaking.

"Are you going to be all right?" she asked. He looked up at her, his eyes glassy.

"I really don't know."

❦

Meanwhile, over in Ireland, across the channel from where Jasper's troupe was scrambling to follow his instructions, the members of Fala's troupe were packing their bags. All their Stoens had been stolen just a few days ago. They had sent word to Tristan and through her to Jasper. Fala had received a reply from Halie. The communication had been brief: "Ours have been stolen, too. Jasper sends a message: We're moving against the Hunters. Meet us in London." The troupe members had picked themselves up and were preparing to travel to England.

Fala perched on a windowsill in the abandoned barn that served as her troupe's headquarters. She looked around the room at her troupe, a raven perched on her shoulder. She stroked his head lightly as she watched her charges. The other six Protectors were busily going through their belongings, deciding what to bring with them. They were packing all sorts of strange things. Nat, Fala's second in command, was standing near the window where Fala sat, looking contemplatively at the window next to hers. On this windowsill sat a row of potted plants. Nat had light hair and slightly tanned skin, both with an odd greenish tint. The expression on Nat's face as he gave the plants solemn consideration was almost identical to the expression he had worn during a conversation they had had the previous day. Fala had a brief flashback to that conversation.

The conversation had taken place just after Fala received the summons from Halie telling them to come to England. The communication had been private, and she had not yet told the rest of the troupe. Before informing them, Fala had pulled Nat aside for a consultation.

"What do you think?" she had asked after relaying the message.

"Well, we have to go, naturally," he had replied. "No question of that. Taking a stand will be dangerous, but it has to be all or nothing if we're going to have a chance. Besides, there's no way we can leave the other Protectors to go against the Hunters all on their own."

"Yes, of course," Fala had agreed. "And I do think we need to take a stand. I've been considering the problem for a while, actually. Doing what we've been doing just isn't enough anymore."

"Do you think this is the right time to do it?" asked Nat.

Fala thought for a moment before answering.

"I don't think we have a choice. We have to stop the Stoenhunters before it's too late. From what we've been hearing, that time seems to be coming all too quickly. Jasper's right. It's only a pity no one did anything sooner. I hope it doesn't come to a confrontation." She glanced away at the other Protectors, worry in her eyes.

Nat put a hand on her shoulder comfortingly.

"Don't worry. We all knew what we were getting into when we signed up. None of us would be here if we weren't willing to take risks. And who knows? Like you say, it may not come to that." Fala had nodded gratefully. There had never been any question in her mind about what they must do, but Nat's words reassured her, easing her worry slightly. He was right. The others knew the danger, and they were prepared to face it.

As if knowing her mind, Nat had patted her shoulder again, smiled, and left her to her thoughts. Later that day, she had made the announcement that they were leaving, relaying Halie's message to the others. After instructing the Protectors to ready themselves for the journey, she had sent Leandra to find a ship headed to London that they could stow aboard. Fala counted on Leandra's persistent nature in situations such as this, and she was not disappointed. Leandra had been relentless in her inquiries. That very night she had found a suitable ship departing the following afternoon. Now, with the preparations made, all that remained was for the troupe to finish packing.

They weren't able to bring much, so the Protectors had to choose which of their few belongings was important or useful enough to bring. Having made his selection from the windowsill, Nat was carefully placing a whole potted plant in his bag. It was a tiny rose that needed constant care to survive. He had raised it from a seed he had received many years ago as a present, and it reminded him of his old home. Genna, an artist never comfortable without drawing materials, carefully and meticulously tried to fit a huge sketchpad into a tiny pack. It contained her favorite sketches and plenty of blank paper. Her little brother, Mica, stumbled by, teetering under the weight of the giant three-volume *Encyclopedia Britannica* carried in his small arms that completely obscured his face. The books were so heavy that he tripped and knocked into Kadin-Lave, making him drop the fistful of metal he was holding.

"Hey!" said Kadin-Lave unhappily.

"Oops, sorry," apologized Mica, peeking around the stack of books. Kadin-Lave bent, annoyed, and started picking up the pieces from where he dropped them, muttering darkly to himself about people looking where they were going. Kadin-Lave, always focused and prepared for anything, was bringing his favorite tool, chosen both for its versatility and its fascination.

Leandra was trying to get a struggling Kaida into a backpack.

"I refuse to be carried like luggage," said Kaida indignantly. "The position is undignified. I will be the laughingstock of my family once I get home," continued Kaida, who knew very well that he would not be seeing his family anytime soon.

"Now, Kaida," consoled Leandra, long hair flying around her head as she struggled with him, "You know you attract attention, and the last thing we need is people staring at us. If we want to stow aboard that ship, we have to be inconspicuous."

"The only reason I attract attention is because I am so good-looking! People marvel at my appearance. It isn't every day you see someone as interesting as me!" he said, stretching and admiring himself.

Nat looked up from the plant he was packing and said, "Oh, Kaida, I almost forgot: on the trip you can't talk to us. Or anybody else, for that matter."

"You must be joking! Tell me he's joking!" Kaida said, looking at Leandra. "Not talk? How am I supposed to maintain the power of speech if I'm not allowed to talk?" said Kaida, clutching his throat.

"Kaida," said Fala, but he cut her off.

"And another thing. How am I supposed to get food? Oh, sure, you *say* you'll slip me scraps from the table, but how do I *know*? How do I know you won't *forget*? Plus, I am a growing individual and I need my strength," said Kaida, flexing a tiny arm. "A few measly table scraps won't do me any good!" he said, gesturing wildly at himself.

"Kaida!" said Fala again.

"Yes, what is it?" said Kaida inattentively.

"We need to get going. Our boat is going to leave in ten minutes, with or without us. This is not up for discussion. Kaida, you have to get in the backpack," said Fala firmly. Kaida issued a stream of protests as he was stuffed unceremoniously into the backpack.

"There we go," said Fala after Kaida was securely sealed in the pack. "Did everybody bring everything? Last chance if you forgot something!" She looked around at their faces. "No? Awright then, let's go." She turned and walked out the door carrying the backpack with Kaida in it. The others followed.

Fala sighed. Sometimes Kaida was more trouble then he was worth. Keeping a young dragon hidden in the middle of Ireland was no picnic, but smuggling one into England was almost impossible.

❦

They arrived at the port with seconds to spare. The troupe sneaked onto the ship mere minutes before it left. They sat panting on the deck as the ship cast off, trying to blend in.

Genna immediately pulled out her sketchpad and began to draw a seagull perched on the railing. It soon flew away, but her photographic memory allowed her to keep drawing. Mica stood next to her, clutching her skirt the whole time. He had never been on a ship before, and he watched the people walking by with a mixture of interest and mistrust. Nat looked green (or more so then usual) and soon leaned his head out over the railing and lost his breakfast. Nat's head reemerged, and Leandra handed him a handkerchief.

"Thanks," he said, and wiped his mouth. Leandra gave him a sympathetic look.

"No stomach for sailing?" teased Kadin-Lave. Nat tried to shake his head, but then he thought better of it. He tried to speak, but closed his mouth immediately.

"It makes perfect sense," said Mica, still holding onto Genna's skirt. Kadin-Lave looked over at him, startled. "Nat's power is controlling and talking to plants," continued Mica. "It's understandable that he'd be more comfortable with earth and roots beneath his feet."

Nat gave Mica a grateful look and then turned his gaze resolutely ahead, attempting to forestall any further motion sickness. Genna looked down at her brother affectionately and ruffled his hair.

Fala stared out to sea, absent-mindedly stroking Kaida's head inside the backpack, which helped to keep him quiet. She was waiting for the raven she had sent to Halie to return. She had told it to deliver the message to Halie and Jasper that her troupe would meet up with theirs in London as soon as possible.

She had also given the bird instructions to bring back a reply from the others with updates should they wish to send one. She anxiously awaited the reply, worrying more and more the longer the messenger took to return.

Seeing her look, Kadin-Lave said, "Relax, Fala. You sent the bird yesterday! It'll come soon." She looked back at him.

"I know. I just wish he'd get back already."

Kadin-Lave shrugged and turned away. Seeing a bucket of water nearby, he decided to practice using his powers. He needed to be ready for anything. By surreptitiously flicking his fingers and staring with varying degrees of intensity at the water, he was able to change its temperature. Kadin-Lave saw a boy not much younger than him was using the bucket of water to mop the floor. He dipped the mop back into the bucket and some water splashed his leg. The boy cried out in surprise, for the water was hot. Kadin-Lave laughed. He hadn't meant to hurt the boy, but the expression on his face as he watched the water in the bucket first turn to ice and then boil over was so comical that Kadin-Lave couldn't contain his amusement.

Leandra, too, was practicing her powers. Under her cloak, she morphed her hand into a paw and back again. She liked her power of being able to turn into any wildcat—it suited her personality.

Mica watched her and Kadin-Lave and sighed. In his brief time as a Protector, Mica had yet to find the Stoen that would unlock his power. The others, the ones who had removed the barrier blocking them from using their magic, were lucky. Fala could talk to birds and even turn into one. Nat could talk to and control plants. Leandra could turn into any wildcat. Kadin-Lave could manipulate temperatures. All Mica could do was follow his sister around and tell people when they were being foolish. Mica knew his talent was a gift in its own right, wisdom was more precious then gold, but sometimes he just wanted to be able to use a magic power of his own. Besides, being wise was tiresome. Mica rubbed his temples. For an eight-year-old, he did quite a lot of thinking.

Glancing up, he saw Fala conversing with a raven that had landed on the railing. One didn't usually see ravens at sea, but wherever Fala was, there were ravens. Crows, ravens, blackbirds would all flock to her side. They brought her news from across the oceans and carried messages to the other Protector troupes, like when they had sent word to Tristan that their Stoens had been stolen. It was strange, the theft. They had gone out for the day, searching out more Stoens, and when they had returned, the Stoens were gone. But none of the locks were broken open, and nothing else was disturbed. Whatever techniques had been used in the robbery, there was no clear way to get the Stoens back.

Mica looked back up at his sister. Genna's drawing of the seagull was finished, and she had started drawing the bucket of water that the boy used to mop the floors. With her drawing the bucket, Kadin-Lave stopped messing with the temperature of the water. He struck up a conversation with Leandra about an old Irish legend.

"No, no, no," said Leandra, "it was the *son* she kidnapped and held for ransom."

"But that wouldn't make any sense!" said Kadin-Lave. "Why would he have been out of the house for the pirates to be able to catch him?"

"That's the way the story goes," insisted Leandra. She began again with, "Grania O'Malley—" but she was cut off by the raven taking off over her head. Fala came over to sit with them. She looked pale. The other Protectors gathered around, concerned.

"What is it, Fala?" asked Kadin-Lave.

"Tristan and the others were captured by Aradia," she said, her voice shaking. The others gasped and looked at her in shock.

"How? Why?" asked Nat, who had come over to join them, as had Genna and Mica.

"We don't know. Two members escaped and are staying with Jasper," she said. "Jasper's rallying support. That's why we got the message. Lisha sent the raven with more information and a warning. They needn't have bothered. We were on our guard anyway, weren't we?" asked Fala, trying to sound cheerful. Her attempt failed miserably. The six of them looked at her fearfully. Leandra looked as if she'd just seen a ghost, and Fala had pretended it was only a bat.

❦

Up and down, up and down. The ship carrying the Protectors swayed every which way as it cut through the open ocean. Fala's troupe had retreated to the cluttered cargo hold to rest for the night. Fala listened to the sound of the waves lapping the sides of the ship. It was a soothing sound, but right now she didn't feel like sleeping. Fala lay back glumly among the barrels and boxes in the cargo hold, her raven hair spread out around her head. Desdemona's face seemed to loom over her out of the darkness, waiting for her to fall asleep. Desdemona, the mysterious woman who was all the more frightening for the secrecy surrounding her, seldom seen, leaving people behind who couldn't remember why they obeyed her. Beside her, Fala felt Aradia's gaze, her expression eerily mirroring the first's. Aradia, the evil witch of darkness, with power over shadows themselves, as malicious as she was powerful.

At least, that was how the others saw them. But Fala knew better.

When she thought of Desdemona, she saw an attention-seeking child, a bully, wanting to be adored yet adoring no one but herself. And Aradia ... trapped, frustrated no doubt, scared.

Fala rolled onto her side, trying to escape the faces, but she could still feel them behind her. Mr. Loxlyheart lurked off to the side, his countenance indistinct.

Fala turned to her other side and looked at the wall. Worried, she tried to calm herself by tracing the lines and scratches in the floor. That portion of the floor had had a fair beating. Fala looked around and realized that it wasn't just that part of the floor. Both walls and floor of the hold were scuffed up beyond repair. Fala shivered as she tried to imagine what had damaged the room so. Although the marks were likely made by boxes sliding around and being dropped heavily by less than gentle carriers, Fala couldn't help thinking that the scratches looked like wounds. One for every Protector?

Either way, it would do her no good for her to worry about it all night. Fala decided she'd ask Halie in the morning. With that thought, she drifted off to sleep.

In an abandoned toyshop, a shadow tossed and turned. It seemed that Fala wasn't the only one being deprived of a good night's sleep.

"Calm down, Rodger. She didn't mean any harm—no... no, what are you doing? Good God, man, what are you doing?"

"I'm taking vengeance, I'm avenging 's death! The child killed If you can call it a child; just look at it! skin. This isn't a child! haunt me destroying love!"

"What are you talking about? A demon? There The child is helpless! She couldn't "

"She can and she did.

"She didn't

For goodness sakes, Rodger, she's only a baby!"

"She's   , I would hardly consider that a baby," said Rodger.

"But she's a child, nonetheless. Can't you see

instant! Rodger, you're scaring me, Rodger! Can you hear me! Put the child down, do you hear me? Put the child down..."

Kiara gasped, and sat up in bed. Panting, she stood and walked to the window between the ground floor and the next floor. Kiara had taken her blanket with her, and now she pulled it close around her. Every night the dream got clearer and clearer, yet it never passed that last part. Whatever happened next, *If*, she reminded herself, *it actually did happen and it's not just a dream*, it had been blocked from Kiara's memory. *What could have happened that was so terrible I've forced myself to forget it? And what were those words I couldn't hear?* She remembered her early childhood well enough. How could she not? Kiara knew *what* had happened, but through the years the "why" and "how" had escaped her, the memories fading away. Kiara had a sinking feeling that the dream was more than just a dream. Whatever it was had really happened. And the memory was starting to return. Kiara shivered as the cold night air came through the cracks around the window. At this rate, she'd never get any sleep. A yawn escaped her. *Maybe I'll just lie down*, thought Kiara. *It was only a dream.* She walked down the stairs and back into her hammock. Pulling the blankets around her she drifted off to sleep.

"No, no don't harm the child, please, I beg of you..."

❧

A carriage splashed through a puddle outside the toyshop. Rain poured down on London, pounding on the roof of the toyshop. Inside, the air was suffused by anxiety. Jasper was pacing across the meeting room, looking angry. Emra was huddled in the corner, curled up in as tight a knot as she could. Lisha was patiently cleaning her forever-dirty fingernails with the tip of a knife. She was sitting at the table with Kiara and Lali, who were making a card tower using a very worn deck of playing cards. Quiet Halie was looking at something in a blue and purple orb hovering in front of her. Kit had gone wandering off to explore the toyshop some more.

"I don't like all this waiting," said Jasper, angrily. "Aradia could hurt Minuette—" he choked back a sob and continued pacing, "and the others. Warrick's and the rest of his troupe have been captured. Who knows who else they've got that we don't know about! Why do we have to wait for Fala to arrive? We should be going out after Aradia, or at least trying to find out where she's going, and for Heaven's sake, Kiara, put those cards away!" Jasper knocked down Kiara's card tower with a single blow from his arm. Kiara looked angry, but Lisha gave her a look that said, *worry about that later.* Jasper paced to the center of the room and glared around at everyone. "Why are you looking at me like that?" he said to Emra, who still sat shivering in the corner. At this, Lisha had enough. She stood and walked right up to Jasper. Lisha towered over him, but he looked up at her, defiantly.

"That is quite enough," said Lisha firmly, enunciating every syllable. "Can't you see that we're just as worried as you are? We are trying to help! Look around at what you've done. The poor girl is scared to death!" Lisha gestured toward Emra. "That card tower took Kiara and Lali five hours!" Kiara glared at Jasper from the floor where she was picking up the dropped cards. "And, damn it, Jasper, I'm fed up." Lali just sighed, examining the queen of hearts. "We know they're are in danger. But we've done all we can right now. There is nothing more we can do without help. We're on our guard. It's not like the Hunters can take us by surprise. But the Stoenhunters and their cronies outnumber us, because the Protector troupes are so scattered. We need backup. Be rational, Jasper. We're all anxious, too. Will you please stop harassing us because the Hunters kidnapped your girlfriend?" Jasper looked taken aback at this. He hadn't thought he'd been quite that obvious about him and Minuette.

"All right, all right, I'll calm down. But I still think there must be *something* we can do instead of just sitting here waiting," said Jasper, throwing his arms up in the air.

"But we 'ave done somethin'," said Lali for what felt like the hundredth time, "We've called for 'elp. We've warned th' others. We've got a plan."

"Then why don't we put that plan into action instead of just sitting here?" asked Jasper.

"It was *your* idea to send word to Fala," reminded Kiara irritably.

"Yes, I know, but I was hoping they could meet us somewhere, I didn't think we'd have to wait for them here." He collapsed into an old armchair next to Emra's corner with his head in his hand. Emra stood slowly. She walked over to Jasper and put her hand on his arm. He didn't stop her. Emra's heart was racing. Jasper was a good person and a great friend, but he scared her when he got like that. Then she remembered why he'd gotten so angry. Her eyes blurred. Now it was official.

"I—I'm sorry. I'm just—" Jasper looked up at Emra pleadingly, his eyes suddenly very shiny. Looking into those eyes, she could see just how much Minuette meant to him. For Emra, there would be others; she could forget Jasper. But for him, there could be no one else. If Minuette died, his heart would die with her.

Deep in the workings of an ancient castle was a dungeon. The sounds coming from it were carried by the wind over the barren landscape. All was still but for the moans and clattering chains coming from the castle and the roar of the ocean. The wind whistled and scattered a cluster of dried leaves over the empty grounds of barren land, which gave way to sheer cliffs. Waves crashed against the jagged rocks. The whole wicked place screamed silently, *death, death.* Suddenly, a light was visible through a window in one of the many towers.

"But why, my dear, must you insist on keeping headquarters here? There isn't another living thing for miles!" exclaimed Julian E. Loxlyheart.

"Then there will be no one to hear the screams. No one to come and take them away, no one to stop us now." Aradia's voice was cold and showed none of the sweetness that it once had.

"Yes, I understand that, but this place is so ...," his voice trailed off, and the wind whispered, *death, death.* He waved his hand to shoo a bat away from his head. "And where, may I ask, is Desdemona?" Aradia smiled wickedly.

"She is away on other business."

"Oh, come come, Aradia, we have a deal you know." Mr. Loxlyheart's eyebrows lifted, and he inclined his head toward her. "And I think that deal includes knowing where everyone is." Aradia's face darkened, and the twisted smile disappeared, the echo of the person she had once been vanishing.

"But I do remember, my good sir. And you would do well to remember that without my abilities you would still be in a cold prison cell with no one to blame but yourself," she said, her eyes almost closing as she floated down the stairs leading to the dungeon. The light from the flickering lantern cast long shadows on the cracked walls.

"I could have bailed myself out," he muttered, but he knew it wasn't true. When you're in jail because of your debts, you can't bail yourself out.

Reaching the bottom of the stairway, they followed along the passageway before stopping in front of a heavy wooden door with many locks on it. Aradia opened the door with the large ring of keys carried in her pale hand.

"And here we are," she said. "The new prisoners." The door swung open to reveal the battered inhabitants. Jordan, Tristan, Minuette, and another person whose face was hidden by shadow were all hanging high up on the back wall, suspended by chains and manacles binding their wrists and ankles, with only a narrow ledge to stand on. Aradia walked up to the fourth person, her eyes blazing with a strange emotion. It was clear that whatever that emotion was, it did not belong on that face. The face still held traces of kindness lingering around the eyes, accenting its old beauty—the porcelain skin, the pale lips—but this was something else. It seemed to come from deep inside Aradia, yet at the same time, it seemed almost as if there were another person inside her looking out through her eyes. It was a look so terrifying that one felt that if a look could kill, it would be that one.

The person she had walked up to also had a shackle around his or her neck, pinning the hood in place so that no features could show.

"Soon you will be dead. Your annihilation is imminent, and there is nothing and no one left who can save you now!" said Aradia.

She is insane! thought Minuette, not knowing that Mr. Loxlyheart was thinking the same thing. Aradia, who had been hovering about an inch off the ground, rose a foot in the air.

"Aradia," said Mr. Loxlyheart. "Aradia! Come back here!" The fire in Aradia's eyes subsided to a dull glow. She sank to the floor reluctantly.

"As you wish."

Aradia floated to the door with Mr. Loxlyheart on her heels. She clicked her fingers and the flickering lamp went out.

Time passed slowly aboard the ship to England, and Leandra was getting very bored. She had counted everything there was to count on the ship a hundred times over, and tried talking to every one of the crew and passengers till she knew more about each of them than she ever wanted to. Kadin-Lave was trying in vain to lighten the mood by telling jokes and riddles. The problem was, he didn't know that many.

"A man walks into a tavern, and he says to the bar tender—"

"Told it," said Leandra.

"All right, all right. Here's a really tricky one. Why did the—" said Kadin-Lave.

"Told it."

"How can you tell I've already told it if I've barely started?" he asked, exasperated.

"Because you only know one riddle that begins like that, and you've already told it to us so many times that we can all recite the answer backward," she said.

"It's not *my* fault! I don't know any jokes or riddles besides the ones I've told you!" said Kadin-Lave defensively. "I was only trying to help!" Leandra was so bored that she didn't even care.

"I suppose I'll practice shape-shifting some more. I'll probably meet you at dinner," she said rubbing her eyes. *Or maybe I'll just go back to sleep.* Until they got to England, Leandra saw no point in even getting up in the morning.

Kadin-Lave watched her leave and then looked over at Genna and Mica. Genna was lucky. Genna had been doing nothing but drawing since they got on the ship. She was the only one who didn't appear bored. Mica just followed her everywhere and hadn't complained once. But then again, he never did. Kadin-Lave watched as Fala walked over to Genna and started a conversation.

When they got on the ship, Genna had furiously scribbled down everything she could see, captivated by the change of subject matter. But after a while she began having trouble thinking of interesting things to draw. She would start drawings and lose interest halfway through, realizing that this drawing was similar to ones she had made before. Now, Genna lazily made ink blotches on the paper, not really caring that the person she had been drawing had gotten up and moved. Genna was relieved when Fala came over. They started to talk about how the journey had been going so far. Genna soon found out that everyone was slowly dying of boredom. Fala even admitted that without all the crows and other birds, she felt lonely and homesick. Genna confided that her creativity had been zapped and that her last three pictures had come out looking like an orange, a fish, and a cloud instead of a ball of string, a shoe, and a sail. This started both of them laughing. Kadin-Lave walked over to them.

"What's funny?" he asked. Genna tried to answer between fits of laughter.

"He he he—I ... drew ... ha ha ha—orange ... ha ha ha—fi—ha ha ha ha!" She fell to the ground, unable to speak.

"You and Drew had an orange fihahaha—what? Who's Drew?" The translation was so far from the truth that Genna (who was just getting up) fell back down to the ground, and Fala sagged over the side of her chair, gasping for breath. By this point, the rest of the Protectors still on deck had come to see what it was all about. Between laughs Fala said, "We ... Genna ... fish ... *snort*," Fala gasped as the snort escaped her and clapped a hand over her mouth. Everyone including Genna went quiet. They all looked at each other and instantaneously burst into laughter. The noise awoke Kaida who, dazed by sleep, forgot that he was on a ship where there were people around and waddled over to them. Mica, who was laughing but not quite as violently as the others, was the first to notice him. He quickly caught Kaida and wrapped him in the blanket the dragon was still carrying. Mica looked around. No one seemed to have seen the baby dragon. He breathed a sigh of relief and put Kaida back in the suitcase in their room.

But Mica was wrong. Someone *had* seen Kaida, and that someone rushed into a shadowed corner of the ship to send a message informing Mr. Loxlyheart that not only were Fala and her troupe coming, they had brought the last roaming dragon on earth.

❦

Mr. Loxlyheart walked up from the dungeon that held the prisoners. He'd never liked it down there. For that matter, he never liked the castle in the first place. It gave him the chills. He preferred his office back in London. It was clean and tidy, and everyone did what he said. His thoughts turned to Aradia. He was starting to really dislike her. He couldn't control her and it disconcerted him. But that would soon change. Once he had the Ultimate Power, he would make everybody in the world respect him. What he was planning was more organized and thought out than anything Aradia or Desdemona could ever do. Desdemona was so concerned with revenge that she had no plans for what she'd do after she had finished with that. And Aradia ... well. He smiled to himself. His plan went much further than one simple revenge. Plus, he was far more clever than they were. He would not implement his plan straight away, and maybe even pretend he hadn't gotten the Power just to confuse people. He would wait until the time was right, and he would be sly about it. People wouldn't even know he was using it. He could slip in some magic here and there. No one would notice. No one would know.

Plus, he had spies all over. Most of them were under fifteen. As Mr. Loxlyheart saw it, it was terribly easy to convince children that they were worthless. After he did that, they would do whatever he said. In addition, they were invisible. No one would notice a child eavesdropping. As Mr. Loxlyheart reminded himself of all these advantages, he began to feel less uncomfortable. He even began to whistle, but he stopped when he realized that some of Aradia's servants were looking at him strangely.

❦

"Put the child down, do you hear me? Put the child down." Kiara gasped for breath, hand on throat as she jerked up in bed.

Kiara stared out the window at the top of the stairs, clutching her blanket. Lisha came up behind her.

"What's the matter?" she said softly, kneeling down beside Kiara.

"It's nothing," said Kiara.

"Some nothing. You've been talking in your sleep something awful," said Lisha. "What's going on? You can tell me. I'm your friend, I can help." Kiara turned away toward the window. Lisha sighed and walked downstairs. Kiara watched as the flickering candlelight faded away, tears in her eyes. Only when the light had fully gone did she allow herself to cry.

❦

Lisha tried to be quiet as she walked down the stairs, but it was difficult with a wooden leg, and she soon gave it up. Instead of going back to bed, she walked into the kitchen and made herself a cup of tea. She sipped it pensively as she sat on a footstool, her peg leg extended in front of her. She rubbed what was left of her leg. Her missing toes itched; Lisha was having phantom pains. She could have sworn her foot was still there and hurting from lack of use. She sighed, stirring the tea. The physical pain she could deal with, but what hurt her more was seeing Kiara like that. Kiara was tough. She could handle herself, and she never showed fear. Now, seeing her helpless, it felt to Lisha like the end. Jasper was falling apart without Minuette. Emra was getting over her feelings for Jasper. Kiara was having nightmares, Halie was homesick (she cried herself to sleep most nights), Lali was bored out of her mind, and Kit was on edge from all the tension around her. As for herself ... Lisha wondered what would go wrong in her life. She was the last one to be affected by the long wait. Lisha's missing foot began to throb. *Ah*, she thought. *I almost forgot.* Her foot always hurt at times like this, when she was worried or under pressure. *I've been working too hard*, she thought. *I should take this time to relax while we wait for Fala and the others.* Lisha stood, put her empty teacup in the dirty sink, and walked out to the street.

It was nearly 6:00 a.m. Several shops had begun to open, and the sun was just beginning to shine its golden rays over the city. Lisha wandered for a while. Finally, she ended up at the river. Lisha breathed in the cool salt air and felt the wind in her hair. Oh, how she longed to be back at sea. On land, the ground was always too hard, too deep, and there were always too many people. At sea, the only other people were your crewmates and any other ships you happened to meet. The water was always fresh and clean. *Maybe I'll go and get the ship ready*, she thought.

On her way back to the toyshop, Lisha found she had just enough money to buy two cinnamon rolls. One for her and one for Kiara.

❦

"All ashore!" Genna loaded up her sketchpad, and Leandra picked up the backpack with Kaida in it. Kadin-Lave and Nat stood up, and Mica clung tightly to Genna's arm. They stepped off the ship, and Leandra, Genna, Fala, and Kadin-Lave immediately began to wobble.

"Sea legs," said Fala as Nat looked at them quizzically. His powers were with plants, so he was always more comfortable with roots below his feet. He had no trouble adjusting to being on land, but on the boat he had been much worse then the others. He barely stood up the whole trip.

Kadin-Lave asked a passerby for directions to the dock where they would meet Jasper's troupe and then proceed to Lisha's ship.

❧

Meanwhile, Jasper, Lali, Halie, Kit, Kiara, and Emra were finishing packing their bags for the long voyage ahead of them. First, to meet Cameron the Stoenmason in England's Lake District to the north of London to find out what they needed to know about the Ultimate Power. Then to Xylon, who would be able to figure out where the Hunters were making their headquarters, so the Protectors could go there and stop them forever.

Emra packed her nightdress and spare robes along with her Stoen. She looked at it. Each Stoen had a category to go with it and only unlocked a person's power if that power fell under the category. This one was an animal Stoen, which meant that it only unlocked a person's power if the power had something to do with animals, like Emra's ability to turn into a snake. Once her power had been unlocked, Emra had no need to hold onto the Stoen, but she felt strangely attached to it. It was a sandy color and fit perfectly into the palm of her hand. The sign on it was beautiful, and the sides curved together elegantly. She traced the delicate carving with her fingers and wondered how old it was. There was so much they didn't know about the Stoens. Where had the Stoens come from? Had humans always had magic? Why had the humans' powers been locked away? The Stoen gazed back at Emra, mute, answerless. Realizing that she would get no information from examining the Stoen, Emra sighed and put it back in her pack.

Lali didn't have much to pack. All she owned had been left behind at her troupe's hideout in France. The only thing she'd had with her when she left was her sister's porcelain hair ornament, which she put in her hair.

Halie, too, had left behind most of her belongings in France, but she borrowed one of Emra's robes for a change of clothing and took her small metal mirror.

Kit had a small satchel of things she had collected while she was with the Protectors. Strange things they were, too. A shiny brass doorknob, a mousetrap, a dry piece of cake, a bright blue ribbon, and a handful of buttons, all of which she tied up in a handkerchief and stuffed into her pocket.

Jasper sat, staring at a picture in a golden locket. Minuette smiled up at him from inside. He sighed. Jasper regretted how irrational he had been lately. He had been ready to put the others in danger to try to rescue her. *What they must think of me now. I've been acting like a child. I'm certainly not fit to lead this troupe. A true leader ought to treat everyone the same. I certainly haven't been doing that ... I think about her all the time. A true leader wouldn't behave as if she were more important than the other Protectors. A true leader shouldn't ... fall ... in love.* As soon as he thought it, he knew it was too late to take it back. It had been too late for a long time now. He didn't *want* to take it back. He closed his eyes tightly, fighting the flood of emotions threatening to overwhelm him. Panic, anxiety, and longing. *If I could just see her one more time ....* There was no use denying it anymore. He loved Minuette more than anything, and he knew that the feeling would never go away. The thought of something bad happening to her was too much to bear. She was sweetness and life and compassion, and his love for her was a part of him now. She was a part of him now. *But that doesn't mean that there's nothing else in the world that I care about. My friends ... my troupe ... my mission...* If the mission to stop anyone from getting the Ultimate Power failed, how would that change the world? Would there even be a world? At least, one worth living in? *Everything that I care about is riding on this. We must not fail.* Suddenly, his determination to save the world matched his determination to save Minuette. Could the two go together? Could he be in love and still be a leader?

In the next room over, Kiara was going through her things to decide what to bring. She didn't have much by way of belongings. She dug through the drawers. A change of clothes, an extra sock, a pistol ... a pistol? She held it up. What was that doing in there? Suddenly, a memory came back to her: Reaching up to the top of the tall cabinet, sliding the weapon off it. She remembered the determination she had felt, the urgency. She remembered holding the gun, large and heavy in her small hands. And here it was again, lying just the same way in her hands, smaller and lighter than in her memory. She blew on it, scattering dust over the room. *Rodger Thornton,* she read to herself. The name stirred something in her memories. *Rodger ... that was the name in my dream! But who is it? And why do I have his pistol?*

"Kiara?" Kiara jumped. Jasper was standing in the doorway. "It's time to leave." Kiara quickly hid the pistol in her bag and hurried after Jasper and the others.

❦

Jasper and his troupe were assembled at the docks. Fala and the rest of the Irish troupe had just gotten off the boat. They were all congregated in front of the *Compass Rose*. Introductions were made as all the Protectors greeted each other and introduced themselves.

Genna, the artist from the Irish troupe, and Kiara started up a conversation about dreams. Genna said that when she had a bad dream, she would sit down and draw everything she could remember to assure herself that it was no more substantial than the drawing. Genna showed Kiara some of her dream drawings and explained the stories behind them.

"In this one, I dreamt that I couldn't draw anymore. When I tried to draw, the drawing just disappeared or turned into something else. And in this one, I dreamt that my little brother, Mica, turned into a brain in a jar. He's so smart, you know. You'll never guess what he brought with him. The *Encyclopedia Britannica*! All three volumes!" Genna shook her head in wonder. Turning back to Kiara, she asked, "What about you? What kinds of dreams do you have?"

At this, Kiara's eyes glazed over. She was about to explain her recurring nightmare to Genna when a nearby person dropped a suitcase and brought her to her senses. There was no way she was about to tell an almost stranger about the nightmare. Kiara looked away from Genna. "I don't remember my dreams."

Emra saw Leandra, the fiery-haired Irish Protector, and struck up a conversation. Emra mentioned how she had unlocked her power, and soon they discovered that both of them had powers that let them transform into animals. This provided common ground and much material for conversation, as neither of them had met many other shape shifters.

"The most annoying part is getting rid of the tail," said Leandra. "Sometimes I walk around for days with it on." Emra shook her head.

"Not me. But sometimes I do find myself changing in my sleep. I wake up and my arms are gone." Leandra laughed.

"Yes, it took me awhile to get used to that, too, but because I turn into wildcats, I'm not so conscious of shifting in my sleep, and sometimes I don't notice until I look in a mirror."

Nat, the assistant leader from the Irish troupe, was talking to Jasper about boats. They found that neither one of them enjoyed sailing because they both got motion sick, though it was worse for Nat because of his powers concerning plants.

Kadin-Lave, the Irish Protector who had control over temperatures, and Lali, the English girl with the nose ring from the French troupe, were arguing about the motives behind some criminal in the news. Kadin-Lave was sure that he was in it only for the money, but Lali thought that there was more to it. Halie listened to them argue.

Kit stood back, shy around all the newcomers.

"I's watchin' the packs," she had said to Jasper when he looked at her questioningly. If the truth were told, Kit was a little nervous about traveling overseas, even though they were staying in England and just traveling up to the Lake District. She'd never even left London, let alone been on a ship! She sat down and leaned on the pile of bags.

A small head poked out from a pack near where Leandra was standing.

"*Pssst! Over here!*" it whispered. Kit was about to scream, but Kaida waved his hands urgently, telling her to be quiet. "*Shh! I'm not here,*" he said and ducked back in the pack as some strangers walked by. Once they had gone, Kaida poked his head out again. The young dragon was about the size of a housecat, with rust-colored scales that faded from red to orange. His wings were folded on his back. Kaida could fly if he preferred rather than walk or climb, but he had been given strict orders not to, as it would make him even more conspicuous.

"Hi. I'm Kaida. Resident dragon. And you are?"

"Kitisha. Kitisha Taylor, but my friends call me Kit," said Kit.

"Nice to meet you, Kit. I was wondering, since you're standing off alone, whether you needed someone to talk to, because if so, I think we can help each other out," said Kaida.

"An' 'ow would that be 'xactly?" asked Kit suspiciously.

"You need someone to talk to, and I need someone to talk to. I'll die if I have to make another journey without speaking to anyone," said Kaida.

"So what do I 'ave t' do?" asked Kit.

"You see this pack I'm sitting in?"

"Uh-huh."

"Well I need to be in a pack so no one will see me. All you have to do is find some way to carry me around on your back so no one can see me and we can keep each other company. What do you say?" asked Kaida. In answer, Kit held out her small handkerchief/ pouch.

"Think you could fit in here?" asked Kit.

"Maybe," said Kaida doubtfully. "Tell ya what. How about I stay under the back of your dress, and you tie that handkerchief around your neck to cover the lump and to hide my head." They tried it. Because Kit's clothes were baggy and loose on her, Kaida had no trouble fitting in the back of Kit's dress. Kit emptied the handkerchief into her pockets and tied it around her neck. The handkerchief proved handy and was just able to cover Kaida's head so they could still converse. Fala happened to glance their way.

"Nice job, Kaida," said Fala, always keeping an eye on her troupe members. "I see you've found a new place to hide." Looking at Kit, she said, "Thanks for keeping an eye on him, um—"

"Kit," said Kit.

"Just in time, too," whispered Kaida. The Protectors were just getting ready to start boarding the ship. The ship was sleek and elegant with two masts and what must have been miles of rigging. Crewmembers bustled around deck or climbed the masts and shrouds, readying to make way. Painted along the side was the name of the ship, the *Compass*

Rose. At the bow, there was a figurehead of a woman dressed in seafarer's clothing, one arm outstretched toward the horizon. Dangling from her outstretched hand by a chain was a compass.

Kit looked at the figurehead's face. She was reminded of someone, though she couldn't quite think who. She peered closer.

"Oh," Kit said as the realization hit her. She remembered Lisha telling her that the ship had been named partly after Lisha's mother. What Lisha hadn't said was how much she and her mother looked alike.

As if on queue, Lisha appeared atop the gangplank in her captain's uniform, the old, beat-up, blue coat blown about by the wind off the sea, the sun glittering off brass buttons, a fancy, feathered, official-looking hat on her head, to welcome the Protectors to her ship. She put on a large, almost joking voice as she greeted them.

"Welcome, welcome, one and all, to the *Compass Rose*. I shall be your captain on this fine day on the Thames. May I present several important members of my crew? The one here is Jasmine, my first mate." Jasmine was beautiful, but not in any conventional way. She was poised and comfortable. She blended in so well with the ship and the sparkling water in the background that it was easy to imagine her simply vanishing if she ventured on land. Her skin was the color of cinnamon and she had dark, almond-shaped eyes with a kind look about them. "This is Isaac, our ship's surgeon," continued Lisha. Isaac was rather tall and formal looking. When he was named, he dropped the suitcase he was lifting. "And Hilda, our lovely new cook." She looked up. Her orange curls of hair were almost entirely hidden beneath a huge kerchief. "This here is Oliver, our boatswain," Oliver grunted. He was rather tall, though not as tall as Isaac, with a flat face and black hair. "And this is Quito, our new cabin boy." A small boy glared at them from the shadows where he was mopping the floor. Mica stared. He looked somehow familiar.

Lisha stopped her introductions and looked down at the crowd, surprised. "Nat?" asked Lisha, staring at the Irish troupe's plant-loving second in command. Everyone looked at him. Lisha stepped forward and walked toward him. "Nat, is it really you?" He nodded, speechless. "Quito?" she said to the new cabin boy, not looking at him. "Please show the Protectors to their sleeping quarters." Her voice shook as she spoke. Quito nodded and motioned for the Protectors to follow him. They boarded the ship, looking back at Nat and Lisha curiously. When the rest of the Protectors had gone, Lisha walked up to Nat and embraced him. "Nat, I've missed you so much." He hugged her back.

"Lisha ... I thought I'd never see you again!"

Lisha held him back to look at him. "Look at you, you strapping young man," she said teasingly, clapping him on the arm. "What happened?" He cuffed her over the head. "Ow!" she said, jokingly. He laughed.

"You haven't changed a bit," he said. She smiled. "And look at you, Captain!" he added, mocking a bow.

"Oh, shut it. They'll be none of that, if you please." They stood there for a moment. He coughed, exaggeratedly. "Oh, how rude of me, welcome *back* to the *Compass Rose*. Please make yourself at home. Once you're settled, meet me in my cabin. We have a lot of catching up to do."

Jasmine, the first mate of the Compass Rose, walked across the deck toward Lisha's cabin, her heart beating loudly. Part of her wanted to turn on the spot and run away, and another part wanted to rush forward as quickly as she could. Somehow she managed to continue on at a reasonable pace, placing one foot in front of the other. Far too soon, yet not nearly soon enough, she found herself standing outside the door to the captain's cabin. Her heart raced even faster, and she found herself rooted to the spot, neither able to turn away nor to enter. Dread mixed with anticipation. Slowly, she raised one shaking hand and rapped quickly on the weathered wood.

"Come in," came Lisha's voice from inside. Jasmine obeyed.

Lisha was seated at her father's old desk, the top of it littered with papers and writing implements. Light streamed in through the windows, making the room bright and comfortable. Jasmine shied away from the comfort, feeling out of place.

Lisha looked up from the papers. A smile broke across her face, and she stood to greet her old friend.

"Jaz," she said warmly, coming over to her. Before Jasmine could stop her, Lisha had pulled her into a hug. "I've missed you," said Lisha, still holding onto her. Jasmine stood rigid in Lisha's arms, her shoulders tense. Lisha pulled away, concerned. "Jasmine? What's wrong?" Jasmine was shaking. She shouldn't have come. She knew it was a mistake.

Swallowing, she said, trying to sound cheerful, "Nothing. Nothing's wrong. It—it's good to see you too, L—Captain." Jasmine bit her tongue. Lisha was still looking at her, concern in her eyes. Jasmine forced a smile. "You ... sent for me?" Lisha nodded, sensing Jasmine's need for a change of subject.

"Yes, I did. We need to start making plans, plot out our course."

"Right," said Jasmine. Lisha motioned her over to the desk, pulling up a chair for her. Jasmine sat while Lisha unrolled a map.

Jasmine found comfort in the old routine. It felt good to be here, to be doing something. They sat together and discussed the voyage, just as they had done so many times before. It was wonderfully familiar and calming, and as they talked, Jasmine felt her worry ease slightly, as if Lisha's very presence banished all bad feelings. Even after they had finished the calculations and decisions that needed to be made, neither one displayed any inclination to conclude the meeting. They talked on, as old friends will do, hardly keeping track of the time, until Lisha absent-mindedly checked the clock.

"Well, would you look at that!" she said, gesturing to the clock. "I've kept you from your work for far too long." They stood together. For a moment, they just looked at each other, Lisha's eyes searching, Jasmine's pleading. Lisha sighed slightly, as if to say, "Fine, you win for now." Jasmine nodded gratefully. As she turned to go, Lisha hugged her again. This time, Jasmine didn't resist. The hug said that Lisha was there if Jasmine ever wanted to talk about what was bothering her. Even though Jasmine knew that she wouldn't take the offer, she appreciated it nonetheless.

Lisha let go, and Jasmine went to the door.

"Thank you, Captain," said Jasmine, turning back to her.

"Of course," said Lisha. "Now, off with you!"

Jasmine's good mood lasted until she got out of the door. As soon as she left the comfort of the cabin, a dark cloud of guilt and shame settled over her.

I really am a horrible person, she thought as she set off to work.

❦

The door to Lisha's cabin opened again and in walked Nat, glancing worriedly over his shoulder.

"Nat," said Lisha welcomingly, making him turn his head. He had a preoccupied expression.

"Hello, Lisha. Is Jasmine all right? I just passed her on the way in, and she looked like she'd just received a death sentence."

Lisha sighed, and her whole body sighed with her, drooping like a sail that's lost its wind.

"I don't know," said Lisha dejectedly. "She won't tell me what's wrong." There was silence for a moment. Then Lisha looked up, straightening herself briskly as if shaking off a heavy cloak. When she spoke again, her voice was lighter, happier. "Well then. Come over here, Nat, and tell me what's happened since I saw you. Tell me everything."

Chains clanged. People screamed. The wind whistled through the ancient castle.

"*D'accord*, bad idea," said Tristan after the captured French troupe's latest escape plan, pulling the chains off the wall by sheer force, failed miserably. "Why not try smashing them against the wall?"

Jordan tested, slamming his manacled wrist repeatedly against the cold stone wall, making horrible clanging noises. Minuette flinched every time he hit the wall, as if feeling the pain herself.

"No good," said Jordon finally, panting from the expended effort. "The chains are too thick."

Minuette hung her head. Misery welled up inside her, and she screwed up her face, pressing her eyes tightly closed, trying to forestall despair. A single sob escaped her, and the sound echoed through the dungeon.

"Do not worry, Minuette. We will get out of here somehow," said Tristan gently.

"I just feel so helpless," said Minuette. "And—and I am afraid." Tristan opened her mouth to say something, but Minuette shook her head. "Not for myself. For the others. Just imagining if the Hunters did this to us, what if," she let out a sob again, unable to stop herself, "what if they went after the others, too, and what if ... what if they hurt—" she broke off, unable to finish. Minuette looked down at the locket that was hanging around her neck, swinging slowly back and forth. She drew a shaky breath, trying to regain her composure, as if the sight of the locket gave her strength. Understanding crossed Tristan's face.

"You really love him, don't you?" Tristan asked. Minuette looked up, surprised.

"Yes ... yes, I do," she said, calm certainty in her voice. She took a deep breath. As she exhaled, some of the pain seemed to go away. A strange sort of peace settled over her. "I am in love," she whispered, more to herself than to anyone else. It felt good to say it out loud. Anything to break that silence. Anything that is, except for clinking chains or the whistling wind. "I am in love with Jasper. Oh, I hope he is safe."

"I hope so, too."

Startled, they all turned their heads to look at the fourth prisoner. They had all but forgotten that there was someone else there.

"You're lucky. You have someone out there thinking about you. I don't have anyone. I'm all alone." She (for it was a she) lifted her hooded head and looked out into the distance. "My only close family member doesn't care about me."

"That is so sad," said Minuette. They both looked out the window. Then Minuette said, "My name is Minuette Geri. What is your name?"

"Laramie. Just Laramie."

❦

"She killed her! She killed her! I'll rip her arms off! I'll tear her hair out! I'll—"

"Calm down, Rodger. She didn't mean any harm—no ... no, what are you doing? Rodger, answer me, Rodger, what are you doing?"

"I'm taking vengeance,

demon! Sent to haunt me after destroying my life and my love!"

"What are you talking about? A demon? There is nothing wrong with the child. The child is helpless! She couldn't kill anyone!"

"She can and she did.

"She didn't k
auses! For goodness sakes, Rodger, she's only a baby!"

"She's three years old. I would hardly consider that a baby."

"But she's a child, nonetheless. Can't you see that you are

she

would have been perfectly FINE!"

"*What do you mean, she would have been perfectly fine? Calm down, Rodger, it's not the child's fault—what are you doing? Good God, man, what are you doing! Stop it! Stop it this instant! Rodger, you're scaring me, Rodger! Can you hear me! Put the child down, do you hear me? Put the child down.*"

A hand touched Kiara's shoulder. She turned. Nat kneeled beside her.

"I heard you get up. Is everything all right?"

"I just—" Kiara, about to lie, looked up into his eyes. They were green and full of concern. They mirrored the ocean stretching for miles in the darkness. She stared. He actually cared.

"I had a bad dream," she said without thinking. His face filled with understanding.

"Do you want to talk about it?"

"What?" said Kiara. She looked at him long and hard. He didn't seem to be making fun of her. She sighed.

"My mother died when I was three years old. I never really knew my father. He spent that whole time away from home, and whatever time he did spent home was with her. She was sick all the time that I knew her. She did her best to raise me. Didn't really get a chance, did she?" said Kiara, attempting a joke.

The laugh died in her throat, and she looked away. "After she died, I went to live with my father's friend, Garron. He was a soldier, and a year or two later, he was called to fight in India. He never came back—" Kiara choked back a sob. "I still don't know much about my father. I don't even remember his name." Tears welled up in Kiara's eyes. She blinked them away forcefully. *No. I can't cry. Not in front of him.* He sat down next to her.

"I know what that's like. My mother died when I was very young, too. And my father—I don't really know what happened to him." Kiara looked at him.

"I'm sorry," she said.

"No, don't be. You've probably had a harder time than I have. You must be pretty strong to have survived that." Her cheeks grew hot. She looked away. "Well, it certainly is a beautiful night," he said, leaning toward her ever so slightly. She leaned sideways until they were almost touching.

"It certainly is."

❦

Emra's eyes squinted against the light. A bell was ringing from somewhere above her. Morning. She sat up, rubbing the sleep from her eyes. Around her, the others were stretching and dressing.

Breakfast was uninteresting. Lisha and the rest of the crew were already awake and busy at work tending the ship. Oliver and Lisha were arguing loudly, shouting across the ship. Jasmine was standing beside Lisha, looking at a map in her hands, confused.

"We're going north," Lisha was saying. "We need to be going south!"

"We *are* going south!" Oliver yelled back. "Been on land so long you've forgot how to read the stars?"

"Been in the taverns so long you've forgot how to read a compass?" she shouted back.

Emra leaned against the railing, watching the crew work as she listened to the Protectors' conversations. When she let her guard drop, Emra found her gaze repeatedly shifted to Jasper. Each time, she'd snap to attention and angrily look away. *No, he's not for you. He loves Minuette. You have no right to be looking at him like that.* Her eyes went to him again. She turned away furiously, heart thumping, and pressed her shaking hands against the top of a barrel as if trying to push the pain away. She drew a deep, shuddering breath and let it out slowly. It was getting harder to ignore her feelings for him. But it had to stop. Letting it go on this long was an exercise in futility. It was done. It was finished. Jasper was never going to be hers. She knew that. She knew that he would never know the way that she felt. He must never know. It would only cause him pain, and that was the last thing Emra wanted. She wanted him to be happy. The best thing for both of them would be for her to get over her feelings, and the sooner the better. But try as she might, nothing had worked. Emra looked around desperately. There must be some way to keep her mind occupied and away from Jasper.

Isaac, the ship's surgeon, passed into her line of vision, pausing to say something to Jasmine. Emra watched him for a moment, tilting her head thoughtfully, emotions still buzzing inside her. He was rather ... not handsome, perhaps, but there was something about his appearance, an almost endearing air of innocence about him. He was tall and thin with neat blond hair and lopsided glasses. He walked with his shoulders stooped slightly, as if bending over a desk. His face had a permanently puzzled look, and without realizing it, Emra found herself smiling slightly. Isaac nodded to Jasmine and started off across the deck, but before he could get more than a few feet, he tripped over a coil of rope and yelped, stumbling back into the side of the ship. He straightened and shook himself. *He's so clumsy!* thought Emra, amused. Suddenly, she found herself giggling. Emra stopped, startled. Slowly an idea formed in her mind. Carefully, deliberately, she mustered all her pent-up emotions and redirected them. Forcefully, she pushed Jasper from her head and shoved Isaac into his place. Isaac's face slid into her mind and did not disappear. She held onto it, adamant. She smiled wickedly to herself. Her eyes followed him as he walked across the deck.

"And some fool bloody well better keep that sail in place!" yelled Oliver. "On deck! What do you think you're doing, wandering around like that?" he yelled as Isaac almost collided with a sailor rushing past and swinging up onto the mast. "Make yourself useful!" yelled Oliver, throwing Isaac a coiled line attached to the topsail. He struggled to pull the sail back in place with the line, but it kept slipping through his fingers. Emra ran up and grabbed it for him.

"Need some help?" she asked. He nodded gratefully. Emra slid in front of him, highly aware of the closeness. She pulled the line tight, slightly changing the angle of the sail, and tied it around the peg on the mast.

"Thanks," he said.

"Don't mention it!" replied Emra cheerfully. *Brown eyes,* she noted deliberately, looking up into his face. They looked at each other awkwardly for a few seconds.

"Uh, you seem to have some skill with ropes, miss, uh ... ?"

"Emra," she prompted.

"Emra. Have you much experience with ships?" he asked. She shook her head.

"Not so far as I can remember," said Emra. It was mostly true. She'd never really been on a ship before, but she'd met plenty of sailors and heard them talk enough to understand the basic workings. "I used to help my family with the farm, and it was one of my jobs to sort out the ropes. When I came to London, I met Lisha, and she taught me some stronger knots." He raised his eyebrows, impressed.

"Indeed," he said. She nodded.

"I barely even know how to swim." That was a lie, and an impulsive, stupid one at that. She could swim in human or snake form, but in case she fell overboard "accidentally," Emra thought mischievously, she wanted Isaac to come and rescue her. He was, after all, ship surgeon.

"How long have you been working on a ship?" she asked.

"Oh, I'd say about—" But before he could finish, Lisha called out, "Oliver! Who do you think you are, ordering my surgeon around the ship? He doesn't know the halyard from the tack! Isaac, come back over here, we've got a question." He bid Emra farewell and went off to help. Emra's heart glowed with triumph as she watched Isaac's retreating form. *I did it.* She suppressed the urge to let out a cheer. *I did it!* No longer would she hopelessly pine over Jasper. All her thoughts had turned to Isaac.

❧

That night, everyone from the three Protector troupes on board and the crewmembers not needed to run the ship were lying in their beds talking. They decided to take turns telling each other stories.

The others quieted down and listened as Kiara started it off. "First things first," she said, flipping onto her front so she was facing Nat. A smile played at the corners of her mouth as she pointed a finger at him accusatorily. "You never explained what the deal was with you and Lisha on the gangplank. When we boarded the ship, she recognized you. I mean, she knows everyone, but that was something different. How did you know each other?"

"That's a fair question," agreed Nat, smiling lopsidedly back at her, "though a better question isn't how we know each other but how we were separated."

"So answer both. Either way, *talk.*"

"All right," said Nat. "Well, Lisha and I have known each other almost all of our lives. We grew up together. My father worked for her father, back when her father was captain. We didn't want to separate any families, so we all lived together on the ship."

Kiara looked at him incredulously.

"You? Grow up on a ship? But you get so seasick you can hardly walk a straight line!"

"Aye," Nat laughed, "I remember Lisha used to tease me about my seasickness. It's gotten worse not being on a boat for so long. I'll have to get used to it again." He paused, glancing at the tilting floorboards and grimaced deliberately, prompting laughs from the listeners. He grinned, and Kiara motioned for him to go on. "There was a chest kept in the captain's quarters, which was always locked," he said, gesturing with his hands as if seeing the scene. "One day, there was some sort of commotion. The captain left his cabin in a hurry to see what the fuss was about. People were shouting, and Lisha found me. Neither of us could understand what they were saying. But instead of finding out, we noticed that the captain had left the door to his cabin open. What did I do? Stupid, adventurous boy I was, I snuck in with Lisha. She kept watch while I looked around. Everything looked the same, but the chest was open. Inside, I found several peculiar stones with strange markings on them."

"Stoens!" exclaimed Emra, hopping forward in excitement. Nat nodded.

"Exactly, but at the time, we didn't know about the powers, so we had no idea what they were. I picked one up. Though I didn't realize it yet, I'd picked the particular Stoen that unlocked my power."

"Ha!" laughed Lali. "Nice work." She propped herself up on her elbows and leaned her head against one hand. "So wot was i'? Wot power did y' get?"

Nat's troupe leader, Fala, answered for him. "Talking to and controlling plants," she said quietly. "Right, Nat?" The others were startled to hear her speak; Fala had been so still that her slight form had blended in with the shadows.

"Aye," said Nat in agreement. "I'd always liked plants," he explained. "I kept a small garden on the ship. I have this theory that a person's power isn't just arbitrary; it has something to do with their character. We're born with the powers, even if we can't use them yet, and no two powers are exactly the same, just like no two people are exactly the same." He looked around at the Protectors' faces, and they looked back. After a moment, he glanced at Kiara. "Where was I?" he asked, slightly disoriented.

"You picked up the Stoen," she said, prompting him.

"Right. It grew hot in my hands and spread a sharp, tingling sensation up my arms and through my whole body. It was unpleasant, but I couldn't let go. Finally, it finished and my limbs were free. I fell to the ground. Lisha called out to me, 'Nat? Nat! Are you all right?' and came over. She propped me up against the desk. There were footsteps, and more shouting. I said, 'Someone's coming,'" He groaned for effect. "Lisha stood, letting me drop to the floor, hearing the footsteps as well. She looked around, thinking quickly. She grabbed me by the arms and dragged me into the corner and threw a blanket over me. I watched through the cloth as she looked around franticly and then hid in the closet.

"The door to the cabin opened," continued Nat. "The captain walked in just as the closet door closed. He saw the movement, as well as the chest still wide open and the Stoen I had dropped on the floor. His features hardened, and he flung the closet door open. Lisha fell out. He bellowed, 'What are you doing in here? Looking through my belongings like a common thief! You will be punished for this!'" said Nat, imitating a deep, gravelly voice. "Her father dragged her out of the cabin. He came back, put away the Stoen, and locked the chest. He grabbed a pistol, probably the reason he came into the cabin in the first place, and headed for the door. On his way out, he spotted the blanket on the floor. But the fight outside was getting fiercer. I didn't know it, but we were being attacked by pirates."

There was a collective intake of breath from the listeners. Nat nodded and went on.

"As soon as he closed the door, I stood. I was still shaken from the experience of unlocking my power, and I still didn't understand what had happened. I opened the cabin door and a pirate's sword slashed across my forehead. I stumbled around, dizzy with pain. I fell to the ground once again. Lisha ran past me, swiping a dagger at a pirate chasing behind her. She tripped him with her peg leg and yelped as another pirate grabbed her and tried to throw her overboard. I was terrified," remembered Nat. "I thought she was dead for sure. I was furious, but there was nothing I could do. Or so I thought. A nearby sack of seeds tipped over in the tussle, and several of them sprouted and curled their roots and vines around the pirate holding Lisha. He dropped her, and she looked at me in gratitude before jumping back into the fight. Somehow she must have known that it was me controlling the plants, even though I myself didn't even know it."

"Wait," said Kit, holding up her small hands. "You c'n do magic without meanin' to?"

"Of course," said Leandra from nearby, tossing her long hair. In that moment, she looked remarkably like the wildcats she could change into. "It's the way lots of people find out about the powers."

"Aye," said Nat. "It was how I found out, more or less. The plants saved Lisha because I wanted her to be saved. Even without meaning to, I was using my power. Anyway, after that, I blacked out. When I came round, I was bound and gagged on the pirates' ship. That's when I truly discovered my power. There was a sack of dried corn in the same room as I was. Several of the plants started to grow and saw at my ropes. When that didn't work, they tried untying the ropes. Soon, I realized that I was the one doing it, controlling the plants. I grew a stalk from one of the corncobs and used it to lift a knife over to me and cut myself free. The door was open, and I flung it wide before stepping out into the sun on the deck of the ship. Unfortunately, there were pirates everywhere. There was a fight, and I ended up chained to the mast. The pirate captain looked at me. He sized me up and, deciding I wasn't a threat, declared that I was to be their new cabin boy.

"That position only lasted several weeks," Nat continued. "At the first port we visited, I ran away. I had no money, so I had to steal to eat. One time, when I was robbing a street cart, a girl saw me and yelled for me to stop." He nodded to Leandra, and she grinned proudly. "I ran. It was right on the edge of town, and I went straight for the safety of the woods. Once there, I used the trees to block the way behind me. But just when I thought I'd lost her, I heard something fast running near me. Then suddenly, a lioness burst through the branches. Too desperate to be surprised, I reacted. I was now quite adapt at using my powers and summoned a nearby bush to strangle her. The lioness broke right through the plant, but it gave me time to escape. When that plant snapped I felt the pain as if it was my own arm being cut off. The lioness pursued me in chase. When I looked back, I noticed for the first time that she was wearing *clothes*. But I had more pressing things to worry about. Before I could give any thought to what that might mean, the lioness transformed into a cheetah. She caught up with me in no time, knocked me over, and a second later she was a leopard. The leopard pinned me to the ground and said, 'That's the last time you steal from my family's shop!' She raised her paw, aiming to kill me."

"How did you escape?" asked Emra. Nat leaned forward, his eyes bright, feeding the anticipation.

"First I cried out 'Wait! I didn't mean any harm. I'm just hungry!' then I moaned to myself, 'I wish Lisha was here.' Well, I got lucky. Those were the magic words that saved my life. Even miles away, Lisha was still protecting me, because as soon as I mentioned her, the leopard turned back into the girl from the shop."

At Nat's gesture, all eyes turned to Leandra, who grinned again.

"That's right," she said. "I'd had my powers for some time by then, and so I acted as a guard for my family shop. I caught this little thief red-handed." She caught Nat in a headlock and ruffled his hair roughly. He called out in surprise and flailed his arms wildly, and the other listeners broke out in laugher and exclamations until she let him go. She settled back into her seat, still laughing. When the others had quieted down, she said, "But I was so surprised to hear him mention Lisha that I stopped attacking him, and asked, 'What?' and just stood there, staring at him."

"Aye," said Nat. "I handed you the bread. You asked me, 'What did you say?' and I said, 'I'm sorry,' completely confused. You noticed then that I was holding out the bread—"

"And I took it," cut in Leandra. "And I asked how you knew Lisha."

"That must have surprised you," said Emra to Nat. Kiara gave her a disparaging look.

"Emra," she said, "if he wasn't surprised to find himself attacked by a lioness while stealing a loaf of bread, and if he wasn't surprised that the lioness could change into other wildcats, and that it wore clothes, *and* spoke English, *and* turned into a girl, why should he be surprised if the girl happened to know his long-lost childhood friend?"

That was too much for the listeners, and they erupted into laughter again. Kiara, an island of dry calm amid a roaring sea of mirth, shrugged in pretend apology at Emra as if she had just informed the younger girl of an unpleasant truth.

Eventually, Emra sat up again and composed herself with difficulty. As the laughter died down around them, she turned to Leandra and asked, "Just for my own curiosity, then, how *did* you know Lisha?"

"*Ev'ryone* knows Lisha," said Lali, sitting up as well, hand still clutching her side.

"Partly because she's been everywhere. Her family used to come trade at the market where we lived," said Leandra, brushing her hair out of her face.

"Anyway," said Nat, "may I continue?" There were murmurs of ascent and Leandra said, "Be my guest." He bowed his head in gratitude and went on with the story.

"So, after it seemed apparent that Leandra wasn't planning on killing me, I tried to get out of there as fast as I could. She wasn't having that, though. So, I told her that I was a friend of Lisha's and explained what had happened, told her the whole story, how Lisha was one of my best friends, how I'd been captured by the pirates and barely escaped and been forced to steal to survive. I was beginning to come back to my senses, so I asked her if she had any news of Lisha. I thought for the first time that maybe I might have a chance at getting home. But no, she hadn't seen Lisha in a couple of years, wasn't it?" he asked, glancing over at Leandra. She nodded. Nat continued, "So, I said that, if she didn't mind, I should be on my way. But she stopped me and said, 'Wait! Where are you staying?' I told her, 'Nowhere, really,' and asked, 'Why?' and then she ... pretty much ... invited me ... to stay with her," he said, as if he knew how odd that must sound. The others who hadn't heard the story before looked at him slightly incredulously. He shrugged. "She just said, 'Well, if you're not staying anywhere ... and you need food ... we have extra food, and Mother's been wanting— an assistant ... so if you'd like to—stay with us...'."

"Just like that?" asked Kiara skeptically.

"I was a bit surprised, too. I was too used to misfortune by then to be taken aback by more disasters, but good fortune really struck me, because I wasn't expecting it. I asked her, 'You'd do that? For me?' She said that she was a friend of Lisha's, too, and that she believed my story. She said, 'It's a mean place, the world. But you gotta get through it somehow. You gotta do what you can to survive. Find a place where you can belong, and people you belong with, and stick together with them.' No one had said anything so nice to me in a long time ... so hopeful. So true. At first I didn't trust it. I looked at her sideways. Why was she taking me in? Was it because I knew Lisha? You know how it works with that—my friend's friend ... you know how it goes. Or maybe she took me in because she realized the bush and trees had been my doing, that I could use magic, too. Maybe she was moved by my heart-wrenching tale." He said this last in an exaggeratedly dramatic way, provoking more smiles from the audience. He shrugged again. "Maybe because of my handsome green-tinted hair." Leandra chucked an empty mug at him from across the room. It bounced of his head with a loud clunk, and he laughed, rubbing the spot. "Just kidding. Anyway, I finally said, 'all right,' and she smiled and said, 'C'mon, let's go then!'" Nat made a beckoning gesture.

"So I moved in with Leandra and her family for a while," he continued. "Her father was off at sea somewhere. I still don't know what happened to my father. I asked Lisha what she knew, and all she could tell me was that he quit his job right after I was captured, and no one's heard from him since." Nat looked down at the floorboards sadly.

He looked up again after a moment, breaking the gloomy silence. "Anyway, Leandra introduced me to Fala and the others, and they explained to me about Stoens and such. With the approval of the Drifters, I joined their troupe of Protectors. Then as fate had it, we ended up here, back where it started. Back home."

Kiara and the other Protectors who'd been listening stared dreamily off into the distance for a few minutes in silence, still caught up in the story. Kit had been completely engrossed, but not too distracted to fail to appreciate Nat's dramatic storytelling ability. *I wish I could do that,* she thought. Then Emra spoke.

"Lali? You and the other Protectors in your troupe knew Lisha, didn't you?" asked Emra.

"Aye, that we did," said Lali.

"How did you meet her?" Lali gave no direct answer, but instead began to tell the story.

"Back in France, where we lived, there'd been a revolution. Th' new gov'ment was doin' bad things, an' we wanted out. I' was a dangerous time. We 'eard of a safe place we could go t' wait i' out, an' we found an abandoned boat tha' we thought we could use t' get there. All seemed well 'nough, 'til we got hit by th' mother o' all storms. It was a storm t' end all storms," Lali said dramatically. "Our tiny boat was tossed to an' fro across th' wide ocean. We should'a known better then t' take an ancient boat wot was left abandoned on th' shore, but we was desperate, an' we didn't think it through. 'Cause of tha', our voyage was about t' come t' an abrupt end. Th' boat was creakin'. Th' wind was 'owlin' in our ears, an' th' rain was poundin' against us. Wind whipped our 'air as we 'eld on fer dear life. Minuette was down on th' deck, strainin' with th 'alyard."

At the mention of Minuette's name, Jasper's heart started to beat hard against his chest, as if trying to break through his ribs. The sound of it was so loud in his ears that he was sure the others could hear it. But remarkably, no one commented, and the story continued.

"Minuette called out, 'I don't think we can 'old on much longer!'" said Lali, trying to imitate Minuette's musical voice. "Halie was up on one o' the shrouds, hangin' on as 'ard as she could, an' down below, Jasper an' Jordan were haulin' on a line. But the ship tipped an' the tack snapped. The line shot across the deck faster than you could say 'Quick, grab it!'" Lali grabbed for an imaginary rope. "Jordan yelled, 'Quick, grab it!' an' Jasper dove after it, catching it up and sliding across the wet deck, still holdin' on." Lali skated a hand across an imaginary deck. "But i' was no use," she said ominously. "The front sail turned over our 'eads, and with it th' ship cut quick t' th' left, tilting almost over on its side. Halie, still 'oldin' onto the shrouds 'alfway 'tween sea and sky, shrieked as the ship spun away and tossed her into the water."

Halie shivered with the memory and received reassuring pats on the back.

"What happened then?" asked Emra.

"I'll tell you," said Lali. "Woll, Tristan shouted, 'Keep working! I'll get 'er!' an' she took off 'er jacket an' leaped overboard. Minuette called, 'Wait!' but i' was too late. Tristan 'ad already fallen t' th' roaring waves. I was still up on a fighting top, but I grabbed a shroud on th' other side and slid down to the deck. I ran over t' give Jasper a 'and with the tack, but the 'alyard slipped out of Minuette's rope-burned 'ands and the topsail unfurled. Jasper's cry was drowned by th' thunder. Th' sky lit up wif lightnin' as Tristan lifted 'erself an' Halie from th' water. Just before they were fully on, th' mast snapped under the wind pressure on the topsail and us keeping th' other one in place. Jordan fell to th' deck an' was pinned down by th' mast."

The audience members winced and made sympathetic noises.

"Was he hurt?" asked Genna, clutching her sketchpad like a life raft. She had one arm protectively around her little brother, Mica, as if to shield him from the storm in Lali's tale.

"We didn't know yet," said Lali. "Tha's prolly wot was worst about th' whole thing, th' not knowin'. Not knowin' if we'd survive, not knowin' if our friends 'ad been 'urt. Anyway, Jasper called out for 'is brother, rushing over to 'im t' see if 'e was all right. But then th' ship tilted over so far that we 'ad to hold on to th' shrouds to keep from drownin'. I tried to hold my breath as th' boat tilted even farth'r, about to capsize. Then, out of th' mist and spray, I saw another ship tossin' in th' storm. It was 'eaded for us. I was distracted by th' ship and forgot t' hold my breath. I was plunged underwater. An' just in time, too. Th' ship capsized an' all of us were dumped int' th' ocean. I sank, 'ardly believin' it was actually 'appening. I can't die now, I thought. Just then, a hand caught my arm. I was pulled upwards. My lungs were about t' burst, an' my mouth was burnin' wif th' saltwater. Th' next thing I knew, I was on board a ship wif my friends bein' lifted out of th' water around me. A strange girl pulled Jasper out of th' water and onto th' ship. I scrambled up an' went over t' check if 'e was alive. He spit water. Then 'e sat up an' started callin' out 'Minuette! Where's Minuette?'" said Lali.

Jasper winced, a tortured look on his face.

Oblivious, Lali continued, "A wave swept over th' boat, re-drenchin' us. Jasper looked around an' 'elped t' pull a drippin' Minuette from th' water. She embraced 'im, throwin' water all over us. Th' deck tilted once again, throwin' me an' Halie almost back int' th' water, but Tristan grabbed me an' I grabbed Halie. It was still rainin' 'ard and th' wind 'ad not let up, but we were onboard. 'Quickly! Get below deck!' shouted th' girl wot 'ad rescued us, grabbin' a line and shoutin' to the crew t' drop the mast. Tristan asked, 'And what about you?' an' she said grimly, 'I'll be all right.' We all went below deck then an' collapsed. Some of us were badly 'urt; others were just tired. Halie was 'alf drowned. Jordan boasted that that 'ad been a cinch and 'e wanted t' go help above, but before 'e got to th' door, 'e collapsed. I just lay down and passed out."

Lali paused to take a drink. The audience waited with baited breath. Lali wiped her mouth with the back of her arm and resumed the telling.

"When I came 'round, several of th' others were already up. There was sun shinin' in from above. I yawned and began t' wring out my still-damp clothes. Th' ones 'o were asleep soon woke up, and th' ones 'urt got taken care of. I was neither, so I was permitted t' go above. I was curious t' meet th' girl wot 'ad saved us face to face, now that th' storm 'ad subsided. I looked around. This ship didn't seem to 'ave been badly damaged, 'specially compared to ours, which had, in fact, sunk, but it was still in need of repairs. And leadin' th' repairs was th' girl who rescued us. Though she didn't look so much like an ord'nry girl anymore. She had on a captain's uniform and was givin' orders to th' crew. I immediately noticed that she 'ad no left leg. I still don't know 'ow she's able to swim like that. She'd jumped in after us and pulled each of us from th' ocean."

"Good old Lisha," said Nat, cutting in. "We always said she could swim like a fish."

"You got that right," agreed Lali. "Anyway, Lisha saw me and smiled, so I walked over an' said, 'Thanks fer savin' me life. That was really somethin', th' way you kept th' ship together an' saved ev'ryone,' but she waved away th' comment. She jus' said, 'I'll never see the day when I let someone drown,' an' then, 'That was some storm, aye?' I said, 'Aye. I ain't never seen any like it.' An' then I asked, 'By th' way, what's your name?' She said—"

Lali stood suddenly, blanket falling to the floor. She planted her feet firmly apart and said clearly, " 'Captain Lisha, at your service,' " and bowed to the audience. They applauded and 'whooped' appreciatively. She straightened and said, still imitating Lisha, " 'What can I do for you?' " Dropping the act, Lali let her posture slump back down, falling back into herself. "So I said to 'er, 'You saved my life. What can I do for you?' But just then, Jasper and Minuette came up from below deck."

Jasper nodded vacantly in acknowledgment.

"We barely 'ad time to meet Lisha's crew before we were dropped off at exactly th' spot we were goin' to," concluded Lali. "We actually arrived a week early. But we did get to know Lisha."

Everyone had been listening while Lali told her story. Now that she had finished, a silence filled the air. People gazed into space, trying to picture that scene. It had an almost magical effect on the listeners. But soon things started to wind down. The magic in the air faded and people started going to sleep.

"That was some story, Lali," said Emra as she crawled into bed.

"Thanks. Y' know, they say th' best stories are th' true ones. Night, Emra."

"Goodnight."

Soon Emra was drifting off to confused dreams about Isaac and Jasper. At first they were separate, but then one's face would transform into the other's, and they merged together so much that Emra could never quite make up her mind who it was she was talking to. First it would be Jasper, but then suddenly, it would be Isaac. Then it would be Jasper again. Emra tossed and turned in her sleep, upset by the uncertainty.

Lali was having a strange dream involving a pirate monkey and edible pink clouds. Halie dreamed of seeing someone's death in a vision and not being able to warn them. Kadin-Lave tossed and turned for quite awhile before he drifted into an uneasy sleep.

Fala dreamed about flying with the crows and then not being able to change back. She was scared, but her friends and family learned to accept her, and Fala learned how to use her beak to communicate using code. Her dream changed, and she was a marionette with Desdemona pulling the strings. In the dream, Desdemona's face filled the sky.

Jasper smiled as he crawled into bed. Lali had left something out from her story.

Nat dreamed of Kiara, and she of him. Leandra dreamed of falling into her favorite childhood story. Kaida dreamed of catching mice, and Kit cried herself to sleep by his side, homesick. Mica dreamed of facing a problem he couldn't solve, and Genna dreamed that all her drawings came to life.

As Jasper blew out the last lamp and drifted to sleep, a small shape came into the room. Checking first to make sure that everyone was asleep, he slipped quietly into a secluded corner of the hold. In the shadows, a girl was waiting for him.

"Are they all asleep, Quito?" she asked.

"Aye, Hilda. All 'xcept some o' th' crew mem'ers an' Lisha."

"I still don't see why you couldn't let me put them to sleep. It would be quicker that way, you know," she said.

"Y' kno' Master's orders. Ye's not ter show yer power er they migh' come ter see ye 're a threat. There's some smart people onboard."

"Do you have the communicator?" she asked. Quito produced it, holding out a glass sphere.

"Excellent," said Hilda. "One of Master's men can let us see him through this to get our next instructions." She took the crystal ball and set it down on the table. It began to glow. A face flickered into view. A face with slick, gray hair and ice blue eyes. The face of Julian E. Loxlyheart. Quito and Hilda bowed low their heads.

"We await your instructions, Master," said Quito.

"Good," said Mr. Loxlyheart. "Everything is going according to plan. I have nearly all the Stoens that I need, and the others will surely come to me soon. However, there is one particular Stoen that eludes me. My sources have informed me that it is unique, that there is only one in the entire world. It is essential that I have it! Without it, I will not be able to unleash the Ultimate Power. And we wouldn't want that, now, would we?" The children shook their heads fervently. "Now, I need you to be on the watch for it, and report immediately if you should find it."

"How will we recognize it?" asked Hilda.

"You will know it by the sign carved on it. The source who told me of this Stoen kindly provided an illustration for me." With that, Mr. Loxlyheart

produced a sheet of paper and held it up so that the
listeners watching through the communicator could
clearly see the sign drawn upon it:

They stared hard at it, eyes wide.

"Look at it," said Mr. Loxlyheart. "Memorize it.
Find it. Keep a low profile and be careful not to get
too close to anyone onboard or you might be reluctant
to betray them."

"Our loyalties lie with you, always, Master."

"Make sure it stays that way. Remember where
you would be without me, where you were before I
found you. If you disobey me, I will send you back
there like the worthless, pathetic children that you are.
Never forget that. Not every rich and powerful man
is this generous to worthless orphans like yourselves,
and you cannot expect such kind treatment from any
other living creature. I shall be in contact." The face
vanished.

Far away, a man watched them leave the room
though a glass mirror. The howl of the wind
drowned his manic laughter as thunder cracked in
the distance.

"She killed her! She killed her! I'll rip her arms off! I'll tear her hear out! I'll—"

"Calm down, Rodger. She didn't mean any harm— no... no, what are you doing? Rodger, answer me, Rodger, what are you doing!"

"I'm taking vengeance, I'm avenging Annabel's death! The child killed her! If you can call it a child, just look at it! Look at that hideous dark skin. This isn't a child! This is a demon! Sent to haunt me after destroying my life and my love!"

"What are you talking about? A demon? There is nothing wrong with the child. The child is helpless! She couldn't kill anyone!"

"She can and she did. Garron, Garron listen to me! You're my friend, my trusted adviser! What would you do if someone murdered your wife?"

"She didn't kill your wife; your wife died of natural causes! For goodness sakes, Rodger, she's only a baby!"

"She's three years old. I would hardly consider that a baby,"

"But she's a child, nonetheless. Can't you see that you are bringing this upon yourself? You want someone to blame, and so you take out your anger on the very being Annabel died to protect! This is not what she would have wanted, Rodger! Rodger, are you listening to me? What are you doing? For Heaven's sake, what are you doing!"

"No more ... no more pain. If I kill her, it will be all right ... Annabel will be ... if it weren't for that thing, she would have been perfectly FINE!"

"What do you mean, she would have been perfectly fine? Calm down, Rodger, it's not the child's fault—what are you doing? Good God, man, what are you doing? Stop *it! Stop it this instant! Rodger, you're scaring me, Rodger! Can you hear me! Put the child down, do you hear me? Put the child down."*

Kiara sat up. Her dream about Nat had ended peacefully, and she had slipped back into the nightmare. This time she was sure she got the whole conversation. It was still blurry, so she couldn't *see* what was going on, but she could hear everything. Finally, some of her questions were answered. Garron was the friend of her father who took care of Kiara for a year until he was called off to war. Annabel must have been Kiara's mother, and Rodger must be her father. The child in the dream must be herself. Kiara grimaced. That was why everything felt so big. Kiara took out the pistol. It undoubtedly belonged to her father. She looked at the name on the barrel. Her father had been trying to kill her because her mother had died. But why would he blame her?

"If it weren't for you, she would have been perfectly FINE."

"She didn't kill your wife; your wife died."

"The very being Annabel died to protect."

That was it. Her mother must have died in childbirth. Kiara sat down with tears in her eyes. *I really did kill her.* Wait. If her mother died in childbirth, then why did Kiara still have memories of her? *She must have gotten sick when I was born and then died several years later. If so, it could have been something else that killed her. Why did Rodger seem so set on my life?*

Kiara got up and stretched. After such dreams, she could never go right back to sleep. She walked up onto the deck and wandered over to the railing.

She looked out over the water. It was so dark, yet so peaceful. Something made Kiara look up. Standing at the railing a little way down was Jasper. He, too, was staring out over the ocean. He jumped when he saw Kiara.

"Why, Kiara! You're awake! Couldn't sleep?" he said awkwardly. "Still having— bad ... dreams?" She looked at him, too stunned to decide how she felt about him knowing.

"How do you know about—"

"You—uh, talk in your sleep sometimes. I was just making a guess."

"Oh," she said. They fell silent. She knew she should feel mad, or at least indignant, but the anger didn't come. To cover up for her confusion, she asked the first thing that came to mind.

"So—uh, what are you doing up?" asked Kiara, deliberately avoiding answering Jasper's question. Just because she wasn't angry with him for knowing about her dream, it didn't mean she wanted to talk about it.

"What? Oh. I just, ..." he glanced away. "Lali's story brought back some old memories, that's all." He paused. The silence was fragile, temporary, as if it knew that there was more to be said. It gave Kiara an odd feeling to see Jasper so unguarded, as if she were looking through the keyhole of the door to his soul. It felt a bit awkward, as if she might be intruding. But she felt that there was something he still needed to say, no matter who was listening. And so she stayed. When he continued, he seemed to be speaking more to himself than to her. "One night, I came up to look at

the stars and found her ... Minuette ... standing here."
He closed his eyes. Then he glanced back toward
Kiara, a wry expression on his face. "I half expected
Lali to mention ... she came up on deck and found me
and Minuette about to kiss." He cleared his throat. "It
was a night just like this one. The ocean was calm,
the stars were all out, and the moon was glowing."
Jasper looked out into the distance. His eyes clouded
over, and he closed them again. "I would do anything
to keep her safe. Anything."

Anything? We shall see about that, thought Quito as
he slipped back into the shadows.

❦

Lisha stood staring off into the night from her place
behind the steering wheel. She traced the constellations
with her eyes, connecting the shining points of light
like pieces in a puzzle. Inside her head, similar
fragments floated around, waiting to be pinned into
place.

First there was the strange Stoen with the sign
she'd never seen before. Working as a longtime
Protector and transporter of Stoens, she had seen
many Stoens in her life, Stoens of many different
types. Many she had seen repeated, some countless
times over. But never had she seen a Stoen like the
one Kit had brought them. The sign was completely
different from any of the others. What kind of Stoen
was it? If only they had some way to find out. But
until they reached their first destination, the home
of a Stoenmason, Lisha would just have to wait. She

brightened at the thought of meeting Cameron, the Mason, and getting some of her questions answered. How exactly did the Ultimate Power work? How many Stoens did you need to unlock it?

And perhaps Cameron might be able to shed some light on other mysteries as well. Such as the mysterious shadow woman who had warned the visiting French troupe of an attack minutes before the witch Aradia arrived. Lisha pondered the vision for a moment. A shadow moving of its own volition ... a mysterious shadow of a woman, a shadow without a body ... a Stoenhunter who had power over shadows... There must be some connection. There must! But what?

And Kaida. What role did he play in all this? The last baby dragon; where had he come from? Had there once been more dragons roaming the earth? If so, then what had happened to them? Were they still around, only in hiding, a secret to be discovered only by those who were trustworthy, like the secret of the Stoens themselves?

Finding no answer in the endless expanse of water and sky, Lisha's thoughts drifted away from these unsolved mysteries.

She thought about her friends, troubled by their troubles. Of Jasper and the anguish he must feel, the terrible uncertainty in not knowing what had happened to Minuette. Of Emra, how frustrating it would be to have the one she cared about not notice and be unable to tell him. Of Kiara and the nameless distress that had kept her up nights. But they were all coping in their own ways. Jasper was focused on the mission, as dedicated and determined as ever.

Emra concealed her pain under a cheerful attitude that she thought no one could see through and allowed herself to laugh and smile. Kiara had been spending more and more time with Nat, and her spirits seemed considerably lighter.

And how good to see Nat again, after so long! One of Lisha's closest childhood friends, snatched cruelly away by pirates, finally to have him back! Abruptly, a cold wind blew past, disturbing her feeling of elation. Lisha shivered, remembering the similar chill she had felt when she thought she would never see her friend again. But all that was gone now. He was home. Nat was back, and they were friends as if they'd never parted.

Lisha looked down from the sky and out across the ocean, her mouth settling into a grim line as she thought of another old friend. Yes, Nat was back. But Jasmine ... what was Lisha to do about Jasmine? Something had changed since the last time Lisha had seen her. They had always been close, ever since they had known each other. They had a certain ... special connection, different from the way Lisha felt about her other friends. But now, suddenly, this distance ... what had happened to change things? Since the beginning, they had harmonized together like... Lisha struggled to put her feelings into words ...like sisters almost, sisters who never fought or disagreed, friends, who could say anything to each other ... but now, more and more, Lisha could feel Jasmine slipping through her fingers, as if somehow she'd been washed out to sea and her only tether to land, to life, was Lisha's grip on her hand. But Lisha couldn't pull her out on her own, and Jasmine's fingers were growing cold and limp, and she wasn't fighting to stay alive, to stay attached to Lisha. How could Lisha help someone who didn't want help?

She glanced down at the compass in her hand and then up at the stars. Neither offered her an answer. A chill wind blew past, ruffling her clothes.

Lisha heard a small noise and looked out across the deck for its source. There were several sailors about, and she could see the silhouette of someone by the railing, standing as still as a statue. She looked closer.

It was Jasmine.

Lisha motioned a sailor over and handed off the steering wheel to him before setting off across the deck. She stepped cautiously, wondering vaguely whether hearts had wings, for how else would they be able to flutter so?

She stopped beside Jasmine, leaning forward watchfully to get a better view of her face. Moonlight shone down upon them, reflecting off of the tears on Jasmine's cheeks. Quietly, ever so quietly, so as not to frighten her, Lisha said, "Jaz?"

Jasmine looked up. Tears swam on the surfaces of her eyes. When she saw Lisha, her mouth opened slightly and she stepped back. Lisha stepped forward, hand held out pleadingly.

"Jasmine," she said again, reaching for her. Jasmine hesitated as if about to take Lisha's hand, but her eyes overflowed again, spilling tears down her face, and she shook her head. She took a step back and then another. Lisha followed after her, desperation in her voice as she said again, "Jasmine, please," but Jasmine turned and ran away into the darkness.

Lisha bowed over the side of the ship, burying her face in her arms. She held onto her shoulders helplessly, uncertain what to do. *Please, come back*, she pleaded silently. *Let me help you.*

❦

The storm came out of nowhere. Emra and the others woke to the sound of shouts and waves battering the ship. Thunder boomed and rain fell like an avalanche. Lisha's voice came cutting through the noise from above deck.

"Hurry! Grab the tack and secure the sails!" The Protectors got up and began running around frantically, trying to help or hide. "Stay below deck!" yelled Lisha. "You're safer there for now." Just then a huge wave crashed over the boat, soaking everyone. Dripping wet, Emra suddenly got an idea. A crazy, foolish idea. She knew it was rash to even consider such a thing, but she didn't care. With a magnificent feeling of recklessness, she stumbled purposefully toward the railing, slipping in the puddles of water sloshing across the deck just as another wave broke over the side. The water washed over her, and she pretended she was being dragged overboard by the wave and screamed at the top of her lungs: "Isaac! Help me!" Isaac, who was just about to go below deck, turned. She felt an exhilarating freedom in finally releasing her emotions and let all her pain and frustration out as she screamed again, "Isaac! Isaac! Help!" Emra pretended to grab for the railing and let herself slip under water. All of a sudden, she realized that she really *was* sliding off the ship. Panic seized her, buzzing in her head as she flailed wildly, trying to stay afloat. She kicked her legs fiercely, willing Isaac to come to her rescue. With each kick, she shouted in her mind, *Isaac! Isaac! Isaac!* until it occurred to her: *He's not going to save me.* Her struggles slowed, weariness seeping through her body, the weight of the water pressing in on her. *I'm going to die.* Her limbs slackened, and she felt abruptly exhausted, as if she'd used up the last of her strength, the last of her will, the last of her endurance. *He doesn't care about me.* Her tears mixed with the saltwater from the sea as she floated downward. And as she drifted toward darkness, it was not Isaac's face she saw. Oh, she'd been a fool, she thought despairingly, a silly impulsive fool. And so naïve to think she could just make herself forget Jasper. Anguish washed over her like the ocean, closing tighter and tighter above her head. Isaac wasn't coming, and Jasper was lost to her. Emra didn't even attempt to swim back up. She knew she wouldn't make it. Her head was pounding and the water was all around her, smothering her. *Yes*, she thought, *let the water crush me, let me freeze and turn to ice.* Her lungs burned, and her face and hands stung from the frigid water. She welcomed the pain, let it wash over her and drown out everything else, filling her mind as she lost the will to live. How nice to just give in and let the water fill her lungs. How peaceful to not have to struggle anymore. Darkness closed in around her.

Suddenly, something sharp and metal hurtled down and sliced her arm open, startling her back to her senses. Emra cried out in pain and lost her supply of air. She choked, convulsing. Blood flooded out around her. Strong hands grabbed her as Emra's world went black.

"Ow!" said Emra as Isaac peeled off the old bandage and began wrapping on a new one.

"Sorry," he said guiltily, not looking at her. She looked down at her other hand.

It had been several days since the storm, and still Isaac refused to look her in the eyes. *What a horrible person*, she thought again. He was a sailor, surgeon or no. He should have at least tried to save her! *Anyone*, she thought, *no matter the circumstances, if they're asked for help should try to give it!* But Isaac, Isaac just worried about himself, getting himself below deck before he ended up like her. He probably thought she was a goner and gave up on her. Emra wondered if he really cared for anyone besides himself. Maybe being a surgeon was a way to try to make himself care, but he still didn't. She, and anyone else he helped, was just another wound to heal, sickness to cure. He didn't worry about people. How appalling, she thought, that she could have been so gullible as to talk herself into being attracted to someone like that. The only emotion he deserved was pity. Pity that he couldn't see people as people. She wondered how many people there were like him, who preserved life but did not value it. Not many, she hoped.

"You should be finished ... right ... about ... now," he said, tying off the bandage. "There you go. All right. You can leave."

Emra stood, gloomily. *Oh, what a wretch I am!* she thought. *How could I have ever seen anything in that—that imbecile?*

Lisha came over, smiling at her. She was the one who had dived in and rescued Emra.

"How're you feeling?"

"Like an idiot. Um ... thanks. For saving my life." Lisha looked at her thoughtfully.

"That was not a wise thing to do," said Lisha.

"What?"

"I think you know what I'm talking about." Emra looked at her feet. Lisha glanced over at Isaac. "Plus," she said, "you could have made a better choice than Isaac. I mean, I suppose it didn't really matter who, but there are a lot of young men on board. Why choose him? He's almost twenty."

"Well, I guess I was just—" Emra looked at her, astonished. "Twenty! I swear he looks seventeen!"

"And you look like you're ten." Emra looked down. It was true she looked much younger than she really was. In truth, she was almost fourteen. She wondered if perhaps Isaac had made an incorrect assumption about her age. She felt even more annoyed at Isaac than before, but at the same time ashamed, for she had made a similar assumption about him.

"Besides," continued Lisha, "you might want to get to know more about someone before you go and do something like that. If you had, you'd know that Isaac can't swim."

Emra looked at Lisha, aghast. Suddenly she found herself doing a reevaluation of Isaac in her head. Perhaps he wasn't quite as bad as she'd thought. If he couldn't swim, how could he have hoped to save her?

"But he could have at least done something!" she thought out loud.

"He did," said Lisha. Emra looked up at her, surprised.

"He did?"

"Yes. He called for me." Emra looked at the deck, mouth hanging open, speechless. "He really can't swim?" she said, starting to laugh.

"No," said Lisha, chuckling. "Hates sailing. I have to pay him double the others' wages just to get him on the ship." Emra shook her head.

Well, that failed miserably, thought Emra after they had parted. *Why didn't I think? I never think things through! He's not all that bad after all, but still it was foolish to assume that he....* She choked back a sob, suddenly reminded of why she had started this in the first place. After all, Isaac had really only been a distraction so she could stop thinking about Jasper. A tear trickled down her chin. It was no use. She still cared for Jasper, far too much. No matter how wrong, no mater how much she hated herself for it, there was just no getting around it. She envied Nat and Kiara, talking so easily on the other side of the ship. Inhaling deeply, she put on a brighter expression and turned her face to the sky, clinging the feeling of the sun on her face and tried to forget her woes.

❧

On the other side of the ship, Kiara and Nat talked easily as Nat steered the ship with one hand and leaned against the railing with the other. It was a calm day. The ocean was still, and the sun shone down warmly, faint breezes whispering by. The two talked about all sorts of things. As it turned out, they had quite a lot in common. Besides their pasts, which were very similar, they both loved to read. As soon as that fact was established, their talk turned to all of their favorite books. They found they had read many of the same ones and discussed those eagerly.

"Let's see ... *Le Morte d'Arthur*," said Nat. Kiara nodded with enthusiasm.

"Yes, I used to love that! I didn't know you'd read it!"

"Of course!" he laughed. "My dad used to bring me all sorts of books."

"Not mine," said Kiara, shaking her head. "He never really gave me anything, but he let me wander around a lot. We had all these books in our home he never looked at, and I just ate them up. I was lucky he let me read them."

"Yes ... yes, I suppose you were." Kiara looked over at Nat. He was looking at her softly, a strange melting look. Their eyes met, and time seemed to dawdle leisurely past, unhurried. Without any conscious effort from either of them, they slowly drew closer.

Suddenly a fish jumped up and splashed down loudly, and the spell was broken. Nat was the first to look away. He cleared his throat.

"They ... they were good books."

"Yes, yes, they were," said Kiara, averting her eyes.

In the shadows, a shape smirked, relishing their discomfort. Quito hated to see anyone feel happy.

❧

That evening it began to rain. The Protectors decided to turn in early due to the weather. While they settled themselves below deck, Hilda stepped into the shadows outside the captain's cabin. Quito was waiting for her there.

"The coast is clear," whispered Hilda. "The captain's busy, and no one's likely to hear us under the sound of all this rain."

"'A know that," said Quito irritably. "Tha's why we picked t'night!" Before she could respond, Quito silenced her with a glare and moved so she could see what he was doing. In his hands was a twisted bit of metal that he was stubbornly using to try to force the lock on the door to the cabin. After another minute of fighting, the lock clicked, and the door swung open slightly. Carefully Quito slipped inside, Hilda following behind. As soon as they were in, she took off her sopping cloak and kerchief and wrung out the kerchief onto the floor, dripping rainwater down onto the carpet. Slipping the kerchief into her pocket, she began shaking out her long, bushy, bright red hair.

"What are y' doin'?" said Quito. "We s'posed t' be lookin' fer th' Stoens!"

"I don't care. My hair's wet," she said with a pout. "If I don't do something about it, it'll stick up something awful tomorrow."

"Yer wastin' time!" he said exasperatedly, beginning to search around. She ignored him, striding forward into the room and leaning against the desk. Glancing around, she spotted a chest in the corner.

"There," she said, indicating the chest. Together, they crowded over the chest, examining it from all angles. "Try the lock." Quito produced the lock pick and started twisting it in the keyhole. After a few tense moments, the lock opened. Hilda forced open the clamps, and together they lifted the top. They let out sounds of triumph as they looked down into the chest. Inside was a collection of Stoens.

"What was tha' sign Master's lookin' fer?" asked Quito, grabbing a Stoen and examining the sign carved into its surface.

"It looked like this." Hilda drew the sign in the dust on the floor. Hastily, they searched through the Stoens, all smooth, flattened spheres about the size of a person's fist, each with a sign carved into one side. "But Master has all of these," said Hilda unhappily, sitting back onto her heels. "That one he's looking for isn't here!"

"We give 'em all to Master anyway," said Quito, disappointment in his voice, as he lifted the Stoens into a cloth bag. Once he had all of them, he stood and closed the chest, putting the clasps back in place.

"What a waste!" said Hilda, her whole body sulking. "All this waiting and hiding is killing me. Working on this ship and pretending to listen to everything anyone says to me. And after all that, we don't find what Master's looking for!"

"Well, tha's not our fault, is it? We did what 'e asked us. Tha's all there is to it." He stood as well, shouldering the bag of Stoens with some difficulty. It was a lot of weight for someone so small to carry on his own. Hilda made no move to help him, leaning against the desk again.

"Oh, you don't understand," she said. "You don't have to cook and make small talk. All you have to do is slink around in the shadows and eavesdrop. You don't have to pretend you're someone else. Lucky little fool. If only Mr. Loxlyheart had—"

"Shhhhhhh!" said Quito. "We're not t' say 'is name else some'un over'eard us."

"I'll say what I please, thank you very much." said Hilda, hopping up to sit on the captain's desk. She shook her hair over her shoulder and began running her fingers through it to get rid of the tangles. Spotting a mirror lying nearby, Hilda picked it up and began fluffing her hair while Quito paced agitatedly.

"No common sense, I tell yer, no common sense. The cap'in could be back a' any minute, an' yer si'in 'ere wastin' time. An' fer wha'? So's ye can whine an' complain 'bout what 'e wants an—an fix yer 'air? Wha's next? Midnigh' snacks?" He stopped pacing and glared at her. She didn't respond. "Well, a's not

goin' ter sit around an be caught with ye. If ye want
to stay 'ere an' be caught, well, a's not gonna be caught
with you. Tha's it. I'm goin'." And with that, Quito
stomped outside and slammed the door, muttering
"Bloody fool."

Immediately, Hilda stopped messing with her
hair. She hopped down off the desk, replaced the
mirror where she had found it, and began scanning
the room with her eyes again. Though focused on the
task at hand, she couldn't keep the smirk of her face.
A fool indeed. Fool enough to trick a fool boy! She
was *sure* that the Stoen Mr. Loxlyheart was looking
for was here somewhere, despite Quito's certainty that
it wasn't. And now, with him out of the way, she
was free to search on her own and take full credit for
whatever she found. She would show Mr. Loxlyheart
who served him best!

She walked careful about the room, scanning the
corners for possible hiding spaces. She riffled through
contents of drawers and cabinets. Nothing. Finally
giving up, she headed for the door. But halfway there,
she tripped on something hard and stumbled forward,
catching herself on the wall. Looking back irritably for
what had made her trip, she saw a floorboard sticking
up slightly. An idea suddenly striking her, she knelt by
the floorboard and carefully pulled it with her hands.
It moved to reveal a thin compartment in the floor.
Elation filled her as she saw a dark pouch lying inside.
She removed it and tipped it over her hand, letting the
contents slip out. She shook the pouch slightly, and
a darkly colored Stoen with a glossy surface fell out
and landed in her upturned palm. Hardly daring to

believe, she turned it over to see the sign carved into its surface.

It was the pattern Mr. Loxlyheart had shown them.

At last. *Finally the spell will be complete. Mr. Loxlyheart will reward me greatly for this!* And with that Hilda slipped the Stoen inside her pocket, put on the dirty kerchief over her newly combed hair, and left the cabin.

Miles away, below the ruins of an ancient castle flanked by sheer cliffs, the weary inhabitants of the dungeon stirred in their chains.

"Tell me about yourselves," said Laramie. "Where are you from, and how did you end up here?"

"We are from France," said Minuette. "The three of us make up most of the French Protector troupe. The two other members managed to avoid being captured along with us. They are probably hiding out there somewhere. Maybe they went to find Jasper," she bit her lip. After a short pause, she said, "I still remember back to before I was a Protector. Maman and I were performers. Singing, dancing. Papa made travel arrangements and introduced us before shows."

"Sounds like fun," said Laramie.

"Oh, *oui, c'est vrai*, it was," assured Minuette.

"What happened?" asked Laramie, picking up Minuette's choice of past tense. Minuette looked down.

"Well ... you see," she said haltingly, "it ... we ... they are dead. My parents. They were k-killed, during the Reign of Terror. There was this man who did not like Papa. The man accused him of treason. *Mon pére* was executed. Maman and I ran. We hid for a long time. But one day, we got caught in this mob. We could not get out fast enough ... Maman told me to hide," she paused, taking a deep breath. "She was trampled—" Minuette choked back a sob. Tristan and Jordan looked at her sympathetically. "Anyway," said Minuette shakily, "Tristan found me, terrified and hysterical, and took me in. She and Halie had already found each other, and the three of us hid out the rest of the conflict together. Somewhere during that time we ran into a Drifter, who told us everything. How every human had a power, but the powers were locked away unless they touched a special Stoen that corresponded to the type of power they had. And how if enough of the Stoens were brought together, one could unleash the Ultimate Power, the power to do absolutely anything you could imagine. She offered us the chance to become Protectors. I am not sure about the others, but the things she said really resonated with me. We had seen what people with too much power could do, what they had done. It was the new government of France that was behind all those executions. So many people, and many of them never having committed a crime! I know if there were a way—if I could go back—if I knew something like that was going to happen, I would want to do everything in my power to prevent it. I had felt so helpless while all of those terrible things happened around me, and the thought that we were not helpless, that we each had a power, and that each was different and each was special, that each human was important ...," she drew a deep breath and let it out. "Anyway, that is my story of becoming a Protector."

She looked over at her companions. Tristan decided to go next.

"My name is Tristan," she said.

"Like the medieval romance, Tristan and Isolde?" asked Laramie.

"Right. My parents liked those stories a lot, and they named me after Tristan because he was brave, a real hero."

"Tristan's an unusual name for a girl," said Laramie. "Was there a reason your parents chose to give you a boy's name?"

"Yes. You see, like many other places, France does not have equality for men and women. My parents weren't happy with the thought that their child should have to live as a lesser citizen just because I was a girl. So, they decided to raise me the way they would a boy. We did not try to hide the fact that I was a girl, but they thought that if I was given the chance, if people could see that I was ... no worse, eh ... not inferior to the boys, then perhaps I would be able to get the same opportunities they would."

"You didn't mind?" asked Laramie. Tristan shook her head.

"Not at all. In fact, I was all for it. Most of my friends were boys, and we all played together, as equals. I was always more interested in sports and playing outside than in cooking or sewing. I had all these hopes and dreams of changing the world, doing great things, inspired in part by my namesake from the legend. My parents loved telling stories, and I heard the legends until I knew them by heart. Getting back to the point, as Minuette said, France was not a happy place to live in for quite some years. There was this writer I admired, Olympe de Gouges. She fought for equal rights for women, among many other things. Eventually she fought a little too hard, and she was executed. We realized then that what we were doing was dangerous. We went into hiding. But we were separated," Tristan paused, staring into the shadows as if they concealed her missing parents. Eventually she shook her head resignedly. "After that ... it was like Minuette said. I discovered other children, and we hid together. And also like Minuette said, when the Drifter explained everything to us, it made me feel stronger, less helpless. I have always been a fighter. I could not be content to just stand timidly by and watch. I would be out there now, if..." she glanced up at the shackles binding her hands above her head, bruises forming where the metal pressed too hard against her wrists. The others nodded. There was nothing more to say. "Well then Jordan," said Tristan finally. "You're the next one." Jordan nodded.

"My brother Jasper and I are from England," he said to Laramie. "Our father was a baronet."

"A baronet?" said Laramie, impressed. "You're nobility?"

"It's a minor title," said Jordan modestly, averting his eyes. "Anyway, his status didn't help him when the government found out about what he'd done." The others all leaned forward, as much as was possible in their chains. "You see," continued Jordan, "my parents were sympathizers with the American colonists. Word came to them from friends across the ocean of the unfair laws and taxes, and the people's cry for liberty. My parents spoke out for them, before and during the Revolution. They were supporters of Edmund Burke, and together they tried and failed to convince King George to make peace with the colonists. When their entreaties were refused for the last time, it seemed that was it. However, several years after the war was over, the authorities connected my father to a shipment of saltpeter that had been intercepted on the way to the states during the revolution. He was charged with high treason for attempting to assist the enemies of the crown. My mother caught word of this before he did, and when they came to arrest him, she pretended to be my father and let them arrest her in his place."

"Why would she do that?" asked Laramie.

"She was trying to protect him. That's just the kind of person she was," said Jordan with a sad smile. "She would always... well, it didn't work for long. They soon figured out what had happened and came after us. We tried to escape, but we were caught. Jasper and I were going to be sent to the workhouse, but our father held off the guards so we could make a run for it. We managed to get away and stowed aboard a ship headed for France. Lali found us there and took us to Tristan." He nodded to her and she nodded back in acknowledgement. "We never found out what happened to our parents," he said more quietly, looking down. "It's not hard to guess, though.

The punishment for treason is severe. There's little hope that we will see them again." He spoke bravely, but his voice broke on the last word.

"I'm sorry," said Minuette, sympathy resting softly in her eyes as if it were accustomed to being there.

"It's all right," he said quickly, his face hidden by shadow. "I knew what I was losing when I got on that boat." The Protectors fell into silence.

"So what about you?" asked Minuette, turning the attention back to Laramie and away from Jordan. "How did you wind up here?"

Laramie let out a sigh.

"It's a long story," she said.

"Well, we're not going anywhere fast," said Jordan. Tristan let out a hollow laugh. Laramie raised her hooded head and looked in their direction. Minuette imagined for one moment that if they could see Laramie's face, there would be a smile on it.

"Very well, then," said Laramie. "What would you like to know?"

"You mentioned your family before," said Minuette tentatively. "I was wondering what happened to them. That is, if you do not mind my asking."

"Not at all," replied Laramie. "Besides, it might be useful for you to get to know a bit about your enemies."

"Our enemies?" asked Minuette, her voice quiet. Laramie nodded.

"Yes. My history concerns them as well."

"What can you tell us about them?" asked Tristan excitedly. "Aradia, Desdemona, Mr. Loxlyheart ... we really know very little about them."

"Yes," agreed Jordan, "for instance, what exactly is Desdemona's power?" Jordan and Tristan launched into an onslaught of questions, so excited that they had someone with answers that they tried to ask everything at once.

"Let her answer one question at a time," chastised Minuette. The barrage ceased. "There," said Minuette, satisfied. "Now, Laramie, you can go ahead. Start wherever you like."

"Thank you," she said, sounding slightly amused. "Let's see ... Desdemona's power. That's the simplest question, with the simplest answer: mind control."

The Protectors' eyes widened.

"Mind control?" repeated Jordan, distressed.

"Yes. Although it's a bit of a misnomer. She doesn't actually control people's minds. Just their bodies. She can turn people into puppets, with her pulling the strings of their actions."

"That would explain why people just stand by and let her steal their Stoens," said Tristan thoughtfully. "And why she is so hard to find. She can probably manipulate people to look the other way when she passes, so no one remembers seeing her."

"Exactly," said Laramie. "And for Aradia, she's a shadow bender."

"We gathered that," said Tristan ruefully.

"Aradia was the one who captured us," explained Minuette, remembering sharply that night in London. The fear and the confusion, the way the dock house had seemed to move about them, the chains binding their limbs, chains made out of darkness. She shivered and tried again to free her chafed wrists from the shackles that held them above her head, rattling the chains that kept her suspended high on the wall. She gave up after only a few seconds, already worn out by the effort. She looked up wearily and nodded to Laramie to continue.

"How much do you know of Mr. Loxlyheart?" asked Laramie. Tristan thought for a moment.

"Let's see ... I have heard he likes things neat and orderly, and he detests uncleanliness and disorder. He does not like the poor, especially homeless street urchins."

"Like us," said Minuette.

"Right. And he owns all these factories, tries to get children off the streets by forcing them to work for him there. He likes power, to have control. I guess that is why he wants the Ultimate Power."

"That's pretty much it, I think," said Laramie. "At least, about as much as I know."

"What else can you tell us?" asked Tristan. "You must have seen and heard things here. Are there other Protectors locked up here? Do you know what happened to the missing Drifters?"

"Yes," said Laramie. "I do. They're all here." Shock lit the Protectors' faces. "The Stoenhunters have been rounding up the Drifters and particularly troublesome Protectors for a while now. Desdemona and Aradia have been plotting this for a long time."

"How do you know so much about them?" asked Tristan. Laramie sighed.

"I know them because I grew up with them. We all lived in the same town. I know because, you see, Desdemona is my sister."

Lisha and Jasmine sat talking in the cabin at twilight. The flickering candles cast light and shadows across their faces. They finished all official business, and Lisha rolled up the maps and stowed them. Jasmine stood as if to leave, but didn't move toward the door. Lisha glanced back at her.

"Would you like some tea?" she asked. Jasmine hesitated. Lisha turned to face her. "Please have some tea." She nodded and sat back down. Lisha made the tea and brought over two cups, one for each of them. Lisha sat, leaned her chin on one fist, and looked at Jasmine speculatively, her tea untouched. Jasmine shifted in her seat. "It's all right," said Lisha gently. "I know something's wrong. You don't have to tell me what it is, though, not if you don't want to. When you want me to know, you'll tell me. I just want you to know that I'm here."

"Li—" the name caught in her throat.

"Drink," said Lisha. "It'll help." Jasmine drank. She drew a shuddering breath.

"I'm sorry, Captain."

"None of that," said Lisha. "Don't apologize. And don't call me 'Captain.' I'm not doing this as your commander; I'm doing this as your friend." That was just too much for Jasmine, and she set the tea down, burying her face in her hands. Lisha went over and put a hand on Jasmine's shoulder. "It's all right. Here, come over here." She led Jasmine over to the bed and they sat together. Jasmine leaned her head against Lisha's shoulder and cried into her neck. Lisha wrapped her arms around Jasmine, stroking her hair and murmuring "Shh ... it's all right. I'm here. It's all right."

By the time Jasmine left, the candles had burned nearly halfway down. Lisha closed the door quietly and turned back toward the room. Glancing down, she noticed a damp spot on the wood as if someone had been wringing out a towel. But then it had been raining earlier; it was likely she or Jasmine had tracked in some water. *Jasmine....* She went back to the bed and sank onto it. As she started to pull the blankets over herself, out of the corner of her eye she saw something that made her stop. Drawn in the dust on the floor was the mysterious sign from the Stoen Kit had found. What did it mean? Her eyelids fluttered and the image blurred. Perhaps the flickering candlelight was playing tricks with her. She must have imagined the sign. As she drifted off to sleep, Lisha thought of Jasmine and smiled to herself. The first step to fixing a problem was always admitting it existed. Perhaps soon Lisha would be able to relieve Jasmine of the burden she carried, whatever it was that upset her so, and see her at last happy and smiling again.

The next day dawned dull and hazy, the sun shining lazily down upon the *Compass Rose*. People reluctantly rose from their hammocks and began chores. Breakfast was fish. Again. No one spoke. No one wanted to.

After breakfast, Lisha began directing the crew to get to their assorted jobs.

"All right, you lot, on deck! To work, everyone! Jasmine, meet me in my cabin to check the map. We need to make sure we're on course."

"I still think this is a bad idea," said Oliver under his breath.

"What was that, Oliver?" asked Lisha, turning toward the flat-faced boatswain.

"I said, I think this is a bad idea, Captain," he said again, more loudly. Several heads turned. He glanced around at the watchers to see if they agreed. "This whole voyage!" he continued. "It's idiotic, practically suicidal!" Turning back to Lisha, he said sarcastically, "Remind me again *why* we're doing this?"

Lisha crossed her arms.

"It's our duty as Protectors to make sure that no one ever manages to unleash the Ultimate Power. Absolute power to do anything you can think of—just imagine how dangerous that is! Things have been pretty quiet for a long time, but now there are three people after that power. Desdemona, Aradia, and Mr. Loxlyheart. With the power, any of them would be a terrible threat. Even without the Ultimate Power, they're all very dangerous already."

"Exactly!" said Oliver emphatically. "And we're trying to find them? The people who want to kill us? How dumb can you get? We should be trying to stay away from them at all costs!"

"We can't do that," said Lisha firmly. "They've captured some of our friends. We have to help them. We have to stop the Hunters and rescue our friends. We're Protectors. That's what we do. We protect people."

"What about us? What about protecting us? You're putting their lives above ours!"

A crowd had begun to gather around, drawn by the sound of raised voices. Oblivious, Lisha and Oliver continued their argument.

"If one of those three gets the Ultimate Power, it'll be bad for everyone!"

"It *could* be. But if we actually manage to find the Hunters, we'll be killed! These people are powerful and ruthless! And even if one of them does manage to get this Power thing, which is unlikely, then as long as we're nowhere near them, it won't affect us. If we just turn around and go home, we can stay safe and far away from all of this."

"What about the people they've captured? You'd just leave them there?"

"Better them than me. Besides, how do we really know they've been captured? I mean, come on. You're going to take the word of some French magical freak girl?"

"Watch your tongue," said Lisha sharply, "or you might loose it. I won't have that kind of talk aboard my ship." They stared challengingly at each other for a moment, each daring the other to yield. Finally, Oliver looked away dismissively. For a moment, the watchers thought that he would let the matter rest, but he continued.

"Besides, even if we could find them, who says we could rescue them?"

"We have to try. Imagine if it was you the Hunters had caught. Would you want us to leave you there and go save our own necks, or would you want us to come and try to help you?" Oliver fell silent. "As long as there's the smallest chance we'll succeed, we're going to try to rescue them and stop the people who captured them from attaining limitless power."

"It's my neck you're asking me to risk, too, you know!"

"We've been through this, Oliver. Everyone knows the risks, but we're all resolved to—"

"Well I'm not!" cut off Oliver. "You yourself even admit there's a risk. I'll tell you what's going to happen. We're going to get there, if we ever find where we're going, and they're going to kill us. All of us."

"No one said you had to risk your life. If you don't want to come, I can drop you off at the nearest port. We can pick you up on the way back ... or not." Oliver paused.

"Is that a threat?" he asked, his voice low.

"Think of it as a warning," said Lisha lightly. Oliver opened his mouth to retort, but Lisha cut him off, saying firmly, "The decision has been made."

"And how come you're the one who gets to make that decision? How come I'm not a part of that?"

"I get to decide because I'm *captain* of this ship and so—" Oliver cut her off.

"Ah, but that's the real issue here, innit?" said Oliver quietly, stepping closer to Lisha. The crew and passengers gaped at him in shock. By now, everyone within ten feet was watching the argument. Lisha merely looked at him, unblinking, her face darkly calm.

"What are you suggesting, Oliver? Choose your words carefully." Lisha leaned forward slightly. "Are you challenging my ability as captain, Oliver?" asked Lisha even more quietly, her eyes narrowing. Her barely masked anger sent a shiver through the onlookers, more chilling than if she'd shouted. But Oliver appeared unfazed.

"And what if I am? I'm sure there's loads of people," Oliver looked out at the crowd gathered around them, "who agree with me in this. I'm sure there are loads of people who are hesitant about risking their lives for strangers. We had no say in the decision to make this voyage. A responsible captain should place the safety of his crew above *all else.*"

"The safety of his crew, or merely that of himself?" asked Lisha.

The listeners made mocking sounds and gestures at Oliver, shouting "Coward!" Oliver clenched his fists, fuming, face twisting and turning red with anger and embarrassment.

"You'll regret ridiculing me when you've been captured and beaten to your knees! You'll see. You'll know I'm right when you're there waiting for your death; you'll regret not listening to me! You'll regret you ever followed the direction of a fool idiot girl what calls herself captain! She doesn't give a damn about any of you! Her and her fool idiot friends! There're all crazy, she's crazy! She's going to get us all killed! Who the devil does she think she is? Who the bloody hell do you think you are?"

"Stop it, Oliver," said Jasmine warningly. Oliver and Lisha looked quickly over at her, startled. Oliver stared at Jasmine for a moment and then began to laugh a cruel laugh.

"You, Jasmine?" he said incredulously. She glowered at him, dark, almond-shaped eyes narrowing. The corner of his mouth twisted into an ironic smile. "I don't believe it," said Oliver, shaking his head slowly. "You're actually naïve enough to trust her? I can't believe it! You really fell for it? How stupid can you get?"

"Enough!" snarled Lisha, startling everyone into silence with the vehemence of her tone. She stepped forward protectively, putting Jasmine behind her, and pointed a finger at Oliver. "I've had enough of your cheek!" she said, over-articulating to make her meaning clear. "You had better learn some respect, or I will teach it to you. This entire voyage all you've done is question me and attempt to order the others around behind my back. Don't think I don't know what you've been doing. Now you insult me and my friends and my crew—" she cut off, too furious to speak. "I've heard enough," she said at last, turning away. The crowd parted to let her pass. She stopped and looked back. "And if I were you, I'd be very, very careful from now on." She turned again and started to walk toward her cabin.

"Like your mother should have been careful," said Oliver in barely more than a whisper. Lisha froze. There were sharp intakes of breath from the crew and Protectors. Lisha whirled around, anger burning in her eyes, and strode purposely toward Oliver. She pulled out a dagger so quickly that it seemed to appear out of thin air into her hand. Marching up to Oliver, she brought the dagger to rest not so gently below his chin, forcing him to tilt back his head.

"You keep your mouth shut, you little weevil, before I permanently attach your tongue to the roof of your mouth!" Lisha quickly turned and stormed toward her cabin, grabbing Jasmine on the way, and slammed the door behind them.

❦

Dead trees moved in the wind. Crumpled leaves chased each other to the window of a dungeon. Inside, the prisoners were listening to a very sad story.

They had heard rumors about Desdemona and Aradia, but now they had a firsthand witness to tell the real story. Laramie, as Desdemona's sister and having also grown up in the same town as Aradia, could tell them valuable information about both of the Stoenhunters.

"It started many years ago when I was just a child living with my sister, Desdemona, and our parents in a small town in Ireland. Aradia lived in the same town as us. Desdemona was older then me and never let me forget it. My entire childhood she bullied me when she thought no one was looking. She was always inventing things to do to me and threatening to kill me if I didn't do what she said. I never really knew why she hated me so much."

"*Ç'est terrible!*" said Minuette.

"Did your parents do anything about it?" asked Tristan. Laramie shrugged.

"Desdemona was her meanest when she thought no one was looking. But I think my parents knew anyway. I think they tried to discipline her several times, but they weren't particularly harsh about it. They didn't really know how to tell her no. Ever since she was a little girl, whenever our parents reprimanded her, she would burst into tears, and they would relent. When she was little it may have been genuine, but as she grew older, she realized she could manipulate our parents that way into letting her get away with almost anything. And I think they felt bad for her also. Desdemona wasn't mean only to me. Petty stealing, playing pranks—everyone got so sick of it that no one wanted to see her. Everyone else shunned her because of the mean things she did. Everyone knew what she was doing, but she was so sneaky that no one could prove it was her. She always came up with good-sounding excuses, and our parents ate them up, wanting to believe anything except the truth. They didn't want to see what their daughter was becoming."

"That might explain why she turned out the way she did, at least in part," said Jordan thoughtfully. "She was spoiled. She always has to get what she wants. The best of everything, I'd guess."

"And that includes the Ultimate Power," finished Tristan.

"Very possibly," said Laramie. "But there's even more to it than that. She doesn't really see other people. The world exists to please her. If she wants something, she takes it. She's completely self-centered, only cares about herself. I don't think she ever developed a conscience. And she absolutely loathes me. But come. You asked of my history. Listen, I'll tell you the story. On my tenth birthday there was a carnival. There was a tent there that was selling Stoens. I knew what they were, because Aradia had already unlocked her power before then. A Drifter had come across her and explained about the Stoens and everything, and she told us. I wasn't quite sure at first that the engraved rocks the merchant was selling were Stoens, so I picked up one to see. Energy surged up my arms and through my whole body. I yelped as the red-hot shock spread into my head. Desdemona turned and grabbed the stone from me. Or she tried to. My hands were stuck to it. I could barely see after that, because the energy filled my eyes, blinding me, but I felt Desdemona's fingers clawing at my hand. Suddenly, the spell was broken and my hands came free. Another girl from the town, my friend Fala, rushed over and caught me as I fell. I lay there—"

"Wait, *Fala* was there?" said Tristan. "The leader of the Irish Protector troupe?" She knew Fala through the network of communication between the different troupe leaders.

"Oh, Fala's a troupe leader? Good for her. Yes, she was there. Didn't you know? *She's Aradia's sister.*" The others gaped at her, but she wasted no time with explanations.

"I lay there in Fala's arms as the energy sank into me. When I regained my eyesight, I saw Desdemona standing there, glowing. She was holding another one of the Stoens from the table. Aradia came over to her. She touched Desdemona's shoulder to see if she was all right, but jumped back and yelped in pain. Desdemona's hands flew off the stone, and it dropped to the ground. She held her head in her hand and staggered backwards until her back was against one of the poles holding up the tent. She slipped to the ground. Aradia knelt beside her and opened Desdemona's hands to make sure they were all right. She turned and said to Fala, "C'mon. Pick her up. We'll carry them home." Fala nodded, but when Aradia tried to lift Desdemona, Desdemona knocked Aradia to the ground with a sweeping stroke of her arm. Desdemona stood and looked at herself. Fala lifted me up, so I stood on my feet and leaned on her shoulder, and we started to walk toward her house. Desdemona looked at me. I froze. That look was so full of hatred. I tore my gaze away. She looked at Fala. Their eyes met. Desdemona raised her hand, and Fala stood, staring at her. Desdemona smirked and moved her hand. Fala walked away from me, leaving me to fall to the ground. She turned and began walking toward Aradia."

"Mind control," said Tristan. "Like a *marionnette* and its master. Just like you said." Laramie nodded sadly.

"Yes. Chance have it, we both found the Stoens designed to unlock our particular types of powers, my sister and I, at the same time."

"What is your power?" asked Minuette.

"I'll get there," said Laramie, a smile in her voice. "Desdemona, unfortunately, realized what had happened before I did. Aradia said to her, 'Desdemona, what are you doing? Let her go!' but Desdemona shook her head. As she did, so did Fala. Fala and Desdemona looked at us, and it was as if they were the same person, for their expressions were identical. Desdemona turned to go and gestured behind her. Fala followed. Aradia ran after her, saying 'Stop!' I ran after them. Desdemona was headed for the docks. Aradia held up her hand, and Desdemona's shadow twisted around her. Aradia moved her hand slowly, and the shadow around Desdemona's arm twisted it, making her fingers point toward Fala. Desdemona's control snapped, and Fala fell to the ground."

The Protectors listening to the story winced.

"Aradia, rushing to her sister, said, 'Fala!' The shadow around Desdemona dissolved. Desdemona smirked and looked straight at me. I snapped upright and began walking. Except it wasn't me walking. She was controlling me. I tried to speak, but I couldn't. She waved her hand and ran off toward the pier overlooking the ocean. I followed helplessly. A dagger flashed in her hand. It must have been in her pocket. We reached the pier with Aradia and Fala hot on our tails. I prayed that they'd catch up. Desdemona beckoned, and I felt myself walking toward her. She handed me the dagger. My hand grasped it and started to move the blade close to my chest. In my mind I was crying, but not one tear escaped my eyes. I couldn't stop myself."

The Protectors gave Laramie sympathetic looks.

"Aradia arrived to see me about to stab myself," continued Laramie. "She stopped in shock and said, 'Let her go! What did she ever do to you?' Desdemona didn't answer. Aradia wrapped a shadow around my hand and forced it back, away from my chest. Desdemona pushed with her mind. Now it was a struggle to see who was the more powerful. I only wished that my life didn't hinge on the test. Aradia was winning. Desdemona was sweating and clenching her fists. But then it seemed from her face that she had come up with an idea. She turned to face Aradia, her eyes blazing. With her concentration down, I was still unable to move, but I was able to speak. I said, 'No, Aradia! Don't look into her eyes!' because it seemed that was how she controlled people. But it was too late. Aradia fought, but Desdemona was able to make her release the spell on the shadow binding my arm. Desdemona kept Aradia at bay, and again I was completely under her control. My hand on the dagger moved closer and closer to my heart, which pounded in my ears. The tip touched my chest, and a dot of blood appeared. Aradia broke out and tried to put a shadow around my arm once again, but Desdemona stopped her in midstep as she walked toward me. Desdemona turned her attentions once again to me, and before anyone could do anything about it, she plunged the dagger into my heart."

"Wait a second. If she killed you, then how are you—" started Jordan.

"Oh, she far from killed me," said Laramie bitterly. "But sometimes I wish she had."

"How can you say that?" asked Minuette. Then she thought back to what Laramie had said about her being lucky to have someone out there thinking about her, and she understood. Laramie had been locked up in this dungeon for who knows how long, feeling abandoned and lonely, with only other prisoners and her hateful sister for company, never knowing what had happened to her friends, family, whether they still thought about her. If they really cared about her, wouldn't they have come for her already? Laramie saw comprehension in Minuette's eyes and continued the story.

"Fala gasped, and Desdemona laughed with glee. I sank to the ground. My head was spinning. But then I realized that I wasn't bleeding. I took the knife out of my chest, and there wasn't even a scratch. Desdemona turned back to me, a look of shock, disappointment, rage, and loathing on her face. She said, 'No—no, it's happened! The prediction's come true!' I asked. 'What prediction?' She told me. She said, 'When you were born, our parents went to a fortuneteller to look into your future. She said that when you turned ten, you would become immortal. I had to stop that happening. Why are you the one who's immortal? It should have been *me!*' Desdemona pushed me to the ground. 'Why do you think I've been trying to kill you all these years?' she asked, walking forward. And then she said, 'Well, if I can't kill you, I can at least make sure I never see you again!' There was a hint of a crazed laugh in her voice. She raised her hand to push me over the side of the pier. Fala shouted, 'Wait!' She ran up and stood between Desdemona and me, shielding me with her body. 'You can't do that! I won't let you!' Aradia yelled, 'Fala, *no!*' and leapt forward; Desdemona's control broken again. Aradia caused a hand made of shadows to lift Fala and me out of the way. She stood before Desdemona. Fala said 'Aradia, no! You'll get yourself killed!' Desdemona stared hard at Aradia. Aradia jerked and twitched and fell to the ground. Desdemona looked at me. I felt myself walking toward the edge of the cliff. Fala couldn't move; she was still under the shadow hand Aradia had created. I stepped off the cliff and fell down into the ocean, where I sank to the ocean floor. I panicked at first, but then I found that I didn't need to breathe. There I stayed for a long time, I don't know how many years, until Aradia lifted me out into this place. I don't really know what happened while I was gone, but things are different. Desdemona seems to be working for Aradia now."

"Wait, wait, wait," cut in Jordan. "Desdemona is working for Aradia? I thought they were *competing* for the power!" He exchanged a look with Tristan.

"What about Mr. Loxlyheart?" asked Tristan. "Does he know about this?"

"Oh yes," said Laramie. "You see, he's working with them as well." The Protectors were struck speechless. Laramie appeared to glance around at each of them and then, getting no more response, continued. "Anyway, I was telling you about Desdemona and Aradia. I don't know what happened to them, but they've changed. Especially Aradia. She's like a completely different person. And Desdemona ... for her to be working for someone else ... it's odd. She's self-centered, but not self-absorbed. She wants to be loved, worshipped. It's not enough that she be the center of her own world, she wanted to be the center of everyone else's as well. Underneath the shell, she's actually very fragile."

Just then the door to the prison opened, and Aradia stepped in. She waved a hand, and shadows sealed themselves over Laramie's mouth.

"Idiotic, foolish girl. I was listening to that lovely fantasy, too, you know. I came to see if I could extract any more information from our prisoners, and lo and behold, I hear my life story being recounted. I listened. I wanted to see if you would get it right. I shouldn't have bothered. Fools, are you really going to trust her? She's been under the ocean for too long, so her memory of this incident is not entirely correct. You can only see so much from one person's point of view. Now, would you like to hear what really happened?" The Protectors' mouths dropped open, but before they could reply, she continued.

"The story of Desdemona starts many years ago. Try to picture it. Imagine what it was like. To be hated and shunned by everyone. Even your own parents don't really like you. Walking through the streets, people avoid you, shoot you ugly looks. Those people deserved whatever they got! And all because of this little rat!" Aradia stabbed a finger in Laramie's direction. "It was all her fault!" she said, fuming now. "She slandered her own sister every chance she got! She deserved to die! But then she had to go along and have that infuriating power: immortal life! Well, if I couldn't kill her—that is, if we couldn't kill—" Aradia faltered for a moment, but quickly recovered. "You see, I was Desdemona's friend, the only one, and I alone saw the injustice done to her, and I resolved to help her be rid of her sister. She told me that I would get to help when the time came, but then on the day of that carnival, she was going to kill Laramie all by herself. It was a painful betrayal at the time, but we've since resolved our differences and remained friends. And we pursue the same goal together now: to kill Laramie! We didn't think it was possible until we found out about the Ultimate Power. It's the only way. We will never be free until we rid the world of that miserable child."

Her story finished, Aradia stood, breathing hard, color still staining her cheeks. She snapped her fingers, and two of the prison guards appeared in the doorway behind her. "I want Laramie moved to a private cell," said Aradia to them. "She doesn't deserve company."

"Yes, Your Grace," said the guards. They unlocked Laramie's shackles and dragged her away. Aradia followed them out the door, locking it behind her.

None of the Protectors dared to speak until Aradia was out of earshot.

"Poor Laramie," said Minuette. "*Quel dommage. What will happen to her?"

"She'll probably get killed as soon as Aradia gets the power," said Jordan miserably. Tristan opened her mouth to say that Aradia wasn't going to get the power, but then realized that their chances of winning were slim and closed it. "Can you believe Aradia, though?" Jordan went on. "She broke free of Desdemona's mind control, which was very powerful even back then! I wasn't sure what Desdemona's power was before. I never would have guessed."

"And who would have guessed that *Fala* was Aradia's *sister*! I did not even know she *had* a sister!" wondered Minuette.

"Mm," said Tristan. She was staring out into space.

"What is it?" said Minuette.

"Oh, nothing. I just thought ... well, maybe there was another reason Aradia had Laramie taken away."

"Like what?" asked Minuette.

"Maybe she took her away because she wanted her not to tell us something."

"Which means there's something we still don't know," said Jordan.

"But what?" asked Minuette, voicing what everyone was thinking. No one had an answer. They looked out the window of the decrepit castle and over the haunted landscape. "Please get us out of here ... please," Minuette whispered to the wind.

❦

"What was that?" asked Jasper. Lisha turned.

"Did you hear something?" she asked.

"I could've sworn that I heard a voice carried by the breeze."

"What did it say?" asked Lisha, checking the compass.

"It sounded like, 'please.' Does that mean anything to you?"

"I'm not sure." The two of then gazed out into the distance. Through the mist, Jasper almost thought he could see a girl's face ... but he couldn't be sure. Lisha turned to him.

"Yes, Jasper. It means something."

For lunch there was freshly caught fish. Kit didn't wait to ask what it was. She just grabbed a plate from Hilda, the redheaded cook, and started eating. A jab at her neck reminded her to slip some to Kaida.

Kaida and Kit had become fast friends and were inseparable.

"'Ow's the fish?" asked Kit between mouthfuls.

"Better than usual," said Kaida, spitting out a fish bone. "Fresher."

"Freshly caught this morning," said a light, lyrical voice from behind them. Kit turned, startled. Jasmine, Lisha's first mate, was standing behind them with a fish kabob in her hand. She had cinnamon skin and hair the color of coffee beans. Her dark, almond-shaped eyes looked kindly down at Kit. Her eyes held a certain bright spark, but also a strange sadness. Kit drew into her shell, raising her shoulders, still shy around strangers. She continued eating quietly. "It's all right. I don't bite," Jasmine laughed, sitting down next to Kit. "My name's Jasmine. I'm sorry, I didn't catch yours."

"Huh? Oh. It's Kit," mumbled Kit.

"Kit? That's a nice name. And who's your little friend?"

"Little!" said Kaida indignantly. Kit quickly put a hand over his mouth and pushed his head farther under the cloth. Jasmine smiled kindly.

"Don't worry about it. I've known about him for a while now. He can come out if he wants to." Kit slowly withdrew her hand, still looking suspiciously at Jasmine. Jasmine tore off a bit of fish with her teeth, oblivious to Kit's stare. "I've been watching you two. He's fascinating. I'm sorry, I would've introduced myself earlier, but Lisha had me working day and night." Jasmine smiled to herself, but her eyes grew strangely sad. Kit relaxed her posture a little. The way Jasmine had said Lisha's name, with such affection, almost tenderness, made Kit feel a bit less uncomfortable. Any friend of Lisha's was all right in her book. Jasmine looked back toward Kit. "How long've you been with Lisha and Jasper and the others?" she asked. Kit looked up into the air, thinking.

"I's been wif Lisha an' wot for—oh, I dunno ... not more n' a few weeks." It was hard to believe, but not much time had passed from when Kit first met Jasper and the other Protectors.

"I've known Lisha since we were children," said Jasmine. "Our families worked together. My parents were merchants, too. I didn't get to know Lisha well though until her father picked me up escaping from the same pirate ship that took Nat."

"Wha' were you doin' on a pirate ship?" asked Kit, beginning to get interested.

"Oh, well, these pirates came and attacked while we were in port. I fought back and tried to stop them, so they tied me up and took me with them. Probably thought they could sell me. I think they were trying to get into the slave trade, but fortunately for me and Nat, they weren't very good at it." Jasmine laughed a little, a laugh that didn't touch her eyes. "I was really lucky they were so incompetent as to attack the same people twice. I might never have gotten home otherwise." Kit nodded her head in awe. She'd heard of slavery but had never been this close to it before. So many brave people, so many sad stories. It seemed so unfair the way that good people had to suffer so much. *Maybe that's why they're such good people,* thought Kit. *Because they've suffered an' all. The difference 'tween them an' th' bad people was that they'd faced the suffering head on, bravely, an' survived it. Mebee bad people are just good people wot didn't make it.* She picked up the fish kabob and turned it slowly. *I 'ope I make it,* she thought. She looked around at the crew and passengers. Each one of them had their own story, every one. *I wish I knew them all. I'd put them all in a box and keep them safe forever, so they'd never be forgotten.*

Jasmine watched Kit, feeling a fresh wave of guilt wash over her. But then she reminded herself that she was doing this to protect them. All of them. What Jasmine had to go through was a small price to pay to keep her friends safe. Even if sometimes it didn't feel like it. But she knew that given the chance, she'd do the same thing again. She would do anything to protect her friends.

❦

Rodger turned from the bed and started to walk slowly toward a man with a child on his knee. He picked up speed and tore chairs and tables out of the way as he advanced toward them.

"She killed her! She killed her! I'll rip her arms off! I'll tear her hair out! I'll—"

"Calm down, Rodger. She didn't mean any harm— no... no, what are you doing? Rodger, answer me, Rodger, what are you doing?" Rodger had grabbed the child under the arms and lifted her up in the air.

"I'm taking vengeance, I'm avenging Annabel's death! The child killed her! If you can call it a child; just look at it! Look at that hideous dark skin. This isn't a child! This is a demon! Sent to haunt me after destroying my life and my love!"

"What are you talking about? A demon?" The man reached forward to try to grab the girl from Rodger. "There is nothing wrong with the child. The child is helpless! She couldn't kill anyone!"

"She can and she did." Rodger moved slowly backwards, toward the open window. "Garron, Garron listen to me! You're my friend, my trusted adviser! What would you do if someone killed your wife?"

"She didn't kill your wife; your wife died of natural causes! For goodness sakes, Rodger, she's only a baby!" The

man, Garron, grabbed Rodger's arm and attempted to draw him back into the center of the room.

"She's three years old. I would hardly consider that a baby," said Rodger, holding the child in the air and out of reach.

"But she's a child, nonetheless. Can't you see that you are bringing this upon yourself? You want someone to blame, and so you take out your anger on the very being Annabel died to protect! This is not what she would have wanted, Rodger! Rodger, are you listening to me? What are you doing? For Heaven's sake, what are you doing?" Rodger had set the girl down and drawn back to the window, holding tightly to her arm. He opened the window and placed his hand on the terrified girl's throat.

"No more ... no more pain ... if I kill her it will be all right ... Annabel will be ..." He was interrupted when the child pushed at his huge hands with her small ones, gasping for breath. Rodger looked at the child and said, "If it weren't for you, she would have been perfectly fine!" With this, Rodger flung the girl down on the floor.

"What do you mean, she would have been perfectly fine? Rodger, it's not the child's fault. What are you doing?" Rodger had grabbed the neck of the girl and slammed her against the wall. "Good God, man, what are you doing! Stop it! Stop it this instant! Rodger, you're scaring me. Rodger! Can you hear me! Put the child down, do you hear me? Put the child down."

Kiara sat up, clutching her throat. She'd felt like he was really strangling her. She composed herself and fixed her thick black hair, which had started coming out of its braids. Now she knew what had really happened, why she had not been able to remember what had happened afterward. She must have blacked out. No wonder she had almost forgotten that night. Awake she knew only what had been told to her. Only a scar remained. But a scar alone was enough.

She looked around. Nat's bed was empty.

Nat stood on the deck. He couldn't sleep. He had lain awake for a long time thinking about Kiara. She intrigued him, even fascinated him. She was so strong in the face of such troubles ... his heart ached to think of her ever being in pain. He prayed that her sad story, a story so much like his own, would have a happy ending. *If only there was a way I could give her that. I would do anything.*

He stared up at the sky, unseeing. He saw Kiara's face in his mind, wearing one of her rare smiles. The corners of his mouth turned up. *I want to see her smiling always. Because I love her.*

He closed his eyes. Yes, he knew it was true. He'd been falling for her ever since he first looked into those dark eyes. Since the first time he saw her smile. *But I can't let her know. If she doesn't feel the same way, it could ruin our friendship, after we've just started. No. I have to put her first. No matter what I feel, I can't take the chance—if I hurt her—*

Footsteps. Nat turned to see Kiara coming up from below deck, wrapped in a blanket. Seeing Nat, she came over to him. His heartbeat quickened. He couldn't breathe. *No! Can't look in her eyes! She'll see. She'll know. Must ... restrain.*

"Nat?" came Kiara's voice. Nat jumped slightly. He looked away resolutely, avoiding her eyes. Kiara came up beside him and carefully touched his face with her fingertips, turning his head toward her. He tried not to look at her. He really made a valiant effort of it.

"Nat, what's—" Their eyes met. She froze, her eyes wide. He looked so vulnerable, like a hermit crab caught without his shell. His expression was so open, so sincere. His green eyes were like windows onto a grassy field. They seemed to be beckoning her forward, like a hypnotist's charm. Nat watched, captivated, as Kiara's face softened, glowing in the moonlight like an angel's. All thoughts flew out of his head as his eyes closed and he moved his face slowly closer to Kiara's. Kiara held very still, scared that the slightest move might wake her from this dream.

Suddenly, Nat remembered his resolution to not give into his feelings, his worry about jeopardizing their precious friendship. He had a sudden premonition of Kiara slapping him and seeing her indignant face for a second before she turned and ran away. Instinctively, Nat jumped backwards. *I can't do this; I—I shouldn't be doing this.* But instead of anger or resentment on Kiara's face, Nat only saw the remnants of anticipation and ... was it longing? Kiara looked at him, still dazed. Confusion showed in her face, then hurt.

"Why ... why did you?" asked Kiara.

"I—I—" Nat looked at her, shocked. This was not the reaction he'd expected. Disappointment painted her features for a moment. Then she snapped out of the spell and looked away. *What am I doing?* thought Kiara. *What have I done?* thought Nat. *She* likes *me! I am such an idiot!* He'd only been trying to avoid hurting her, but his efforts had backfired.

What was I thinking? thought Kiara. *People like me don't do stuff like that with people like him. He doesn't actually like you. He just feels sorry for you. Besides, he's— he's too good for you, you—you don't deserve him, he's—*but why? Why couldn't she give in? Just this once?

But the moment was broken. Now was not the time. Kiara turned, blinking tears from her eyes. *No—I can't cry. He can't see that I'm upset.* She couldn't take in anymore and ran back downstairs.

"Kiara! Wait! I didn't mean—" It was too late. Nat sat, his head in his hand, and cried like he hadn't since he was a little boy. *I can't believe I hurt her.* Little did he know that right below him, Kiara cried. Their tears would mix with the ocean air, and tomorrow the red eyes would be gone. Neither would ever have to know.

You don't deserve her.
He's too good for you.
You'll never—
Never—
Never get your happy ending.

It was a rainy day with nothing for most of the passengers to do. Various members amused the rest with their powers. Leandra, the fiery Irish girl from Fala's troupe, was up first. She laid a blanket on the floor and crawled under it. Under the blanket her form changed. Something growled and threw off the blanket. Standing there was a leopard wearing Leandra's clothes. Then she morphed into a tiger and began pacing in a circle, swiping her claws threateningly at the onlookers. Halfway around the circle, she changed into a white tiger. Leandra leaped at the nearest person and changed in mid-jump into a panther. She landed beside the person she was aiming at. Walking to the middle of the circle of people, Leandra lay down. Then she was a lioness. She bared her sharp teeth and reared up on two legs. Turning into a cheetah, she began to run around in circles at amazing speeds. Soon, she was moving too fast to see, merely an orange blur. Then it stopped, and there stood Leandra, fully clothed, just morphing her paws back into hands. Her audience cheered as she took a bow and returned to her seat.

Kit turned her head toward the shoulder where Kaida perched and whispered, "She's amazing!"

Kaida leaned toward Kit's ear and said, "Crazy girl. Too much spirit, if you ask me."

Fala, the black-haired leader of the Irish troupe, was next. The Protectors gasped as she flew into the room in her raven form and circled above them before perching on the edge of a chair. People watched it. The beautiful black feathers were almost blue in the light, and the eyes were intelligent. The raven looked out at the crowd. She took a pencil and paper from a desk and began to write.

"'Ow can she do that?" asked Kit.

"It's not so hard. So she can write, *I* can—" but Kit never found out what Kaida could do, because at that very moment, the bird swooped over her head and handed the paper to Mica. Then she took out a piece of cloth from the drawer and a needle and thread. The raven began to sew. Within a minute she had finished. The raven held up her finished work. Embroidered on the fabric was a picture of the sign on the animal Stoen. She flew once around the room with it and then sat, or rather stood, at the back of the room. The raven flapped her wings, sending clouds of dust over the crowd. Everybody started coughing. When the dust cleared, Fala stood where the raven had been. She quietly took her seat, and the audience applauded.

"She's so—I dunno, quiet. Polite. Distant. Modest. I can't explain it," said Kit.

"Hmm. Makes you wonder what her past was like," said Kaida.

"Or her family," said Kit.

Next up was Nat. He took a sack of seeds into the center of the circle.

"I'll need a volunteer," he said. "Kiara?" She looked up, surprised. Kiara stood slowly and stepped into the circle.

"Just look at him. It's obvious he likes her," muttered Kaida to Kit.

"Nothin' wrong wif that," said Kit. "An' you 'erd that from Lisha." Kaida looked uncomfortable.

"So what if I did? A dragon's got his right to eavesdrop on people."

Nat told Kiara to stand in the center of the floor. Then he opened the sack of seeds. Nat raised his arms above his head, letting his hands bow down toward the sack. Vines glided silkily out of the bag. They curved in a circle around Kiara and rose gracefully into the air like the necks of swans. More vines began to flow out of the bag and follow the others. The first vines grew almost to the ceiling in a circle around Kiara. Kiara watched them, wide-eyed. Nat twirled his fingers, and the vines spiraled together from the top in an elegant cascade, forming a teardrop-like shape around Kiara. She watched in wonder as the vines swirled around her. Nat smiled, excitement in his eyes as he moved his arms in an almost dance. The tiny vines lifted upward, spinning in the opposite direction, and wove themselves in with the other vines in intricate patterns. The intertwining stems formed a delicate teardrop-shaped basket around Kiara. Nat touched his fingers together and pulled his arms apart. As he did, all the vines stretched outward. Tiny holes appeared between the vines and a shape—Kiara—was visible within. The vines, as thin as fingers, were woven into an intricate and beautiful pattern. All around the room people gasped. Kiara looked around her with an open mouth, wondering at the beauty. Flowers and sprites were depicted in the tapestry of vines. Leaves shaped like hearts decorated the image. Then she noticed something. Nat saw her shift positions through the tiny holes filling the design and smiled, his heart racing. For encoded into the pattern so that only Kiara could see were the words

I Love You.

Kiara brought her hands to her mouth. Her cheeks grew warm, and she felt a smile stretch across her face as she struggled to stifle sudden tears. The vines soon dried and contracted, fading into the air like spider silk. Everyone applauded as Nat took a bow. He grinned at Kiara, and she smiled at him, both blushing faintly. They sat down in the shadows where no one could see Kiara put her hand in his.

Emra got up next. She went under the blanket that Leandra had used in her performance. But instead of just one snake, three emerged. The crowd stared at them.

"Oh!" said Mica, the wise young Protector from the Irish troupe. "She wants us to guess which one is her!" Comprehension dawned on the faces of all present. They began to systematically examine the snakes. They were identical in every way.

"I know how to figure it out!" said Leandra. She changed into an ocelot and began hunting around, still wearing her dress. Finally, she changed back with something in her hands.

"A mouse?" asked Jasper.

"No human girl would willingly swallow a whole live mouse," said Leandra. All the girls around the room murmured their assent, and the boys laughed.

Leandra took the mouse and dropped it into the circle. Nat formed a wall with vines so it couldn't get out. All three snakes slithered toward the mouse. One struck first and unhinged its jaw to swallow the mouse. Another one grabbed it out of the first one's mouth and slithered away. The third one chased after the second one halfheartedly, but soon gave up. It slithered under the blanket again, and Emra came out, clutching the blanket around her. Everyone clapped as Emra took a bow.

"I wonder where she got the other snakes," whispered Kaida suspiciously. Leandra and Nat shook hands on a job well done. Lisha stood up and walked to the center.

"Anyone else?" asked Lisha.

"How about Genna?" suggested Mica, gesturing toward his sister. Genna looked at him reproachfully.

"Mica, you know I haven't unlocked my power yet," she said quietly.

"No power? Ha! Have you *seen* her drawings? And no normal person has a memory like that!" said Kaida, startling everyone.

"Go on, Genna, draw something!" the Protectors encouraged her.

"All right, all right, I'll do it." Genna stood up and walked slowly to the center of the room, carrying her sketchpad. "What do you want me to draw?" Everyone began making suggestions.

"Draw the boat!"

"Draw Mica!"

"Draw me!"

"She doesn't want to draw you."

"Well, why not?"

"Because she *should* be drawing *me*!"

"Draw Leandra changing into a lion!"

"Draw the Stoens!"

The last request drew Genna's attention.

"All right, then. I'll draw the Stoens," she said. She was about to begin to draw from memory when Jasper asked, "Emra, can you go get them?" Emra stood before Genna could protest that she remembered what the Stoens looked like. Lisha tossed her the ring of keys. Emra caught it and ran up the stairs. She was gone for a while. When Emra finally returned, she was white as a sheet.

"Well, did you get them?" asked Jasper. "Emra, what's wrong?"

"Jasper ... Lisha ... they're gone!"

❧

The next day brought with it views of a world carved out of the side of a mountain. Houses on stilts linked by spindly stairways lined the cliff face. The crewmembers and the Protectors gasped as they gazed around, their worry over the missing Stoens momentarily forgotten.

"We're 'ere!" cried Lali, the sun glinting off her nose ring. Emra was smiling broadly. "I've never been to the Lake District before!" she said excitedly.

"All ashore!" called Lisha as they reached the dock. Lisha hopped down from the mast and leaped out over the gangplank onto solid land. She stood and breathed in the air off the mountain. The rest of the Protectors filed off the ship. The crew stayed aboard, leaving Jasmine in charge until Lisha returned.

Jasper released the Protectors into the city to explore and to find out surreptitiously if any Stoens had been stolen lately. Lisha and Jasper set off purposefully toward the mountain. Lisha turned.

"Kit, you'd better come with us." Kit looked at her questioningly and then raced to catch up. She followed them up the maze of streets and alleyways. The sky was getting cloudier and the streets were badly lit. No, that wasn't it, the sun still shone brightly on the other side of town. Then Kit saw the clouds of fog coming out of a large mill at the top of the mountain. They began climbing a stairway up the mountain, and a cold wind blew through Kit. Kaida climbed over to the front of her dress. Kit held him tight. Being a reptile, Kaida was more susceptible to the cold than Kit was, and she did her best to keep him warm. Kit lost track of how long they'd been walking. It felt like hours, and it kept getting colder. Eventually, Lisha and Jasper waited for her to catch up, and Lisha draped a blanket around the three of them. Soon they hit a pocket of fog. They began to cough.

"What's in this stuff?" asked Kit between coughs.

"Cotton dust. Come on, just a little further," said Lisha, pushing on. When Kit looked up again, they were right in front of the mill. Lisha walked up to the big doors and knocked hard. A slot opened and two eyes were visible.

"We're here to see Cameron. Will you let us in?" yelled Lisha above the howling of machinery from inside.

"No visitors. Company policy," said a man's voice.

"This is a matter of great importance. I need to speak with Cameron," yelled Lisha.

"No visitors!" He was about to shut the slot, but Lisha stuck a shilling in the hole. The eyes widened, and he took the money. "Door to your right. I'll let you in." The slot closed. Kit glanced at Lisha, who looked carefully straight ahead.

"Where did you get that?" asked Kit.

"I heard that Cameron was working at the new mill up here. They've been springing up all over the place, what with the flying shuttle and all that making work so much more efficient. It's disgusting really, the way the workers are treated, but it pays better than whatever they were doing before, so they do it. The rules are strict, so I thought we might need a bribe to get us in." Kit looked at Jasper, who hummed to himself exaggeratedly, glancing purposefully in the other direction. Kit giggled, but the sound was lost to the roar.

There was a sound like metal scraping metal, and the door swung open. Lisha led the other two inside.

Kit looked around. They were in a fairly large room, damp and badly lit. Surrounding her, Kit could make out the source of the roar: huge machines filled the room, spinning and weaving dangerously fast. Groups of people monitored and worked on the machines, workers so dirty they were barely distinguishable from the machines they worked on. Kit started, realizing that the majority of the workers were children, some much younger than her. A hand touched Kit's head. She jumped.

"Stay close," said Lisha. The man led them to the back of the room, where a woman with orange-streaked blond hair and a crushed nose was bent over a spinning machine. Her hair was tied up tightly in a gray cloth the same color as her apron. She looked up as they came over.

"Someone to see you, Cameron," shouted the man, trying to get above the noise. She stood and took in these three strange people. For a moment, Kit was afraid she didn't recognize them.

"Lisha?" Cameron stared. "My—it's so good to see—" She broke off, glancing around. Her expression darkened. "You shouldn't be here," she said under the noise of the whirring machines.

"It's all right," shouted back Lisha, then, more quietly, "I bribed the guard." Cameron glanced over at the manager, resolutely facing away from them. "We've got something to talk to you about. Important." Cameron's brow furrowed as if she were teetering on the edge of a decision. Then she nodded and led the three of them out a back door. They emerged behind the factory to find an assortment of small houses piled nearly on top of each other. As soon as she shut the door behind them, Lisha said, "We have some questions to ask you. What—"

"Shh!" said Cameron, looking around. "It's not safe to talk here. Follow me." With that, she started walking quickly, yet carefully, past the dangerously dilapidated houses. The others followed her. Kit looked around and hugged Kaida even closer. The houses were like those of a ghost town, barely habitable, yet shapes stirred inside. After awhile, they reached a small hut. Cameron opened the door and led them through to a stairway at the back. Down, down they climbed. Kit felt growing trepidation as she watched the long shadows thrown on the wall by the lanterns. Finally, they reached another door. Cameron opened it, and the others followed her through. Kit felt as if she were stepping through a portal into another world. Suddenly, the sun was up. They were in a sculptor's workshop. Lying around on tables were tools, which Cameron quickly shoved onto shelves or into drawers.

"Sorry," she apologized sheepishly. "Ever since the Stoenhunters shut my shop down, I haven't found time to clean up."

"The Stoenhunters shut you down?" asked Jasper, concerned.

"Yes," said Cameron. "Mr. Loxlyheart came and built the mill you just saw. Everyone said he was crazy for trying to start a factory on the edge of the Lake District, but he said that if a town could survive here, then so could a factory. When he found out what we were all up to, he shut down the whole operation and press-ganged us into working for him." A somber silence ensued, and Kaida took that moment to poke his head up from inside Kit's dress. Upon spotting Cameron, he crawled up to Kit's neck and yelled, "Cameron!" Kaida jumped off Kit's shoulder, catlike, and landed on the table. He ran on all fours to Cameron and leaped toward her. She stepped back, surprised, but realizing who it was, embraced Kaida. Pulling him from her with two hands and holding him out in front of her, she looked Kaida up and down.

"Kaida! Boy, have you grown! What are you doing here?" she asked.

"Well," preened Kaida, "after I went to live with Xylon, I met his adopted niece, Leandra. Crazy girl. I tried to follow her home; living in the forest can get a bit dull. But Xylon caught me. I asked him if I could go stay with her to get out of the woods for a while. Eventually he agreed. Through Leandra, I met the rest of the Irish troupe. When they went to meet up with some Protectors from England, I went with them. There I met Kit," he gestured toward Kit with his thumb. *Dragons have thumbs?* thought Kit.

"I thought you might want to see each other, so I brought Kit with us. The two are inseparable!" said Lisha. Kit nodded inwardly, understanding. She had been wondering what she was there for.

"So wo' *were* you up to tha' Mr. Loxly'eart 'ad t' come 'n stop ya?" asked Kit.

Kit caught Lisha smiling to herself and resisted the urge to glare.

"Well, you see," Cameron began, sadly. "I belong to the Guild of Stoenmasons," she said, pronouncing the two syllables in the word Stoen.

"Don't you mean, 'stonemasons'?" asked Kit. Cameron smiled. Kit noticed again how crooked her nose was. *It must have been broken*, thought Kit. Cameron appeared to be in her early thirties, but Kit couldn't be sure. The bent nose made her look older.

"Stoenmasons don't work with stones. We work with Stoens. Make them, actually." She wiped her forehead with the back of her hand. "Well, we can't just make as many as we want any time we want. The magic laws governing the Stoens dictate that there must be a certain number of each type in the world at a time. We maintain that number. Repair or replace broken ones, help the Protectors watch over the ones that are out there, you know." Kit gaped at her.

"Woll, I s'pose they must've been coming from somewhere," said Kit.

"Anyways, what was it that you wanted to talk to me about?" asked Cameron.

"Yes, that. The Ultimate Power," said Jasper bluntly. Cameron stopped and looked at him. She drew the curtains closed and sat the three of them down on couches in the next room. Cameron sat expectantly, resting her chin in her hands.

"We need to know a few things about the Power, so we can stop the Hunters from getting it," said Jasper.

"The Drifters have all disappeared, and no one seems to know that much about how the thing actually works," continued Lisha. "Do you need all the existing Stoens to complete the pattern to get the Ultimate Power or just one of each type?"

"Each type?" repeated Kit questioningly.

"Oh, you know," said Cameron, "the way it works is that even though there are many different powers that people have, the powers can be sorted into groups along with ones similar to them. Each group of powers has a Stoen needed to unlock the powers in that group. But there is more than one of each Stoen, depending on how large the group is. For example, one group is powers having to do with animals. All the specific powers that people have that fit under that category are slightly different, but they are all related to each other as they each concern animals. The animal Stoen unlocks the powers of people in that group. But since it is such a large group, there are several animal Stoens in the world at a time. Anyway, let me see," Cameron paused to think. "I believe that to unlock the Ultimate Power you need one of each type.

That is, one Stoen from each of the different groups, categories, of powers."

"And how many would that be?" asked Jasper.

"How many different types of Stoens are there?" asked Lisha, leaning in. "How many different groups of powers are there, different categories?" Cameron stood up and took a large leather-bound book from a high shelf. She blew dust off the cover and took it over to the couch. Cameron opened it and flipped through the yellowed pages one by one. Kit watched pictures of wings and what looked to be an alphabet fly by. Cameron finally came to a page with sketches of symbols with cramped, handwritten notes in the margins.

"I believe there are ... twelve types of Stoens." The three of them stared at her in disbelief. Only twelve?

"Only twelve?" asked Jasper. "But ...." Mr. Loxlyheart, Desdemona, and Aradia only needed to collect twelve rocks to be in control of the world. It seemed so ... easy.

"Tell me, Cameron," said Lisha, putting on a show of calm, "if someone did get the Ultimate Power, is there any way it could be removed? Undone? Taken away? Defeated?" Cameron flipped through the book. Again, Kit saw brief glimpses of illustrations, barely there long enough for her to see what they were.

"There is. Actually, it's quite simple. It says here, 'In the event that an individual obtains the Ultimate Power and the individual is rendered unconscious by unnatural means, then the Power will be removed and returned to the pattern to be claimed by the next person who touches it,'" Cameron read. "Either that, or the person with the Power would have to give it up freely. And once someone has had the Power and lost it, they can't ever have it again. That particular person, that is."

Lisha thought for a second.

"That's good ... but not good enough. Is there a way to permanently destroy the Ultimate Power?" asked Lisha. Cameron turned another page.

"It seems that the Ultimate Power, instead of being transferred into a person, can be transferred to an object. If that object is destroyed, then the Ultimate Power will be as well," said Cameron. Jasper's brow furrowed.

"That doesn't make much sense," said Jasper. "If an object had the Ultimate Power, wouldn't it be invulnerable?"

"Actually, no. You see, the object itself does not *have* the power; it is merely *carrying* it. This way, the Power could be taken far away from the place where the Stoens were arranged and given to someone. This would be much easier than them having to assemble the Stoens themselves," said Cameron.

"So that means," began Lisha, but she stopped. There was a low knocking sound coming from the other room.

"One second," said Cameron. She stood and left the room. Kit ran her fingers down the armrest of the couch. Suddenly, Jasper jumped and grabbed Lisha's arm, pointing to the wall. Kit looked up, startled, and Lisha gave Jasper a questioning look. He pointed more forcefully and the girls followed his gaze. At first Kit didn't take in what she was seeing. She blinked several times before the realization hit her.

"Is—is that?" stuttered Jasper.

"The shadow woman," said Lisha in a whisper, just loud enough so the others could hear. Cast on the wall beside them was the shadowed silhouette of a woman, the very same bodiless shape the Protectors had seen in the image Halie had shown them of the night the French troupe was attacked.

"What does it mean?" asked Jasper.

"She's trying to tell us something," said Lisha, peering intently at the shadow woman. Quickly, the shadow woman began writing words on the wall with her finger.

"Wot's it say?" asked Kit impatiently, more annoyed than ever with her inability to read. Lisha leaned over sideways and whispered the words in Kit's ear, never taking her eyes off the wall. The writing said:

It's a trap go now before she comes back

But at that very moment, Cameron reentered the room and the shadow woman darted away to the darkness behind a bookcase, erasing the words in her flight. Kit tried to stand, thinking they would make a rush for the door, but Lisha held her back. She faced Cameron calmly, continuing their conversation as if nothing had changed.

"So, Cameron, what was all that knocking about?" asked Lisha.

"Woodpeckers. Awfully annoying, always tapping at the walls," said Cameron. "Sorry about that."

"Right. Well, thank you for all your help," said Lisha, standing. Kit and Jasper stood with her.

"So, is that all you wanted to know?" asked Cameron casually.

"Just one more thing," Lisha said. "How did Mr. Loxlyheart find out about the Masons?" Jasper looked at her sharply.

"I—I," Cameron stuttered, startled as if she hadn't thought of that before. "I don't know," said Cameron.

"D' y' know wo' Mr. Loxly'eart's planin'?" asked Kit. "An' does 'e know 'bout this book o' yours?"

"I—" Cameron started to say. She was interrupted, for at that moment, the door at the back of her shop was slammed open. Five men stepped in and walked toward Cameron.

"Are these the ones?" asked the first man. Cameron nodded curtly, not looking at anyone.

"I'm sorry," said Cameron in a monotone. "I tried to warn you. I didn't want—" she drew a quick breath. "But they find ways to make you do what they want." Kit and Jasper looked at her, horrified, and then at each other. Kit could tell that they were both thinking the same thing: the shadow woman had been right, for the second time. Lisha's features settled into a resigned expression for a moment before shifting to attack mode. The men moved slowly toward them, brandishing weapons.

"Surrender and your lives may be spared," one of them said. The three Protectors were caught between the couch and Mr. Loxlyheart's men.

"On the count of three," whispered Lisha. "One—three!" On the word "three," she kicked one of the men in the face and, while he was recovering, pulled out a pistol. Lisha fired once, reloaded, and shot again. There was a thud as another man fell to the floor, clutching his arm. Two of the remaining men grabbed for Jasper, but he ducked and swung a candlestick at their legs. A man raised his hands above Lisha and was about to strike down when—

"Lisha! Above you!" yelled Kit. Lisha looked and jumped onto the couch, tipping it over. The man only succeeded in knocking another to the ground. Lisha looked at Kit from behind the upturned sofa and her eyes said, *Thanks, Kit.* She reloaded the gun, but it was knocked from her hand before she could fire. Kit slipped nimbly under people's legs until she came to the table. She closed the big, dusty book Cameron had been reading from and slid it off the table. Kaida jumped to her arm like a falcon, and Kit put the book under her dress.

"Lisha! Jasper! This way!" yelled Kit at the top of her lungs before jumping for the door. Lisha looked around and motioned to Jasper. A man reached out and caught Lisha by the throat and lifted her in the air. It would have been over for her if Jasper hadn't stepped in, whacking the man over the head with the candlestick. There was a dull thunking noise when it hit, and the man dropped Lisha and collapsed to the floor. Lisha fell to the ground. She had a clear path to the door, but a group of the men had circled around Jasper.

"Er, Lisha," he said, "little help here?" Lisha pushed off a chair and jumped to the middle of the circle.

"Duck," she said, as she planted the chair to the floor and leapt up, kicking out in a circle at the men, knocking them to the ground as she went. Lisha grabbed Jasper and bolted to the door. Kit, who was already outside, stepped to the left as the door swung fully open, and Lisha and Jasper tumbled out into the street. The men inside got up and started for the door. Lisha and Jasper braced themselves for another attack, but before the men got to them, Kit slammed the door in their faces and shoved a broom handle through the crack between the bottom of the door and the threshold. There were loud thuds as the men slammed into the other side of the door. The broom splintered but held. For a moment, Lisha and Jasper just stood, looking at Kit in utter amazement. Lisha shook her head, smiling.

The three of them ran the short distance to the dock where the *Compass Rose* waited ready to cast off. The crewmembers gave them quizzical looks as they looked down from the deck. Lisha put two fingers in her mouth and let out a shrill whistle, and soon all the other Protectors gathered. The rest of the Protectors stared at Jasper, Kit, and Lisha. All three had attained injuries of varying degrees of severity. Lisha wiped blood off a cut across her cheek.

"Come on, folks, all aboard, quickly now!" The Protectors were brimming with questions, but at Lisha's instructions, they all hastened to board the ship. "Come on, come on, hurry up now," said Lisha, ushering them along. They heard a shout from far off. The yells got closer and closer. "Quickly, get on the ship," said Lisha frantically. The voices got closer. Finally, Kiara and Nat stepped aboard. They were the end of the line.

"Cast off!" yelled Lisha. The crewmembers, already in their positions, made no delay before lowering the sails and shooting the ship off into the wide, blue ocean. Several of the men who had attacked them, limping and bleeding, clustered around the dock. A moment more and they would have made it onto the ship. Lisha breathed a sigh of relief before slumping down onto a crate.

"Leggo! I's fine! Leggo!" Kit pulled away as Isaac tried to examine her. She was the last to be examined by the surgeon, as she was the least hurt. Lisha, aside from the cut on her cheek, had a mildly twisted ankle, a cut lip, and a bruised neck from when the man tried to strangle her. Jasper had the beginnings of a black eye, and the fingers on his right hand were bleeding at the knuckles from where they'd hit the bottom of the candlestick he'd been fighting with.

Kit had gotten off easier than they had. Most of the blood on her wasn't her own, but she had been scratched up. One man had even managed to nick her ear with something sharp, and she'd scraped her knee in the rush to get back to the ship, but that was the worst of it.

Finally, Isaac let Kit go above deck. She was greeted with warmth.

"Kit!"

"You're better!"

"What happened?"

"Are you hurt bad?"

"Tell us everything!"

And so she did. Everything from the walk up the mountain to Cameron's betrayal, leaving out only the details about the Ultimate Power. As she told the story, her audience was captivated and didn't take their eyes off her once.

"Kit, you're amazing!" said Genna.

"An' such a great storyteller!" put in Lali.

"Thanks," said Kit modestly.

"Tell us another story, Kit!" said Leandra.

"Mebee tomorrow," said Kit. She would have loved to keep on telling stories forever, but it was getting late and she was exhausted.

On the way to her bed, Kit was stopped by Lisha.

"Hey, Kit. Tomorrow, come to my cabin for the meeting with the others. Oh, and by the way, thanks." Kit smiled shyly, and when she went to sleep she had the sweetest dreams.

❦

The following morning, several of the Protectors met in Lisha's cabin to discuss their next course of action and to hear what Jasper and Lisha had learned the day before. The two troupe leaders, Jasper and Fala; Nat, Fala's second in command; Lisha; her first mate Jasmine; Kit; Kaida and Halie sat around Lisha's cabin, sitting or leaning on various pieces of furniture. Jasper spoke first, his black eye standing out sharply against his pale skin.

"At this time, I *would* ask for you to tell me what you found, but I can guess. Mr. Loxlyheart has built a mill atop the hill and has, I'm assuming, taken any and all Stoens he could get his bony hands on. Well, friends, I've good news and bad news. The bad news is that we have lost another ally to Mr. Loxlyheart." Shocked looks passed around the room.

"Who is it?" asked Fala, trying to sound calm.

"Cameron. She's a Stoenmason," said Lisha sadly.

"A Stoenmason?" asked Nat. Apparently Kit hadn't been alone in her ignorance.

"Yes," said Jasper.

Jasmine turned to Nat and explained. "They're the ones who watch over the Stoens, fixing or replacing them as the need arises." Kit looked quizzically at Jasmine, wondering how the first mate of a ship knew so much about Stoenmasons.

Nat got up.

"Wait a minute. You're telling us that there are people who make Stoens, and one of them is working for the Hunters?"

"It's more complicated than that, but yes, in a nutshell. Calm down. She's no longer such a huge threat to us. Kit made sure of that," said Jasper, smiling at Kit. Fala looked at her.

"What did you do?" she asked curiously, kneeling down so she was at her level. Kit thought for a minute before saying, "I stole 'er book. Th' one 'bout Stoens."

Kit held up her prize. Fala reached forward and took it. Flipping through the pages, she said, "This is it. It has everything. I don't understand why Mr. Loxlyheart didn't take it from her." She closed the cover and looked at Kit with new respect.

"Nice job, Kit!" said Nat.

"Aye!" said Jasmine. "Good, quick thinking!"

Kit beamed.

"So, that's the good news?" asked Halie quietly.

"Yes," said Jasper. "We now have the tools we need to defeat Mr. Loxlyheart, Desdemona, and Aradia. We know a way to permanently destroy the Ultimate Power." The group gathered closer together as Lisha and Jasper explained how that would be done.

Just outside the captain's cabin, there was a sharp intake of breath from a shape hidden in the shadows. But it was a breezy day, and the gasp was not heard by anyone who could know what it meant. If only the wind had been blowing in the other direction, maybe things would have turned out differently.

"What next?" asked Jasmine.

"Well, since Cameron betrayed us, I'm not so sure we can trust what she told us. Next we need to find Xylon. He's a Stoenmason, too, and he'll be able to verify our information and tell us how close to their goal the Stoenhunters are," said Jasper.

"Ah, yes, Xylon. Why didn't we just go straight to him?" asked Fala.

"Because he's a hermit, and no one has seen him for years. I'm not quite sure where he is," explained Lisha. "He's difficult to keep track of. Halie, after the meeting I want you to stay with Jasper and me and see if you can find him. Fala, if you could fetch Leandra? She *is* his niece. Maybe she'll know where he is. The rest of you are dismissed." On that note, the meeting ended. Not thoroughly productive, nor useless. But there was an important change: Victory was no longer out of their reach.

🖤

Kit's eyes opened in the dark. She could feel the ship rocking beneath her as they sped on through the night. Quietly she stood and walked toward the stairs. She tiptoed across the deck and cautiously touched the door to Lisha's cabin. It was unlocked. Carefully she opened the door and stepped inside. Lisha wasn't there. Kit looked around for a minute before she saw it: the book she had stolen from Cameron. As she sat, pulling the enormous book onto her lap, she felt as if there was something important concealed in its pages, something even more important than defeating the Hunters. She opened the book to the middle. There was a large drawing of a castle and beside it some small houses. On the next page held a picture of two dragons, not small dragons like Kaida, but huge dragons, bigger than the *Compass Rose*. The next two pages were stuck together, and Kit was unable to pry them apart. Next was a picture of a battle. Humans were throwing spears and arrows at the dragons. There was a huge pit opening up below them. Turning the next page, completely engrossed in what she was doing, Kit didn't hear someone walk into the room until that person was right in front of her.

"Enjoying the book?" asked Lisha. Kit jumped and her face turned red.

"I just thought—I din't mean—it was only—th' door was—"

"That's all right. It's natural to be curious. So," Lisha paused and looked down at her, "what have you learned?" Kit shook her head.

"Not much. I's jus' lookin' a' th' pictures." Lisha sat down beside her.

"It's an interesting story," said Lisha. Kit looked up.

"Do you know what it says?"

"Somewhat," was the reply. "My family's always been involved in this whole mess. This very ship's been used to transport Stoens for a long time," she said, gesturing around the room. Kit looked around at the shadows dancing on the wall and shivered. "But, no," continued Lisha. "I don't know the whole story. Not very many people do. It's a safeguard, a form of protection. We each know our role and what we need to do, but we're not supposed to know too much about the other jobs, the other pieces of the puzzle, and certainly not the whole picture. Sometimes, we have to do things without knowing why. But we each have our part to play, and somehow the pieces fit together. It's not a perfect system; sometimes we're missing information that we ought to know. Sometimes, we have to step up and do more than our share. Sometimes, we find things out that we're not supposed to know." Kit looked down guiltily. Lisha leaned over and patted her head. "Some things happen for a reason, even if we can't see it at the time," she said. "And though we may not be able to see where the wind will take us, we need all of us to steer the ship."

"Wot's my part, then, Lisha?" asked Kit. "I'm just a kid. I don't know nothin' 'bout magic or anything else. 'Ow can I 'elp?"

"Oh, but Kit, you've done so much already! Your quick thinking and resourcefulness and courage have been invaluable," said Lisha appreciatively. A small smile stole across Kit's face at the praise, and her cheeks grew warm. "Listen." Lisha counted off on her fingers. "You brought us a Stoen. You stole Cameron's book. You helped us get away from the Hunters. And, though you may not know it, you've been given one of the most important jobs of all." Kit looked up at Lisha, eyes wide. "Guardian."

"Guardian?" asked Kit. "Of wot? Woll, the Stoens, o'course, but all th' Protectors protect them." Kit's brow furrowed in confusion.

Lisha smiled. "It's true that all the Protectors protect the Stoens. But you've been given the task of protecting something far rarer and of far greater importance." The light from the lantern gleamed mysteriously on the captain's face. She leaned in close and said in a low voice, "Kaida chooses who he stays with. Whoever he picks, it's their job to look after him. Kaida's a very important piece in the puzzle."

"Why's 'e so important?" whispered Kit.

"I don't actually know," admitted Lisha. "I just know that he's important and must be protected at all costs. I probably shouldn't know even as much as I do, but it's a good thing I do, because now I get to tell you. But enough secrets. You should be in bed.

We should arrive at our destination in Larne, Ireland, soon. You'll need your sleep." She patted Kit on the back and rose. Kit rubbed her eyes and headed for the door. As she closed it, Kit saw Lisha bending down to pick up the book. Kit was too tired to even contemplate what she had discovered, and before she knew it, she was asleep.

❧

"Minuette," said Jordan, breaking the cold silence of the gloomy dungeon. "Could you sing something?" She looked up.

"I have been hanging on this wall as long as you have, Jordan. I do not know how good my voice will sound."

"It doesn't matter. I just—I think it might help." She nodded.

"What should I sing? *'J'ai perdu mon boheur'*[1]? *'O mort! Termine mes doulers'*[2]? *'Adieu mes amours'*[3]?"

"How about that English one, you know, the one we all used to like."

"All right." Minuette waited a moment before beginning to sing, tentatively at first and then with growing confidence:

[1] "I Have Lost My Happiness," from *Le Devin du Vilage*, a French opera by Jean-Jacques Rousseau, first staged at Fontainebleau in 1752.
[2] "O Death! End My Sadness," from *Tarare*, a French opera by Antonio Salieri and Pierre-Augustin Caron de Beaumarchais, first performed in Paris in 1787.
[3] "Farewell, My Loves," Medieval French folk song from the late 1400s.

Alas, my love, you do me wrong
To cast me off discourteously,
For I have loved you so long
Delighting in your company.
Greensleeves was all my joy,
Greensleeves was my delight.
Greensleeves was my heart of gold,
And who but my lady Greensleeves?

Outside the dungeon cell, three guards looked up from their game of cards to listen.

"That music..." said one of the guards, Mr. Thornton, setting down his mug of ale.

"Is tha'... is tha' one o' th' pris'ners?" asked Mr. Bumbleweed. Mr. Tweeble nodded.

"Th' French girl, sounds like. I 'ad a son once. Would've been about 'er age by now."

"You 'ad a son?" asked Mr. Bumbleweed. Mr. Tweeble nodded. "What happened to 'im?"

"I ain't seen 'im fer, fer a long time," he said quietly. "Dissapear'd, 'e did. There was a pirate attack, an' no sign of 'im since. I quit my job to go look for 'im. Joined up 'ere t' pay th' bills." There was a pause. "Wha' abou' you two?" he asked.

"I'm 'ere fer the same reason," said Mr. Bumbleweed. "'Ave t' pay the bills. Signed up as a worker fer 'is factory." No one had to ask who "he" was. "I 'ate seein' th' way 'e treats them kids," said Mr. Bumbleweed with surprising passion. "All those children workers ... t'ain't right. An' even lockin' this lot up like they was criminals. I sometimes wish I could do somethin' about it, but wha' can I do? Can't do nothin' a' all. I'd leave if I 'ad anywhere t' go."

"Rodger?" asked Mr. Tweeble, friendly as always, addressing Mr. Thornton. Rodger Thornton took a long time answering.

"I had a string of bad luck. Lost everything. I mean, everything. Sold the house, didn't help. Needed a job. You can guess the rest." They nodded sympathetically. He grimaced. "Made more money, took some more jobs, eventually bought the house back. But it's no good. What's the point of a big house with no one to live in it?" He took a drink from his mug.

"No family?" asked Mr. Bumbleweed kindly. Rodger flinched.

"My wife—" Rodger said finally, the words catching in his throat. "She died. Many years ago."

"Kids?" asked Mr. Tweeble curiously. Rodger shook his head slowly and then nodded.

"Yes. There was a child." He sighed. He had never acknowledged that fact before. But that music ... at first it had touched him because it made him think of his wife, whose death he had never really gotten over. But then, suddenly he had been reminded not of the woman he had loved so much, but of a small child he should have loved more. "Alas, my love, you do me wrong, to cast me off discourteously," he murmured to himself.

He fell silent, and the three listened for a moment more to Minuette's song.

If you intend thus to disdain,
It does the more enrapture me,
And even so, I will remain
A lover in captivity.
Greensleeves was all my joy,

> Greensleeves was my delight.
> Greensleeves was my heart of gold
> And who but my lady Greensleeves?

Several days later, the Protectors found themselves docking at the port in Larne, Ireland. With the combined efforts of Leandra, Xylon's niece, and Halie, they had at last located the hermit's home. Once again, Jasper sent the Protectors to see if Mr. Loxlyheart, Desdemona, or Aradia had been around to steal the Stoens. Lisha and Jasper, along with Kit and Kaida, went to find Xylon.

The journey was not quite as bad as the last one. Instead of climbing up a mountain, they simply had to hike through the woods. Kit looked back as the small town disappeared between leaves and branches. This time Kaida trotted beside Kit. Kaida hadn't been permitted to fly for so long that he preferred to walk. Old habits die hard. But Kaida was extremely pleased to be let out and pranced around, pouncing at bugs and small animals. Kit watched him, laughing.

"Kaida, spit that out, it's poisonous," said Lisha sharply. Jasper turned to see Kaida gagging on a yellow-leafed plant like a cat throwing up a hairball. He spit it out and hopped quickly toward Kit. She picked him up and ran to catch up with the other two. They had reached a rough-hewn stone cottage that was in need of repairs. They heard sounds coming through the forest. As they got closer, Kit realized that someone was cutting wood. *Chop, chop.* Lisha stepped into the clearing, holding her hand above her eyes to shield them from the sunlight.

"Xylon? Is that you?" she said. The man turned aside from the log he was cutting to look at her.

"Lisha!" he exclaimed, coming over. "It's been awhile. How ya been?" Xylon was an old, white-bearded man with skin like folded parchment and kind gray eyes. His clothes were tattered and frayed, with patches where they had ripped apart. He took off his glasses and cleaned them on his shirt before coming to meet them.

"I'm still alive," replied Lisha cockily.

"And Jasper, right?" he asked. Jasper nodded politely and shook the hermit's hand. "Hey, you all right?" asked Xylon, noticing Jasper's black eye. "What happened?" Jasper exchanged a look with Lisha.

"We had a run-in with some Stoenhunters a few days ago," said Lisha.

"Stoenhunters, eh?" he said. "You'll have to tell me all about it." Then Xylon saw Kit holding onto Kaida.

"Kit! I was hoping I would see you! And Kaida," he said, lifting Kaida out of Kit's arms. "He's smaller than I remember. Have you been shrinking on me?" Kit was dumbfounded. Xylon, this strange, old hermit, recognized her? And even more, he was looking forward to seeing her? This was just too strange.

"Xylon, we're here on rather urgent business," said Lisha awkwardly as Xylon greeted Kaida.

"Oh yes, how rude of me! Please come inside!" He beckoned them into his cottage.

Kit soon found herself sitting on a rock at a wood table with no two legs the same length, drinking homemade tea made from a mixture of sap and herbs. Kaida was given his tea on a saucer, like a cat. "So what brings you all the way out here to my humble cottage?" asked Xylon. Lisha placed the book Kit had stolen from Cameron on the table.

"We need you to verify the information we've obtained. And we'd like to use your map," said Lisha. Xylon began studying the book.

"Indeed. Oh, the map, of course." He left the room and returned with a parchment map, which he handed to Lisha. "There you go. You do remember how to use it?" Lisha nodded and took the map to the floor where it could be fully opened. She got down on her hands and knees and spread it flat. Kit came over and sat on one side to keep it down, and Kaida sat on the other. Jasper stayed at the table, talking with Xylon as they watched the girls and the dragon. Xylon flipped through the book as they talked, presumably checking its accuracy and seeing if anything had been tampered with, while Lisha explained the map to Kit.

"This is not an ordinary map. If you touch the compass rose and say the name of a person or object, the map will show them to you. Watch. Kit!" Kit looked down and noticed that there was a now tiny red dot on the map. Her eyes opened wide. She jumped back from the map, and it rolled back into a scroll. Lisha laughed. Kit knelt down, embarrassed, pulling the map flat. "This map has many useful purposes. One could find a buried treasure, a sunken ship, a lost relative—a great number of things. Perhaps the most useful thing you can do with this map is—look. Stoens!" Suddenly, multicolored dots appeared all over the map. Kit realized that each color represented a different kind of Stoen. "Now, Kit, Kaida, help me look for a place with the highest concentration of different Stoens," said Lisha. Kit and Kaida immediately began doing just that. Lisha sat on one side of the map, so Kaida was free to roam around. One place caught her attention. Lisha and Kaida noticed it at the same time. Kaida pointed to it with a claw and declared, "Stonehaven. That must be it! Now isn't that ironic? Oh well, we'll have to go there, I suppose." Lisha rolled up the map and put it back in the other room.

"Lisha? That map ... is that how he knew I'd be coming?" asked Kit when she returned.

"Halie isn't the only one who can see things happening at other places," said Lisha mysteriously.

"But I thought Jasper said that no two people 'ad th' same power," said Kit, confused.

"No, no two powers are exactly alike, but some come close," Lisha explained.

Wow, thought Kit. *This power stuff is even more compl'cated than I thought.*

Kit and Lisha joined Jasper and Xylon at the table. Jasper looked up when they arrived.

"Ah, good. I was just about to explain what Cameron told us. I'm worried that she might have been lying, since she did betray us to the Hunters."

"Good idea," said Lisha. Jasper explained to Xylon what they had learned.

"So, Xylon, is that right? Will transferring the Power into an object and smashing it really destroy the Power?" Xylon stoked his beard thoughtfully.

"Well, I suppose that's one way of doing it." Jasper looked at him sharply.

"What do you mean?" Xylon looked off to the side as if trying to remember something.

"Ah, well, it's just that ... well, I suppose it *might* work. But destroying the Power that way is like shredding a book to keep anyone from reading it, where you might just as well burn it." Jasper looked at Lisha, uncomprehending. Xylon sighed. "What I mean is that destroying the Power this way *may* make it permanently inaccessible, or it may just make it a lot harder to unlock. Y'see, there's no way to truly destroy it. Listen, I'll explain." He took a drink and then began to tell the story.

"I've never understood why no one passes down the story anymore. Do the Drifters think it's unnecessary? Maybe. Maybe they think it's too dangerous. But I think that knowing is better, knowing so you can be prepared." He looked around at the Protectors seriously. "See, many years ago," he continued, "a long, long time before you were born, that innate magic inside every human was not locked away from us. Anyone could learn to use their power. Not everyone did. It's like reading, or some skill like that. Back in the ancient world, places like Greece and Rome and the like, they thought too scientifically to be completely open to the idea of humans having magic, so very few people learned to use their power.

But if they wanted to, they still could. How do you think the Oracle predicted the fall of Croesus?"

He looked around at them as if expecting some response, but when the Protectors remained silent, he shrugged and went on. "But then in the Middle Ages, when science fell back aways, people were more accepting of the idea. Most people could learn to use magic. Oftentimes it wasn't particularly flashy or impressive; it was just a part of life, like cooking or sewing. In addition, in this time of acceptance, magical creatures could be believed as well, and it was then that the dragons felt safe to reveal themselves. At first, they were worshipped, sought after for their wisdom. But the knights, proud and hungry for glory, started hunting them. And they were, I must say, rather good at it," said Xylon ruefully. "Shocked at this betrayal, the few remaining dragons cursed the human race, locking away our powers deep within ourselves so we could never use them to hurt again. Then they disappeared."

"Now wait a sec," said Kit. "If th' dragons locked away th' humans' powers so we wouldn't 'urt 'nyone, izzat really a curse? They were doin' it t' protect people!"

Xylon looked uncomfortable.

"Well, the point's debatable," he said. "Anyway, the dragons did one final act before disappearing. They recognized that there were still some decent humans left in the world, humans who used their magic for good, and decided that they shouldn't be punished along with the rest. The dragons chose some trustworthy people to become the first Stoenmasons.

They taught them the dragon magic necessary to make the Stoens, magical items that would allow humans to gain access to their own powers again. See, the way it works is this: the dragons have a collective of magic, one pool that all the dragons use."

Xylon drew a circle on the tabletop with his finger. "That pool of magic wants to stay together," he explained, "but the dragons can dip into it and use some of the magic."

Xylon pulled Cameron's book over and started flipping through it, stopping on the page with a chart of all the different types of Stoens and the signs carved into them.

"The twelve signs identifying different types of Stoens are ancient dragon runes," he said, pointing to the chart. "When a human touches a Stoen of the type that corresponds with the kind of power they have, the Stoen creates a temporary link from the human to the dragon magic collective."

"How does that let a person use their power?" asked Jasper, confused. Xylon scratched his head.

"Think of it this way," he said. "Imagine that a human's power is like a tangible thing inside them, but it's surrounded by a wall of dragon magic preventing the human from accessing it. When the human gets connected to the dragon magic collective, however, the little piece of dragon magic preventing them from using their power gets sucked back to the collective, leaving the human free to use their power."

"That makes sense," said Lisha, sipping her tea. "But where does the Ultimate Power come into it?"

"Well, y' see, the dragons and the original Stoenmasons didn't realize at first that in using dragon runes to connect the Stoens to the collective power of the dragons, they had accidentally provided a way for a human to access that power themselves. The power of the dragons is a power not meant for man. We're too greedy—too shortsighted. It's too much for a human mind and body to handle. We found this out the hard way. That's another story. So, the Masons scattered the Stoens though the world and assigned Protectors to make sure no one ever got this power, and Drifters to choose the Protectors. When they were gone, they chose successors to become the new Stoenmasons and carry on their work."

"I see," said Jasper, eyes wide with wonder.

"But," said Lisha, "that still doesn't answer our question." Xylon shook his head tiredly.

"No, I suppose not. Forgive an old man; my memory is not what it used to be. I know this though: containing the Power in an object and destroying it will merely lock it away, kinda like the humans' powers were locked away. And things that are locked can be *unlocked*. Even if the key is difficult to come by."

"So," asked Lisha, brows knit, "are you saying that there's a better way?"

Xylon opened his mouth, but at that moment there was a roar from outside and a great bang as something was flung against the door to the cottage. In an instant, the Protectors were on their feet.

Through the window, they could see that a large group of men stood outside, trying to break through the door. The foremost were bruised and injured, and Kit recognized them as the men who had attacked them in the Lake District.

"Oh, lovely," said Jasper sarcastically. "They've brought reinforcements." Lisha reached for her dagger, but Xylon caught her arm.

"No, go," he said urgently. "You must get out of here. You must stop them!" The door splintered, and the men charged through into the cottage. "Go!" he yelled as the men surged forward and grabbed him. "You have to know! You must give—" Xylon was clonked on the head—hard—by the first man's fist and knocked to the floor, unconscious.

"Come on!" said Lisha, grabbing Cameron's book. She and Jasper turned for the back door.

"Wait!" cried Kit. "We can't jus' leave 'im 'ere!"

"We have no choice," said Jasper. Before she could offer further protests, he grabbed her and dragged her out of the house, Kaida scrambling onto her back.

Kit struggled all the way back to the ship, where the others were already waiting on the dock, the crew ready to cast off. Nat met them on the gangplank.

"Not *again*?" he asked as they rushed past him. Lisha grabbed his arm.

"On board. Now." Nat shouted to the others as he was dragged up to the deck, and the Protectors hurried onto the ship. As they cast off, Jasper finally let go his grip on Kit. Tears streamed down her cheeks.

"We've abandoned 'im," she said quietly. *Just as I abandoned my family.* As the wind rushed past, whipping the tears from her eyes, Kit felt guilt and longing pressing in on her. She thought of her mother and little Charlene. It felt like an eternity since she'd seen them. Kit wondered where they were, whether they were all right without her; on the streets, anything could happen. Kaida looked up at her, worried, before snuggling up against her neck. She hugged him.

Jasper came to kneel beside her.

"Kit," he said gently. "I know you're upset. Believe me, I regret having to leave Xylon there as much as you do. But it's up to us to stop the Hunters before they do something terrible to the world."

Kit sniffed. "You fought in Cam'ron's shop," she said through her tears. Jasper looked down.

"Yes, well, there were only five of them then. There were a lot more of them this time, and it's unlikely we could have beaten them all. And if we tried to carry Xylon with us, we would have been too slow to escape."

"We could've tried," said Kit. "Now they're gonna kill 'im." Jasper put a hand on her shoulder.

"No. No, I don't think so. He's too valuable for them to do him any harm."

"You don't know that," she said accusingly. Jasper paused for a moment.

"You're right," he said at last, uncertainty showing in his face for the first time. "I don't know that. But I do know that he wanted us to go and keep fighting, use the information that he gave us. And don't worry—the old man still has a few tricks up his sleeve."

Across the deck from them, several Protectors were solemnly consulting. Jasmine came up to Lisha and put an arm around her shoulders. Lisha looked up at her and smiled wearily.

"Where are we going next?" asked Jasmine.

"Scotland," replied Lisha. "They're gathering at Dunnottar Castle. In Stonehaven." Emra's eyes widened.

"Is i' far?" asked Lali.

"About a week if the wind's good," said Lisha.

"Will we return alive?" asked Kiara. Lisha looked out to sea.

"I hope so."

A week later, the ship reached its destination. Even from a distance, the Protectors could make out the ruins of a mighty fortress on a high piece of land flanked by cliffs on all sides.

"There! There it is!" shouted Lisha.

"Stonehaven," murmured Fala. Lisha jumped down from a mast and stood before the Protectors and crew, calling for their attention. Jasper strode to her side, taking charge. The black eye had almost completely faded, leaving only a slight discoloration on his pale skin.

"All right, gang. This is it. I hope you're ready."

"Of course we're ready!" called Leandra. "That's what we came here for!" There were cheers from the Protectors lining the deck. Jasper smiled.

"That's the spirit! So, to the plan. We'll have to split up. Kiara, Quito, Kaida, and I will go and rescue the prisoners," said Jasper.

"What?" said Kit. "Y'mean me 'n Kaida 'ave t' split up?"

"I'm sorry, Kit, but we need Kaida's help on this mission and yours on another," said Jasper.

"But," Kit said, looking at Lisha. Not go with Kaida? *But I'm supposed t' protect him,* she thought. Kit saw from Lisha's face that she understood. But Lisha merely shook her head and mouthed, *It's all right.* Before she could protest, Mica, the wise little boy from the Irish troupe, stepped forward and said, "I should go with them."

"What?" demanded Genna, gaping at her younger brother. "Mica, it's too dangerous! You'll have to wait on the ship."

"No," said Mica. "They need me. I can help free the prisoners. I can pick the locks. I won't make any trouble," he said, turning to Jasper. Jasper looked at Lisha, and then at Mica, and then at Genna.

"He's right," said Jasper. "We really could use his help." Genna looked at Mica. He held her gaze.

"All right," she said at last. "But be careful!"

"Now," continued Jasper, "Nat, Emra, Genna, Lali, Kit, and Halie are going to try to find where they're keeping the Stoens. Steal them if you can. No Stoens, no Ultimate Power." Emra nodded firmly. Nat looked longingly at Kiara, and Genna tried *not* to look at Mica. Kit looked at Lisha again, who gave a small nod and pointed to her forehead. Kit remembered Lisha's praise of her resourcefulness and admitted reluctantly that perhaps the time she had spent on the street had given her skills that would be useful in trying to find and steal the Stoens. The others would have to protect Kaida for now.

"That leaves Lisha, Jasmine, Oliver, Leandra, Hilda, and Kadin-Lave. You lot are going after Mr. Loxlyheart, Desdemona, and Aradia. See if you can keep them busy while the others try to find the Stoens; take them out of the picture if you can. Just try to keep them from unleashing the Power."

"What about Isaac and me?" asked Fala. Jasper turned to them. Addressing Fala he said, "You are going to circle the castle in your raven form and make sure everything's going all right. If something goes wrong, caw three times and try to come find me or any of the others."

"And what about Isaac?" she asked.

"He will stay to guard the ship, along with the rest of the crew," said Jasper slowly. "Now, does everyone know where they're going?" Everyone murmured a general yes. "Good. Then we'll split up as soon as we land. I'd say we've got, what, Lisha?" Jasper asked.

"About five minutes," said Lisha looking up at the sky. "Jasper, I do think it's going to rain."

"Enough of that for now. Five minutes, everybody. Five minutes."

Jasper leaned against the railing as the crew and Protectors dispersed. Lisha approached him.

"Well, you sure seem to know what you're doing," said Lisha. Jasper let out the breath he'd been holding in and deflated. He leaned, head down, against the railing. "Or ... not." Jasper looked at her sideways. She leaned against the railing next to him and put a hand on his shoulder. "Don't worry. We'll do fine. And if we don't, we'll go out with a bang. Everybody trusts that you've made the right decisions, and—"

"But what if I didn't?" demanded Jasper suddenly, getting up. "What if someone dies?"

"I don't doubt that might happen," said Lisha. "But no one will blame you if it does." Jasper turned and looked back at Lisha. It struck him what an amazing person she was. Lisha, who never let her friends down. Who dove into the ocean in the middle of a storm to save complete strangers, even though she was missing half a leg. Lisha, of all people, had known Jasper and Minuette were truly in love before even they had. She had trusted Kit immediately, a dangerous judgment call that had proved invaluable. Lisha seemed to know more about people than they even knew about themselves. Nat and Kiara, Minuette and Jasper, Emra, Kit, the list went on and on. All the people she'd helped... He just hoped that it wouldn't end now on account of him.

❦

When the ship had come as close as it could, the Protectors were loaded onto the dinghies and rowed ashore. As they passed the sheer, rocky cliffs framing the platform of land on which sat their desolate destination, all were filled with a sense of foreboding darker than the clouds forming in the sky. The crumbling black towers of the ancient fortress of Dunnotar Castle loomed high above them. They hit the shore and pulled the boats onto the beach. Lisha stood, hands on her hips and chin thrust out in determination, gazing at the thin path snaking up the cliffs. The Protectors milled around on the beach, torn between anticipation and dread. They busied themselves with helping each other make preparations for their various tasks, readying themselves for the trial ahead. Soon the Protectors began splitting into their assigned groups. It was time for saying farewells.

"Kaida, be careful awrigh'? I couln't bear if you din't make it back," said Kit.

"Same goes for you, Kit Taylor. I'm—I'll miss you if you don't come back," said Kaida between sobs.

Kit hugged Kaida close, tears in her eyes. Kaida's claws dug into her shoulder.

Genna was lecturing Mica about taking safety precautions on the mission.

"Sometimes they have booby traps at places like this," she said, looking earnestly into his face to make sure he took in what she was saying. "Watch where you walk and don't step on anything out of the ordinary. Also, when approaching guards, try not to be too obvious about what you want. Oh, and don't make too much noise." Mica nodded. He already knew all of this, but he listened to it because he knew it would make Genna feel better. Truthfully, it made him feel better as well, just to know that she was thinking about him.

Nat and Kiara stood slightly away from the group. They talked from several feet apart, their eyes averted.

"So ... I guess this is it," said Nat.

"Guess so," said Kiara, not looking at Nat, her voice uncharacteristically high.

"I—uh, I—be careful out there. Um," stammered Nat.

"Right," said Kiara, trying to keep her voice from trembling. "You too."

"C'mon, Nat, we 'aven't got much time!" yelled Lali.

"Coming!" said Nat. He turned back to Kiara, and before he could decide against it, leaned forward and kissed her. As he was about to pull away, she wrapped her arm around his neck and pulled him back in.

"Kiara! There's no time to lose!" Reluctantly they fell apart.

"Well—uh," said Kiara, blushing. "Good luck."

"Good luck." They turned quickly and ran after their groups.

The Protectors set off on the trail up the cliffs. At the top, the groups all went separate ways.

"Let's go this way," suggested Oliver, pointing off to the right. Lisha and her group broke off and walked across what might have been an old jousting field situated just before the castle. Two sides of the square field dropped off into sheer cliff faces. Ahead of them lay the ruins of one wing of the castle, blackened and bleak against the gray sky. An eerie wind blew through the ruins as if the castle were drawing a raspy breath. Dead trees bent in the wind, and a few brown leaves blew through the air.

Lisha stopped them once they reached the center of the field. She surveyed the space in front of her with concentration, squinting at the area before the castle.

"That didn't take long," she said.

"What?" asked Leandra. Lisha glanced back at her.

"Well, we haven't found Mr. Loxlyheart, or Desdemona, or Aradia," she said. "But I do believe we've found the Stoens."

Sure enough, on the field in front of them, perhaps twenty paces away, was a group of guards forming a perimeter around ... something.

"Come one, we might as well," said Lisha, calmly waving them forward. "There's no telling where the others ended up. We should keep going. If we can take out the guards, or distract them somehow, we might be able to make off with at least some of the Stoens."

"Actually, this is the end of the road," said Hilda calmly. As if out of nowhere, armed men advanced on them. "I'm sorry," she said, not at all sounding it. She pulled off the dirty kerchief holding her orange curls in check and flicked it to the ground in disgust. She put her hands on her hips and leered at the Protectors. Frantically, Lisha, Kadin-Lave, and Leandra looked around for a way out but found themselves surrounded. Lisha looked up as she heard the sound of a bird cawing three times. The guards muttered to each other in low voices.

"What're we supposed to do with them?" one asked.

"Just hold 'em here until *they* arrive," said another.

"What—how did they—" stammered Leandra, angry panic edging her voice. Her gaze flicked from the crewmembers to Hilda's malicious expression and then to Lisha standing dumbfounded at her side.

"Isn't it obvious?" said Kadin-Lave. "She's a spy."

"*You're* a spy?" said Oliver incredulously.

"Who are you working for?" demanded Leandra. Hilda looked at her as if she had asked an ignorant question.

"Why, Mr. Loxlyheart, of course!"

Meanwhile, Oliver had been edging toward the circle of men. He went up to one of them and asked, "Where's Aradia?" The man looked at him incredulously. "No, I'm serious," said Oliver. He sighed. "Do any of you report to her?" Several of the man raised their hands. The Protectors looked around, mouths open. *What?* they all seemed to be thinking. Oliver pointed to one of the men. "You," he said. "You can tell Aradia that we've done as she asked. We brought her the Protectors, led them into the trap, just like she told us. Now it's her turn to fulfill her part of the bargain, not to harm any of us. That was the agreement. We've done our part. We couldn't stop them splitting up, though. The other two groups went off toward the castle. One was looking for the prisoners, so they'll be near the dungeons. The other's wandering around in there somewhere, looking for the Stoens. Isn't that right, Jasmine?" he said, glancing over at Jasmine. All eyes went to her.

She looked at the ground, refusing to meet anyone's gaze, and nodded quickly as if the simple motion pained her greatly.

"You were spies, too?" asked Hilda, surprised. "We're working for Mr. Loxlyheart; you're working for Aradia." She glanced at the remaining Protectors. "I don't suppose any of you're working for Desdemona?" No one said anything. Lisha was looking at Jasmine, dismayed comprehension dawning on her features.

"That's what you were so upset about," she said in an almost whisper, her voice strangely gentle. Jasmine lowered her head even further, touching her chin to her chest.

"It—it must have been a week before we set off with you that she found us," said Jasmine, trying at last to explain what had happened, "and it was just Oliver and me, getting the ship ready so that we could leave as soon as Fala's troupe arrived, and then suddenly, a woman appeared on the pier. At first we didn't realize, but it was Aradia. She told us who she was immediately, and we drew our weapons, making ready to attack her or defend ourselves, but she held up her hand to stop, said she didn't come there to fight, said she wanted our help. We refused. In fact, we even yelled some insults at her, we—we said we would never help her and that she was a horrible witch, and all sorts of other things. And then," Jasmine shuddered at the memory, "the shadows came alive and bound themselves all around Oliver, lifting him off the ground, wrapping around his neck, choking him. It—it was horrible! I shouted 'Stop! You're hurting him! Stop it right now!' and she said only if we agreed to what she wanted us to do. I—I didn't know what to do. I couldn't let her kill Oliver! So I said, 'Fine, we'll listen,' because that wasn't really promising anything, and I had to do something! 'What is it that you want?' I asked her. She smiled then, a horrible, horrible smile, and the shadows lowered Oliver to the ground, and he collapsed, gasping for air, and I helped him to his feet. She told us. Heaven help us! She told us that she—she wanted us to—to betray you, all we had to do was lead you to them, and none of us—none of you—would be harmed."

"So you agreed?" demanded Leandra. "You actually believed her?"

"No!" cried Jasmine defensively, looking up. "Of course not! She's an evil liar, a wicked, cruel monster! We said absolutely not! She was asking us to betray the Protectors, our friends, betray the world! She was asking me," Jasmine's voice became very soft, almost inaudible, "she was asking me to betray Lisha. I told her that was something I could not do." She shivered. "She," her voice cracked. "She lifted Oliver again, and his face was bright red, and his hands were starting to bleed from clawing at the mass, and I couldn't—" She paused for a moment, unable to continue. "She said that if we didn't bring you to them, hand you over smoothly and painlessly, that she would seek you out herself and kill you. And that—that if we brought you to them, they would leave you alive. My head was tearing apart. I didn't know what to do! I was so afraid. I was filled with this horrible panic burning in my ears. I asked, 'How can we believe you?'" Jasmine's voice squeaked, and she swallowed before continuing,

"'How can we believe you?' and she told us that they needed you alive for the spell to work; there needed to be witnesses who understand what is going on, otherwise it won't work, and I said but then how can you threaten to kill them? And she said—she said that they didn't need *all* of you alive," she closed her eyes as if trying to block out the memory, "that if they wanted they could easily kill some of us, like," she gulped, "like Jasper, she said, or—" Jasmine pressed her hands against her face, shaking.

Oliver stepped in.

"I think her words were, 'Like Jasper, or—or your precious Captain.'" Oliver looked at Lisha then, and there was something like pain in his eyes. Lisha turned to look at Jasmine, her face showing every soft emotion.

"You did this to save me," she said. Jasmine looked up at her, tears still streaming down her face. "Jaz," said Lisha, "you know that I would rather die than let one of the Stoenhunters get the Power." Jasmine's gaze slipped downward again.

"I know," she said shakily. "But I couldn't live with myself if I let you die, not when I had a chance to save you." She drew an unsteady breath. "I'm sorry."

Lisha gently put her hand beneath Jasmine's chin, pulling her face up so she had to look at Lisha. Lisha wiped some of the tears from Jasmine's cheek.

"Don't be. You did what was right by your conscience," she said. They stared into each other's eyes, unable or unwilling to look away. For a long moment, no one moved. As the silence stretched on, Oliver cleared his throat and continued the story. "So, we asked again, 'How can we trust you?' And she said, 'Do you really want to take that chance?'"

"What about the chance that one of them gets the Ultimate Power and does something terrible to the world?" interrupted Leandra. "Do you have any idea what you've done? Saving one person doesn't matter if the whole world's destroyed! You've given them the keys to absolute, unlimited power!"

"No, we haven't!" said Jasmine suddenly. "I didn't agree to what Aradia told us to do until I figured out a way to stop them while still doing what she said! I made sure that they wouldn't be able to unleash the Ultimate Power! I hid one of the Stoens so they won't be able to complete the pattern."

"But there isn't just one of each type of Stoen!" said Leandra exasperatedly.

"There is one Stoen, a special Stoen, of which there's only ever one of in the world at a time," said Jasmine earnestly. "I know because my family has the job of keeping it safe. It's called the Dragon Stoen. It's different from the rest. It doesn't unlock a person's power; it gives people the little bit of dragon magic you need to become a Stonemason, but only if you've been specially chosen as a Stonemason's apprentice and successor. You can't complete the spell for unleashing the Ultimate Power without it. The other Stoens, they create a link from a human to the dragon magic collective so that the dragon magic stopping the human using their power rejoins the rest, but that's all it does. It's a one-way connection, human to magic. The Dragon Stoen is the other way around: it's one way, from the magic to the new Stonemason. Without it, you could have one of each of the other Stoens and you still wouldn't be able to get the Power. Because even though together they create this really wide bridge to the dragon magic, it's still only one way. You need the Dragon Stoen in order to let dragon magic into this world, into a human."

"Why didn't you tell us this before?" asked Kadin-Lave. "If you knew all this, you could've saved us the trouble of going to find a Stoenmason!"

"Well," said Jasmine reluctantly, "I didn't actually know all of that until recently. I just knew that it was a special Stoen, that there was only one of it, that you needed it to unleash the Ultimate Power. I didn't know why, though; that part I learned from Cameron's book. But anyway, I knew that it was really important," said Jasmine. "That's why it's assigned a special caretaker. That's me now. And I made sure the Hunters wouldn't be able to use it to unleash the Ultimate Power. I put it in a safe place where no one would ever think to look."

Hilda stepped forward.

"Oh, I wouldn't be so sure about that," she said. She held out her hand. For one horrible moment that stretched into eternity, the Protectors all stared at it, shocked. In her hand was a Stoen.

Jasmine's eyes bulged wide. Her jaw dropped.

"How, how did you?"

Lisha was silent for a long time. Finally she spoke.

"That's the one that Kit found, that first day." The Stoen with the unfamiliar symbol Lisha had been puzzling over. Now she understood. Without looking up, she said softly, "Jaz, where did you hide it?"

After a moment, Jasmine said, "I—I gave it to a jewels merchant. Not to sell, just to have on display. I figured that the safest place for a Stoen was with other precious stones. I thought that right in the open like that, right in the most obvious place ... that no one would think to look there."

"Well, someone did," said Lisha. "Kit picked it out from amongst all the others and stumbled upon us. We brought it with us on the ship."

"Maybe Kit was a spy, too," said Kadin-Lave.

"Don't be ridiculous," said Leandra. "If she were working for the Hunters, she would have just brought it to them instead of to us. How was she to know that Jasper's troupe would take the Stoens with them?"

"Maybe it was an accident. Maybe she didn't mean to run into the Protectors."

"If she were one of Mr. Loxlyheart's spies, she wouldn't have dropped the Stoen as she did, even in panic," said Lisha in the same soft, certain tone as before.

"Enough," said Hilda impatiently. She began to hum a sweat melody, and the Protectors felt a sudden fatigue set in on them. They struggled to maintain consciousness, sagging toward the ground as they fought against Hilda's magic. Lisha collapsed to her knees, and as she looked around, she saw Leandra and Kadin-Lave fall to the ground beside her, the anger in their eyes giving way to drowsiness. Guards swarmed around them.

Lisha knew somewhere in her mind that she should feel afraid for what was going to happen, but she couldn't. She was still numb from the recent revelations, and all she could see were memories flashing through her head. Everything was starting to come together. Jasmine's pain, her unwillingness to talk to Lisha, Oliver's mutiny and cowardice, his attempts to get them to turn back, Hilda and Quito, the traitors, the missing Stoens, and the mystery of the unfamiliar Stoen that had kept Lisha wondering many nights, the Dragon Stoen, finally explained. But there were still pieces that had yet to make sense. What of the shadow woman who had come to warn the Protectors, and why were some of the guards working for Aradia and some for Mr. Loxlyheart? All these thoughts flashed through Lisha's head in a matter of seconds. With the drowsiness sinking in on her, she also began to absorb the grim reality of the situation. She felt her emotions rush back, flooding the empty space that had been filled by numbness. She felt panic for the first time, fear of what would happen, and outrage at the Hunters for all they had done. But there was one thing she didn't feel. She couldn't be mad at Jasmine, especially when her intentions had been so pure. But to think that the Hunters could force Jasmine to betray Lisha in order to save her ... they must have known what it would do to her. She knew this. She knew they needed her off balance so she wouldn't be able to think straight. But the simple cruelty stabbed through her as she looked at the faces blurring around her, and she let herself slip into darkness.

There was a scratching sound coming from outside the dungeon. The three prisoners watched breathlessly as the lock on the door strained against frantic hands.

"Darn this lock! That's the third one so far. How many locks can a castle like this have?" said a voice.

"Keep working at it. I think this is the one," said another voice.

"It took us twenty minutes just to find the entrance, another fifteen to find the dungeon, and now we get stuck here because of this stupid *lock!*" Suddenly, the lock clicked open and Jasper fell in. Mica was still clinging to the lock as the door swung open.

"Jasper!" called Minuette. Kiara put a finger to her lips as she followed Jasper into the room along with Quito and Kaida.

"Quiet," she whispered. "We're going to get you out of here." Mica, who had picked the lock, proceeded to use the lock pick to open the shackles chaining the prisoners to the wall, Kiara holding him up so he could reach the locks. Mica gave a spare lock pick to Jasper, who immediately rushed to free Minuette. Kaida climbed up to free some of the prisoner's wrists that were too high up for the others to reach. Jasper freed Minuette, and she dropped to the floor in front of him. She kissed him quickly and followed Kiara and Quito to the door, rubbing her wrists. Tristan raised her eyebrows at Minuette. She, too, jumped down from the wall and ran to the door. Jasper stared after Minuette. He'd have liked to have kissed her longer.

"Come on, let's go free the rest," he said. Jasper peaked around the side of the door to their dungeon. "The coast is clear." But as he spoke, they heard a bird caw, once, twice, three times. The Protectors exchanged worried looks. "Stay quiet," said Jasper. "We don't want anyone to—" Suddenly, someone grabbed Jasper and pulled him away from the others.

"Jasper!" cried Minuette as he struggled against his captor. Several more guards appeared in the doorway. They caught the other Protectors and dragged them up the stairs and out of the castle. The frightened Protectors looked around and saw that the other groups, including Lisha's crewmembers, had been captured and stuffed in cages. The guard holding Jasper shoved him in a cage with Tristan. There was no great struggle; they had been caught off-guard and had little time to defend themselves. The Protectors all cautiously checked to make sure their companions were all right. Strangely, Quito was not put in a cage.

He smiled darkly at them and followed the guards out. The cages were arranged at the side of what might have been an old jousting field. The remnants of stands lined the side of the field between them and the ruins of one wing of the castle. On the other side was a sheer drop to the ocean. The ground was hard and rocky, with only a few spots of sad-looking dried grass left. On the ground was spread out an incomplete circle of Stoens, each with a different sign carved into its face. Quito and Hilda brought over a sack and emptied it. As the Protectors looked on in horror, they realized where their missing Stoens had gone. Quito hurried to fill in the missing spots in the circle. Jasper counted, his heart sickening. Twelve. The Stoens had been set up to unleash the Ultimate Power. They all felt the scent of doom in the air, and a distant storm boomed on the horizon. The Protectors looked around for some shred of hope and saw only each other's scared faces behind bars.

Jasper suddenly saw Mr. Loxlyheart standing on the ruins behind the cages, watching the scene take place with a smug grin upon his pale face. Leandra changed into a lioness and leaped at the bars of her cage. She fell backwards with a sickening thud. *It's over*, thought Minuette. *We've lost.*

Not quite yet, said a voice inside her head. But it wasn't hers.

Jasper looked defiantly toward Mr. Loxlyheart. *It's not over yet*, thought Jasper. *It's only just begun.*

Suddenly, all eyes turned to watch as a lithe, darkly gowned form emerged onto the field. Mr. Loxlyheart welcomed Desdemona as she arrived. A murmur passed between the prisoners at her appearance. Most had only ever heard about her before, and only sparse details at that, and the sight of her standing before them sent chills through the observers. Her dark eyes were narrowed, lending her expression a mix of anger, slyness, and condescension. She had death-pale skin that looked unaccustomed to the sun. Aradia soon joined her, carried on a cloud of shadows. In contrast, Aradia had a face that seemed unsuited to the derisive look upon it. It was a face that led you to expect kindness, and the cruelty present instead was all the more terrible because it was unexpected.

Minuette watched Aradia's approach, brow furrowed.

"Curious," she said.

Lisha, who had been sitting very still and staring off toward Jasmine's cage since regaining consciousness, looked up from her thoughts, pushing them to the back of her mind and forcing herself to concentrate on the current situation. "What's that, Minuette?" she asked. Minuette pointed.

"Aradia. She does not have a shadow. See?" Sure enough, it was true. Before they could remark on it further, however, they were interrupted by shocked exclamations from the other Protectors at seeing the three supposedly feuding Stoenhunters greet each other warmly, or as warmly as was possible.

"You were working together?" yelled Jasper before he could stop himself. His enemies grinned back at him.

"Is it so hard to believe? We knew if we competed with each other, then neither of us would get the

Power. It worked out so much better this way," explained Desdemona. She smiled cruelly for a minute, surveying the damage done.

Their various minions were assembled around the sides. Mr. Tweeble, Mr. Bumbleweed, and Mr. Thornton, along with Hilda and Quito, were guarding the prisoners. Kit watched as Desdemona stepped in front of Aradia and began to speak quietly to Mr. Loxlyheart. Aradia simply floated to the side as if she were a deflated balloon. She hung there in midair while the other two talked. Then, with a final word to Desdemona, Mr. Loxlyheart moved purposefully toward the pattern. Suddenly, Aradia snapped to attention. Her shadows caught him and pulled him back.

"And just where do you think you're going?" said Aradia.

"I am going to claim my prize," said Mr. Loxlyheart, moving backwards toward the pattern.

"And since when is it yours to claim?" asked Aradia.

"Since I hired you to steal the Stoens for me!" said Mr. Loxlyheart.

"Oh, really?" said Desdemona, stepping in front of Aradia. "My recollection was that we would share the Power, that we would split it, fifty-fifty." *Fifty-fifty?* thought Nat. *But there are three of them.*

"You know as well as I that the Power cannot be divided. We have fooled ourselves long enough. One of us will take the Power, and I mean that person to be me," said Mr. Loxlyheart casually.

"Fine with me," said Desdemona, stepping aside. Aradia stepped forward, her eyes empty, yet blazing. Shadows bound themselves around Mr. Loxlyheart and began to lift him into the air.

"Wait, stop! She's mine, damn it, mine!" said Mr. Loxlyheart, suspended off the ground by a fist of shadows.

"As I recall, it was *I* who found her, *I* who stole all the Stoens, *I* who did all the work. If you want the prize, you have to work for it first." said Desdemona, fire in her eyes. *What?* thought Kit. *Desdemona and Mr. Loxlyheart arguing over... Aradia?*

"This is not fair, Desdemona, I tell you it isn't fair!" screamed Mr. Loxlyheart.

"*Fair?*" shrieked Desdemona, "*I'll* tell you what's not *fair!* My own *sister* getting *eternal* life and me stuck with this stupid, useless power! What, I ask you, is the point of being able to control people's bodies if you can't control their minds? They all hated me, and it was all her fault! I waited years to get rid of her, but what do I find? Not only can she not die of old age, she cannot be *killed!* But with this power, I will be able, once and for all, to take what was rightfully mine from the start and rid the world of that useless *pig!* I am the elder sister, it is *my* right to get the Power, and I—"

"*Your* right? I am the one who did all the work to get where I am today! You make other people do the work *for* you. You never bother with things that you could just as easily make other people do!" said Mr. Loxlyheart.

Jordan and Lali exchanged bewildered looks, unable to believe that Desdemona and Mr. Loxlyheart were having such a childish argument moments away from one of them possibly getting the Ultimate Power.

"Oh, you, you, you. It always has to be about *you*, doesn't it?" snarled Desdemona. "Mr. Loxlyheart. Ha! You're more like Mr. Hypocrite! You never did a day's work in your life. If you want some thing done right, you have to do it yourself. Well guess what? *I* want the Power, *I* deserve it, *I* earned it, and *I'm* taking the Power, and there's nothing you or anyone else can do to stop me!"

At that moment, the sun slipped below the horizon, plunging the whole field into complete darkness. There was slight confusion and then cries of surprise as a giant flash of light illuminated the field. Circles of light rippled out into the sky from a center point, growing wider as they did. Then a haze of light and swirling colors of pure energy coalesced into the form of a shimmering dragon, the visual embodiment of the Ultimate Power, hurtled down the tunnel from the sky, and hit the origin of the light circles.

Everyone's focus was on that center point, and no one noticed Aradia collapse to the ground or saw the shadow that had been holding Mr. Loxlyheart up in the air disappear, dumping him unceremoniously on the field next to her.

There was another brilliant flash of white light, brighter than the first, and a rumble as if from an explosion. A voice, magnified to a hundred times its original volume, boomed over the field. As the fog from the explosion started to clear, a shape, roughly human, emerged from the dust above their heads.

"YES I 'AVE DONE IT! I 'AVE TAKEN TH' ULTIMATE POWER. ME! NOW I CA' USE I' TO GET RID OF ALL EVIL IN TH' WORLD!"

"Oh joy," said Lali sarcastically. "It's Mr. Bumbleweed." The others looked at her and then back at the sky in shock. Indeed, it was true. Hovering one hundred feet in the air was the unmistakable figure of Mr. Bumbleweed.

"YES, MY FRIENDS. I SAID 'RID TH' WORLD OF ALL EVIL'! I NEVER WANTED T' WORK FER THEM STUPID COWARDS! ALL MY LIFE I'VE 'AD T' WORK FOR WICKED PEOPLE, AND NOW I CAN PUNISH THEM ALL! STARTING WIF YOU!" He pointed toward Mr. Loxlyheart, Desdemona, and Aradia. Suddenly, they were locked in cages, not unlike the Protectors'.

"AND YOU!" All of Mr. Loxlyheart's, Desdemona's, and Aradia's cronies were suddenly locked up as well. Mr. Tweeble, standing guard near the Protectors, yelped as bars sprang up around him.

Nat jumped at the cry. Looking around for the source, Nat's eyes grew wide as his gaze fell on Mr. Tweeble.

"No, no, it can't be," he murmured. Leandra turned into her human form and stared at him from the next cage.

"What?" she asked. He nodded toward the scrawny figure of Mr. Tweeble.

"That man looks oddly like—" but he was cut off by Mr. Bumbleweed.

"MY NEXT ACT WITH THIS ULTIMATE POWER WILL BE TO FREE THE PRISONERS! MY ENEMY'S ENEMY," he said, looking down at Mr. Loxlyheart, "IS MY FRIEND." The Protectors couldn't believe their luck. Lisha was suddenly reminded of how, when she had been captured, Mr. Bumbleweed had been reluctant to tell Mr. Loxlyheart where she was. Perhaps he really *had* been trying to protect her.

Mr. Bumbleweed waved his hand, and all their cages disappeared.

Nat, however, seemed not to notice.

"But, that couldn't be him," said Nat to himself, still looking off toward the caged Mr. Tweeble instead of up at Mr. Bumbleweed hovering in the sky.

"What? Who? What are you talking about?" asked Leandra. Nat turned to her in a daze. He gestured incredulously to Mr. Tweeble.

"My father," he said. She gaped at him.

"HEY, THIS IS PRETTY COOL!" shouted Mr. Bumbleweed. He snapped his fingers, and the castle was suddenly repaired and decked with gold. *Fft!* He snapped his fingers again. A horse drawn carriage appeared. *Fft!*

"HEH, HEH. ON SECOND THOUGHT." *Fft! Fft!* The next thing they knew, all the Protectors were in cages again.

"I wouldn't want any o' you t' do anything sneaky t' try t' get rid o' th' power, would I?"

"Oh no," said Genna.

Fft! Fft Fft!

"HEY, I COULD GET USED TO THIS! HA-HA-HA-HA! HA—" Before he could finish his malevolent laugh, a dark disk of energy spread from the cage holding Mr. Loxlyheart, Desdemona, and Aradia. The energy knocked Mr. Bumbleweed clear out of the sky and against a tree. It also destroyed the cages holding the three Stoenhunters and their men.

"That blast!" called Emra. "It looked almost like—" Aradia stood shakily, her eyes turned to the Protectors.

"No way," said Leandra, shaking her head in awe. Aradia had changed. Her eyes were gentle and filled with fear, wonder, and surprise. All the hate was gone as though it had never existed. Her lips opened in wonder.

"I—I'm—" she looked down at herself, flexing her fingers.

"No, no!" Mr. Loxlyheart screamed. "Desdemona! How *could* you let down your guard like that? Now look what you've done! She's *free!*"

"I'm free," said Aradia softly.

"What's going on?" asked Kadin-Lave.

"Oh!" said Minuette with dawning comprehension. "Aradia was being mind-controlled by Desdemona the whole time! Laramie was right! She *is* on our side!" Jasper looked at her in amazement. "Seriously?" he exclaimed. "Ha! That's absolutely brilliant!" Lisha's eyes widened in sudden revelation.

"The shadow woman!" she exclaimed. Jasper looked at her quizzically. "The shadow woman! The one who came to warn us before the attacks! It was Aradia! Minuette noticed earlier that she didn't have a shadow! Desdemona could control Aradia's body, but not her mind. Because Aradia's power is bending shadows, when her body became Desdemona's puppet, she became trapped in her own shadow!"

But their attention was suddenly turned back to Mr. Bumbleweed.

The glowing dragon shape of the Ultimate Power that had leaped from the sky now emerged from Mr. Bumbleweed's chest and dove into the ground covered by the Stoens.

"'In the event that an individual obtains the Ultimate Power and the individual is rendered unconscious, then the Power will be removed and return to the pattern to be claimed by the next person who touches it'," quoted Lisha, remembering Cameron reading to them from her book. Lisha looked excited and scared at the same time. "Fala!" she called through the bars of her magically made cage. The other Protectors looked at each other. They had forgotten Jasper's instructions to Fala to keep watch in her bird form and intervene if things went wrong. But now their eyes turned to the sky, where a circling raven paused in mid-flight and looked down. "Do whatever necessary to prevent anyone from touching those Stoens!" called Lisha to the raven. The raven, who was indeed Fala, cawed in recognition and rocketed toward the ground. Mr. Loxlyheart looked up just as Fala pulled out of her dive and began pecking at his face.

"Aaaugh!" he said, trying to throw off Fala.

Desdemona looked around and saw that no one was watching her. Slowly, she edged toward the Stoens.

"Fala! Get Desdemona!" shouted Lisha. Fala turned and flew at Desdemona. Desdemona whipped around and stared into Fala's bird eyes. Her wing froze, and she spun out of control. Desdemona bolted for the Stoens. Fala desperately tried to regain control of her wings before she crashed into something. Aradia was still looking around, dazed, but when Fala nearly hit her, she snapped to attention. Lisha could see Aradia's mind cleverly working through what to do. She gathered some shadows and threw them at Fala, attempting to catch her and tow her to safety. The shadows missed, and Fala bounced off a tree.

"Hey! Little help here!" yelled Nat. Aradia turned, and with one hand still throwing shadows at Fala, she raised the other and broke the locks on the cages. Protectors rushed out onto the field.

"Get them!" Mr. Loxlyheart shouted. All of the men standing behind him suddenly raised their weapons and stampeded forward. But as they approached the Protectors, they hesitated. A murmur when through the crowd: "Children ... they're just children." The Protectors paused, facing their enemies. For a moment, they stared at each other, no one making a move.

"Charge!" yelled Mr. Loxlyheart. They charged. Lisha shouted instructions to the Protectors.

"Aradia! The weapons!" she yelled. Aradia raised a hand and began sending shadows forward to grab the enemies' guns and daggers. She moved tentatively at first, still not used to such freedom of movement.

"Keep them from getting the Power!" called Lisha over the noise of the battle. "Defend yourselves! Don't kill unless you have to." Desdemona, cut off from the Stoens, began looking for a new route out of the mob. Leandra immediately changed into a lioness and leaped on one of the men. Emra became a snake and proceeded to strangle two men at once, choking them until they dropped to the ground, unconscious. Nat brought roots up from the ground to trap the advancing forces. Lisha's crewmembers joined the fight as well. Lisha pulled out two pistols and threw one to Jasper. Kiara took her father's from her pocket.

"This is just too easy," said Kadin-Lave, smiling, as one man fell to the ground before him, shivering.

Then one man shot lightning from his eyes.

"You had to say it, didn't you?" asked Lisha, kicking a man in the face. All around them, the henchmen countered the Protectors with their own powers.

Lisha pushed her way through the crowd, trying to get to Mr. Loxlyheart, but a creature halfway between a man and a bird swooped down from above and picked her up in his talons.

"Lisha!" shouted Jasmine. She grabbed a rock and threw it into the air. It hit the creature, and he let go of Lisha. Jasper and Minuette fought back-to-back as a group of henchmen surrounded them. A man grabbed Kiara and tried to strangle her. She raised the pistol and shot him in the shoulder. He fell to the ground, still holding onto her. She wrestled against his strong arms and eventually broke free. Reloading the pistol, she ran forwards, dodging past Protectors and the Stoenhunters' men.

"Kiara!" shouted a voice. She looked around. Two men were holding Nat, one preparing to shoot him. Kiara shot the first man in the leg with her father's pistol and ran up and punched the other in the nose. Then she rushed over to Nat to make sure he was all right. He smiled gratefully, but then his eyes widened.

"Look out!" he yelled. Kiara started to turn just as Rodger Thornton crashed into her, struggling to shake off one of Aradia's moving shadows. She stumbled forward and whirled, fighting to regain her balance. She raised the pistol and pointed it at Mr. Thornton. Kicking off the shadow, he looked up to see who he had crashed into. Kiara saw a puzzled expression form on his weary features as his gaze fell first upon her face and then upon the gun in her hands.

That pistol, he thought. *That's my pistol ... but how could she? But no, it couldn't be. Could it?* He looked at her again, scrutinizing her features.

"Kiara?" he asked, hardly daring to hope it was true. Her grip slackened on the gun, letting it dangle loosely from her fingers.

"Dad." Her voice showed no sign of the resentment that had built up over the years. He walked unsteadily toward her. Arms outstretched hesitantly, he let the gun drop from his hand.

There was a loud **bang** as it hit the ground, and Kiara watched, horrorstruck, as Rodger fell at her feet.

Kiara knelt by the man who had left her to wander the streets because of an accident and the color of her skin. But none of that mattered anymore. "Dad, I'm sorry," said Kiara.

"I'm the one who should be apologizing," he said with difficulty. "I was a terrible father. I realize that now. I deserted you, my own child. I thought I'd never see you again."

"It's all right, Dad. It's going to be fine," Kiara said.

"Kiara, you look so much like your mother ... those dark eyes—"

"It's all right. I'm going to get you out of here." Kiara lifted him with difficulty. Nat saw her struggling and came over.

"Here, I'll help you," he said. Together they carried him to one side of the field. They lay him down away from the fighting.

"You'll be safe here. If anyone tries to hurt you, tell them you're with me," said Kiara. Nat and Kiara walked back toward the fight.

"I don't see why you had to do that. Who was he, anyway?" asked Nat as they walked.

"He's my father," she said. Nat stopped. She turned back to look at him.

"Your father?" he said in astonishment. "You found your father here, too?"

"What? What do you mean, I found my father, too?" Suddenly, Nat jumped up, eyes back on the mob. "Damn! That reminds me—" He ran off toward the fight. Perplexed, Kiara took off after him.

Leandra found herself face to face with Hilda. Her fists tightened.

"How could you betray us? How could you join him?" she asked.

"Mr. Loxlyheart was the only one who saw anything in me. I would be dead if it wasn't for him," replied Hilda.

"We could have helped you. We could have—"

"No! No one could have helped me! I was weak. Mr. Loxlyheart found the goodness to take me in. Anyone else would have let me die." There was fire burning in her eyes.

"Is that what *he* told you?" Leandra shot back. Hilda glared at her. Strange music filled Leandra's head, and she fell to the ground, drowsiness overtaking her.

Nat ran through the field, pushing people out of the way, Kiara close behind him. Finally, he found what he was looking for. Mr. Tweeble was crouched next to Mr. Bumbleweed, who was still lying where he had fallen from the sky when Aradia's blast knocked the Ultimate Power out of him. Nat stood still for a moment, not sure quite what to say.

"'Ey, mate," Mr. Tweeble was saying, shaking Mr. Bumbleweed's motionless form, "wake up, now, ay? We go' a ge' ou' o th' way!" Still oblivious to Nat's presence, Mr. Tweeble leaned down to check for a pulse. Nothing. His face turned white. He sat back on his heels. "Dead? No, ay, 'sno' righ'. 'E deserved be'er 'n tha'. Musta been th' fall wot done i'. 'E was up so 'igh ... poor devil. Poor, poor devil." He shook his head sadly.

Nat came forward.

"Um ... hello," he said. "Uh ... it's me. Nat." Mr. Tweeble looked up. His eyes fell on Nat and he froze. He stared, speechless.

"Nat?" he said after a moment, standing, "is tha' really you?"

"Aye," said Nat, trying to keep his voice steady. "It's me." The goofy grin that broke across Mr. Tweeble's countenance took ten years off his face. Tears came to Nat's eyes as they hugged and Mr. Tweeble kissed the top of his head.

Kiara caught up with Nat quickly. When she saw who he was with, she stopped dead in her tracks.

"*Him?* But why—" Kiara started to say. Nat looked up at the sound of her voice.

"Kiara, sweetheart, I would like you to meet my father," said Nat.

"*He's* your..." she started.

"Yes. Nat ... Nat Tweeble."

Desdemona froze two people and made another two begin to clear a path from her to the Stoens. Kit was the only one who seemed to notice her.

"No!" she shouted and ran after Desdemona. Kit jumped in front of her just as she had almost reached the Stoens. "You want th' Power? Then you'll 'ave t' go through me!"

"Very well," said Desdemona. The next thing she knew, Kit found herself on the ground several feet away, her arm bent in a painful position. She winced from the impact and fought to get her breath back. Suddenly, everything stopped. Everyone ceased fighting and looked around, confused. Realization dawned simultaneously on Protectors and henchmen alike, who all looked toward a single spot. The dragon form of the Ultimate Power had appeared again from the pattern and vanished almost instantly. Kit stared. Desdemona was glowing. She grew until she was three times her previous size.

"FINALLY, AFTER ALL THESE YEARS," Desdemona said, her harsh, piercing voice cutting through the air like a crack of lightning. Thick clouds gathered in the air above her. The castle went back to its ruined state at the slightest glance from her wicked eyes, and all the other luxuries Mr. Bumbleweed had wished up disappeared. She smirked haughtily as she walked along through the crowd. Her tattered gown was mended and shining like new satin. Her black hair flew around her shoulders, and her catlike eyes stared down at everyone as if they were grasshoppers. Her purple lips curled into a smile.

"MR. LOXLYHEART, YOU OLD FOOL. DID YOU THINK YOU COULD OUTWIT ME? WITH A WAVE OF MY HAND, THE WORLD COULD BE UNDER CONTROL."

Far below, Halie's mind was working. She'd always been quiet and shy, but now panic emboldened her. She could not be content to stand by and watch while Desdemona took over the world. *I have to warn everyone,* thought Halie. But how do you warn the world? Halie screwed up her face and clenched her fists. A small orb formed in front of her totally by accident. *That is it!* thought Halie. It now occurred to her that with her powers of projecting images of events happening at other places, she might be the only one who could help. *I do not have to tell them. I can show them! I will project an image of what is happening here at Stonehaven into the mind of every person around the world! Everything I can see, they will see.* She'd never tried to project an image directly into someone's mind before, but she knew she had to try. They had to be warned. She shut her eyes tight and then relaxed. She saw clearly in her mind Desdemona's wicked face grinning at them. Around the world, people stopped to stare as a vision appeared before them, all showing the image of a cool face with purple lips and greedy hawk eyes. Around the world, people stopped their conversations or stirred in their sleep and listened as the booming voice began to speak.

"YES. AFTER ALL THIS TIME, I CAN HAVE ALL I EVER WANTED. NOW I HAVE THE ULTIMATE POWER. ANYTHING I CAN THINK OF, I CAN PERFORM."

Desdemona looked down. And smiled.

"WHY, HELLO, JASPER. GLAD YOU COULD MAKE IT." He stared, trying not to let the fear show on his face.

"You know me?" he asked. She laughed, a terrible laugh.

"OF COURSE I KNOW YOU! YOU'RE THE ONE WHO ORGANIZED THIS," she looked around, smirking, "LITTLE GET-TOGEATHER. YOU'VE BEEN A REAL THORN IN MY SIDE. I WAS RATHER WORRIED FOR A LITTLE WHILE THERE. BUT THAT'S ALL OVER WITH, NOW THAT I HAVE THE POWER. I CAN DO WHATEVER I WANT." She raised her hand menacingly over Jasper's head. He stared at it, frozen and entranced.

Minuette rushed forward and grabbed Jasper's arm, holding him tight.

"Leave him alone!" she said, eyes burning so fiercely that Desdemona was taken aback. However, she quickly regained her composure and leered down at them.

"AH, YOUNG LOVE. THERE'S LITTLE I HATE MORE. BUT FIRST THINGS FIRST. I HAVE SOME UNFINISHED BUSINESS THAT HAS WAITED FAR TOO MANY LONG YEARS."

A terrible sound was heard issuing from the castle. A struggling form with chains around its whole body crashed through the wall of the castle. Several of the chains broke on impact, and the person's hood fell back. Laramie made no sound as the shackle around her neck fell and clattered to the ground. Strands of hair so light they were almost white flowed out in front of her face. Jordan, Tristan, and Minuette were all thinking the same thing: she obviously hadn't aged a day since she got her power and was thrown into the sea. She had the body of a ten-year-old, yet her mind was older. Her head tilted back, and her eyes opened to reveal one gray eye and one copper eye. Laramie's skin was as pale as her hair from not having seen the sunlight for so many years, and her limbs were as thin as a skeleton's.

"YOU ARE IMMORTAL, AND SO CANNOT BE KILLED BY ANY NATURAL MEANS. BUT BECAUSE I HAVE THE ULTIMATE POWER,

I CAN DO ANYTHING. I AM STRONGER THAN ALL OF THE PROTECTORS IN THE WORLD COMBINED AND CAN EASILY STRIP THEM OF THEIR POWERS. FIRST, I WILL TAKE AWAY YOUR IMMORTALITY, AND THEN I WILL KILL YOU!" No one made a move to stop her. No one could. A trail of smoky black and purple dust flew from Desdemona's fingers as if carried by a strong wind. It hit Laramie in the chest and began to burn green flame. A huge gash formed where the fire burned away at her heart. Then, blue light flowed through Laramie's body as if carried by her veins. It filled her out to her fingertips and toes, making eerie blue lines across her face and arms. Her eyes blazed blue, and her hair billowed around her head like sails in a great wind. The magic retreated into a glowing sphere around the hole in her chest, and Laramie's limbs and head drooped. The blue light brought back with it a sprinkling of gold: her power. The gold dust mixed in with the sphere.

"YES ... AFTER ALL THESE YEARS." Desdemona's eyes lit up as she raised her hands above her head. "DIE!" Red flames blossomed from her fingers. She shot rays of white lightning at Laramie. They hit the sphere around her chest and began to work their way through to her. But the force of the blast sent Desdemona tumbling backwards, straight into the ground. Laramie absorbed the sphere of green fire, blue liquid, white lightning, and golden dust and fell through the air. Aradia broke through the stillness and caught her with a shadow net, which lowered her slowly to the ground.

"The backlash from Desdemona's attack knocked her out!" exclaimed Emra. "Desdemona must've lost the Power, too!"

"There's some poetic justice in that," said Lisha. "Revenge is a two-edged sword, they say."

Meanwhile, Minuette and Aradia rushed to Laramie.

"She absorbed Desdemona's poison," said Aradia in wonder.

"Do you think she will recover?" asked Minuette.

"She seems to have also taken back her own power along with the blast. They may counter each other," said Aradia thoughtfully.

"So she will live?" asked Minuette hopefully.

"I believe so, though she may have lost her immortality. That's what she wanted, anyway."

Jasper walked up and stood before the crowd.

"It's time to end this. Once and for all." Fala, still in raven form, cawed and dropped something down to him. He caught it; it was a conch shell carried up from the ocean. "Cameron told us that the Ultimate Power could be stored in an object, like this shell, and that if the object was destroyed, the Power would be inaccessible," said Jasper to the crowd, trying to show them more confidence than he felt. He took a handkerchief from his pocket. "To keep the Power in the shell," he explained, "we have to make sure no one touches the shell itself. Because if anyone were to do so, the Power would go to them." He wrapped the shell in his handkerchief with only a corner showing. "Now, to put the Power in the shell," he said, more to himself than to anyone else. Carefully, he touched the exposed corner of the shell to the circle of Stoens. The dragon of the Ultimate Power slipped quietly from the circle of Stoens into the shell. "As long as this handkerchief is around the shell, no one can get the Power. And when I destroy this, no one will be able to get the Power. Ever." Thunder crashed closer and closer. Trees swayed and branches broke with the incoming storm. Rain started blowing through the air.

Kaida looked at him disbelievingly. "But you can't just destroy it! Think of all the good things we could use this for!"

"If there's one thing I know," said Jasper seriously, "it's that absolute power corrupts absolutely. Just look at what it did to Mr. Bumbleweed! He barely had it for five minutes before he started using it for selfish reasons. And now look what's happened to him."

"He's dead," said Nat. Heads turned to look at him. "He didn't protect himself, because he thought he was invulnerable," Nat continued. "Aradia's blast knocked the Power from him, and without the Power, he had no hope of surviving such a fall. Power's useless without wisdom. And absolute power requires absolute wisdom to wield it. No human has that. So no human can handle the Ultimate Power."

"It must be destroyed," proclaimed Jasper. Everyone looked toward Jasper in silent agreement, some nodding affirmatively. Jasper raised the shell above his head...

...and Desdemona dashed up and snatched it. She grabbed Minuette with her free hand and ran to the edge of the cliff. Minuette let out a cry as she was dragged along, surprised by the strength of Desdemona's grip. Jasper and Mr. Loxlyheart sprinted after them. Desdemona reached the far corner of the cliff and whirled around. She held the shell high above her head with one hand and clutched Minuette's arm with the other, keeping her dangerously close to the edge.

"Choose, Jasper!" yelled Desdemona. "Either you let Mr. Loxlyheart take the Power while you save your girlfriend, or you fight him for it and let the girl shatter on the rocks below! Choose carefully! You may not be able to win a fight against a grown man. It doesn't matter to me which of you gets the Power since I can't have it." Thunder boomed above and lightning lit the horizon, illuminating Desdemona's crazed face like a candle at midnight. An insane excitement shone upon her features. It was disturbing to watch.

Mr. Loxlyheart still ran toward them, having started farther away, a wild look on his face.

Jasper knew he had to think fast. Mr. Loxlyheart would reach them in a minute.

Minuette looked at Jasper, terrified of what would happen next. What had she done, letting Desdemona know about them? She had given the witch a weakness to exploit. Jasper looked from one to the other. He couldn't think straight. Was there a way he could save both? He'd thought he'd resolved his internal conflict between being in love and being a leader. He'd thought he'd found a way the two could exist together. Did he now have to choose between them? Choose one of the two halves of himself and let the other die?

"Oh, sorry Jaspy. You took too long. Hope your hands can catch faster then your head can think!" Desdemona pushed Minuette toward the edge. Her foot slipped, and she started to fall.

"Minuette! No!" Jasper started to run after her, but he stopped himself with difficulty. This was no time to be selfish. The questions he had been asking himself were the wrong ones. It wasn't about him and Minuette. He had a responsibility toward the world. No matter how important she was, the Power had to be stopped no matter what. If he saved her and let Mr. Loxlyheart get the power, what kind of world would it be for them to live in anyway? He had created a dichotomy where there was none. The decision was excruciating, but it had to be made. The answer was clear. He knew what he had to do. Jasper darted forward just as Mr. Loxlyheart reached them, feet hitting the ground and propelling him forward like springs. Determination in his eyes, Jasper gathered all his strength and anger and shoved against Mr. Loxlyheart, shouldering him in the chest. Mr. Loxlyheart was knocked backwards. He was so surprised he didn't make a move as Jasper leaped forward and grabbed the shell. Desdemona released it into his grip with a sly grin. Too late he realized that Desdemona had pulled off the handkerchief.

His fingers touched the shell.

❦

"Jasper," Minuette murmured as she fell through the air. The cliff face rushed past her, wind whipping her hair. Tears flew upward from her eyes. He hadn't saved her. And now she was going to die.

"I love you."

Suddenly, she stopped falling. Something caught Minuette in midair and lifted her back up the cliff. It set her down gently.

Desdemona was standing by the cliff, a mysterious smug smile on her lips. Mr. Loxlyheart was sprawled on the ground, dazed.

Jasper was holding the shell.

He opened his eyes.

"Minuette! Are you all right?" he asked desperately. She turned her head away. She knew perfectly well that he had likely just saved the world by stopping Mr. Loxlyheart from getting the Ultimate Power, but she couldn't shake the thought that she had come second.

The next thing she knew, Jasper's lips were pressed against hers. That almost made up for the whole thing. Almost.

Jasper and Minuette slowly made their way back to the group.

Jasper stood before the assembled crowd, all watching them as the rain started to fall.

"I willingly relinquish the Ultimate Power into this shell," yelled Jasper, loud enough so that everyone could hear. The dragon emerged from him and sank into the shell. He raised it above his head.

"This will be the end of the Ultimate Power. No one shall have absolute power again. Let this be a lesson to all the world." Little did he know, of course, that the whole world was indeed watching him. He raised the shell high, and—

"Oh, Jasper. I forgot to mention," Desdemona said from behind him as if she'd just remembered to buy milk. Her mouth twisted in a wicked grin. "A little loophole that might make you reconsider." He turned to face her. Her eyes narrowed gleefully as if to say, *I've got you now.* "If you destroy that shell, everyone who has ever had the Ultimate Power will die. And that includes you."

Minuette and Jasper looked at each other. There was resignation in his face, as if he'd always known this was coming. Minuette shook her head in denial, her eyes wide with terror. Something broke inside her as she looked at Jasper and felt him begin to slip away.

"No," she said in barely more than a whisper.

"Minuette," he said softly, and she saw from his face that he had already accepted his fate. Perhaps he had accepted it a long time ago. She shook her head again.

"Don't do this. Please don't do this."

"I have to. It's the only way. Please understand, Minuette."

"No! You do not have to do anything! There must be another way. We can think of something else!"

"We don't have time. We have to destroy the Power before someone uses it to do something terrible."

"*This* is not something terrible?" she asked, her voice breaking over the words as her insides splintered, the world collapsing in around her. "Look," she said, and swallowed, "*look.*" She took his face in her hand

and stared deeply into his eyes. In a heartbeat, their minds were connected like they had been before, thoughts floating freely between them. Minuette pictured an image and held it up for him to see: The two of them side by side, all grown up, hands interlocked like links in an unbreakable chain. She felt his pain at the sight, how his heart ached alongside hers. But as his thoughts washed over her, she realized with him that their dream was out of reach. He sent his fears to her, fears of what would happen if the Power weren't destroyed. Images floated to the surface from both of their pasts: Jasper's last sight of his father fighting the constables as his children ran to escape the workhouse, Mr. Loxlyheart's factory with the noise and the dirty workers, Minuette's father being led to the guillotine where so many of his countrymen lost their lives, the dungeon cell where Minuette had been imprisoned, her mother trampled under the feet of an angry mob.

I understand, she told him.

This is what people do with power, said Jasper in their shared mind space. *Even if their beginning intentions are good—get children off the streets, overthrow an oppressive government—they become corrupted.*

At the same moment, their minds went to the possibility of repairing the tragedies and injustices of the past with the Ultimate Power. But then, as one, they dismissed the idea. *Although there is always a possibility that it wouldn't happen, that good would come of it, the dangers are too great,* thought Jasper, underscoring the point. *And that's why we can't even consider trying to fix these problems ourselves with the Power. The only thing we can do is try to provide for the future. Destroy the Power here and now.* The temptation for misuse was too strong; they both felt it. If not for them, then for someone else. Power has a way of changing allegiances on a dime. Besides, who were they, they wondered, to meddle with the past? Any action they took would have unseen repercussions that would undermine their very purpose. No, no good could come of the Power. It had to be destroyed.

They came out of their premonition with desolate resolve and insurmountable regret.

"I'm sorry," said Jasper earnestly. "I wish it didn't have to be this way."

In answer, Minuette leaned forward and kissed him. Suddenly, it no longer mattered that she had come second.

"I will miss you, Jasper," said Minuette after pulling away. "I will not forget you. *Je t'aime, mon chéri.*"

"*Je t'aime*, Minuette. I will always love you." Jasper turned to the crowd. "Lisha ... Jordon ... Emra ... Kiara ... Kit..." He looked around the crowd and murmured each of their names as his gaze fell on them, lingering especially on his brother, their eyes saying more than words ever could. "Minuette," finished Jasper, turning to face Minuette and taking her hands as he said her name. "I just wish I could have had more time to spend with you. All of you. All the Protectors who have bravely risked death and worse to bring us to this moment. But now it's time to do what we came here to do. And although my journey ends here, yours continue. I wish you all the best fate imaginable. We've stopped what could have been the worst disaster of all time, but that doesn't mean you can just sit around now. This is your chance to go out and make a better life. Wherever the wind may take you. May you all find happiness and be forever surrounded by people you care for and who care for you. Enough. Goodbye, my friends. See you on the other side." And with that, Jasper smashed the shell.

The dragon exploded forth from the broken shell, screeching and screaming toward the sky. Sparkling scales fell like petals from a dying flower and broke upon the ground. The majestic shape made of the tangible liquid magic of the Ultimate Power solidified for one moment into a gleaming sculpture in the sky and then burst into innumerable shards of blue crystal, falling down around the people like crystallized rain.

"What have you done?" came a shrill cry from the edge of the field. They all turned to face Desdemona, who had forsaken all pretense of unconcern, an expression of shock on her face to discover that her gamble hadn't paid off. How could she have been wrong? She had known he would chicken out at the last minute! She had *known* it! How could he sacrifice himself to save others? She couldn't understand it. But before she could wonder at it further, she felt something strange happening to her feet. Looking down, she saw them begin to disintegrate. With a cry of shock, she stumbled back and fell to the ground. Her waist quickly disappeared into a growing pile of sparkling purple dust flaking off her. Her feet and elbows likewise dissolved. The world became a blur.

Mr. Bumbleweed had almost completely dissolved into a shimmering heap of green dust. Jasper was disintegrating much more slowly because he was standing, but his feet were turning to light blue glitter, which fell like sand in an hourglass, leaving a sparkling pile around his ankles. He turned to Minuette.

"Minuette, I love you."

"Jasper, I—" Jasper dove forward, and Minuette followed him into a passionate kiss. Emotion filled their ears like a burst of music as their spirits met. In their minds, the sun rose, sparkling with lines of multicolored lightning. The sky between them was lit with such colors that the dawn would be jealous. The sun rose and set over and over again in a dazzling dance, and they felt their lives slipping past them, as if aging until they were very old. They saw themselves for one moment as they had looked in Minuette's vision: the ageless couple joined forever by the bonds of true love. They drew apart, and their eyes met one last time. Then, as suddenly as it had started, it was over. Minuette was fourteen again, as was Jasper. Their lifetime together was over before it had even started. His arms slowly slipped from around her, and he sank toward the ground. Her arms trailed after him, tears welling from her brown eyes and falling on him as he slowly dissolved into a pile of sky blue glitter that, in turn, broke into miniscule grains of sand, which spread and scattered across the earth. Finally, all that was left was a blue stain in the hard ground and a gold locket. No one came near. Desdemona and Mr.

Bumbleweed had long dissolved, and Mr. Loxlyheart had run off. Everyone stood silently as the last of the shimmering magic faded from the air and the last of the shards of the shattered dragon of the Ultimate Power came to rest. Minuette collapsed and started to shake with weeping. Several people tentatively reached out a hand, but no one broke the invisible, wide semicircle around her. Slowly, people began to depart, and all around the world, people were wiping their eyes and holding each other close, moved by the vision Halie had given them. One by one, the crowd at the castle dispersed, leaving only Minuette. Her crumpled form slowly faded from their view, but the image remained in many of their minds long after.

Epilogue

That was the last that anyone saw of Minuette. After the fight, the Protectors regrouped and freed the rest of the prisoners. We found Warrick and his entire troupe in the dungeons, as well as the missing Drifters and countless others. When we rescued Xylon and told him what happened, he was furious. He was in such a state that we let him calm down and never asked what was wrong, and he didn't tell us, saying it hardly mattered anymore. On the way out, we realized too late that Minuette was not on the ship with us. We turned back, but our search of the island proved fruitless, and we were forced to leave without her.

From there, the Protectors went our separate ways. Lisha had agreed to take us to wherever we were going, dropping off the different groups at our respective countries. She was going to return to London with the remainder of the English troupe.

I went back home to see my family.

Kiara went to stay with her father, Rodger Thornton, at his old house.

Nat also went to spend time with his father, Mr. Tweeble.

Lali and Jordan both joined Lisha's crew, as she was short a few members after sacking the traitors.

Halie went to stay with Xylon to learn more about her powers and the Stoens.

Kaida (naturally) stayed with me.

Fala, Laramie, and Aradia went back to the town where they once had lived.

The others I'm not entirely sure of. Mr. Loxlyheart, for instance, disappeared as mysteriously as did Minuette. I'm sure most of the Protectors are probably safe, though. What could happen to them now?

But what, you wonder, happened to them after Lisha dropped them all off?

I have in my possession several letters sent from the former Protectors to each other. These I will enclose. Some people I have lost track of or contact with, though I have tried my best to discover the whereabouts of as many of them as I can.

This first letter, from Kiara to Nat, was one of the first letters I was able to find. Once Nat heard about what I was writing, he immediately sent this to me. I have kept it a secret, as Kiara will mostly likely kill me when she figures out what I'm doing, and I hope to have the story published by then.

I think this letter is really quite sweet and it shows another side of Kiara. Ever since she met Nat, she hasn't been the same paranoid, cynical person she was when I met her. And we have long since reconciled our differences and remain close friends.

Dear Nat,

I've missed you so much. I guess there's no easy way to say it: my father died today. I barely had a few weeks to get to know him. He told me all about my past and about my mother. I think he rather liked having a daughter after all. He couldn't stop apologizing. And I thought he'd never change! I guess he was just angry. He loved my mother very much. I wish I could have known her. She sounds wonderful.

But all good things ... you know how it goes. It seems that the injuries my father received in the fight were too much for him. He never quite recovered from them and almost never left the house. The least I can say is that he died peacefully. I only hope my own death can be as gentle.

Anyway, enough talk of death. Life is so much more important. Without imposing, I would like to take you up on your invitation to come stay with you. My father's house holds too many sad memories.

Please get back to me, or I'll simply show up when you least expect it!

With all my heart,
   Kiara

Mira Singer

I am, I admit, slightly embarrassed to print this next one, but it can't be helped. I had hoped that no one would need to see all the spelling mistakes I made and how silly I was, but Lisha insisted I keep it as is. This was a long time ago (well, not a long time ago, but it feels that way). It may not seem silly to you, but, well ... I'll let you decide that for yourselves.

Dear Lisha,

I havent sean you cince yu droped mee off in Londen wif Emra. I've bean spending time withe my mother and sister, Sharlene. Remember her? Its nice to bee home. I'm staying with Emra at the toyshop for a wile. Emras been teching mee how two rite and read. Emra has lots of frends that com bi somtims, and I'm making new frends to. I've been thinking a lot about everything that's hapend. Yu se, I was wondering wot to do with the rest of my life. I nevr rely thout I could amont too any thing be coze I grew up on the strets, but now that I've sean and done things so much biger then I am, my dreems hav also grown. Looking back, the thing I engoyed the most was coming back from seing Camron and teling every one what hapend. I've always liked teling stories. Ramembring that, I can't believe I didn't think of this sooner. I want to be a writer! Peple can com to mee with exciting tru storys and adventores like ours and I can rite them down for them. Ive alredy started working! Some of my friends here have bean giving mee storys they want me to rite. But the first story I'm gonna rite mite bee the most important. My own. I'm sending the first draft to you with this leter. Do you like it? I want you too read it over and make sure

274

I got al the details rite. Emra's bean helping me with speling. She would've fixed this leter, but she thout the miss-takes wer cute. I hope you don't mind. Kidas here, of corse, and hes bean fine. Come vizit soon if you can. We rely mis you!

Kit

This next is a letter from Lali to Halie, written while we were still in the process of redistributing the Protectors to their successive destinations. Halie was one of the first to be dropped off, along with Xylon, as the cottage where he lives was the closest destination.

I am thankful that I have this letter, because there are many parts of the story that I can't know simply because I wasn't there. I've been able to reconstruct much of it through interviews and perhaps a little magic, but it's good to have a firsthand account of sorts.

Dear Halie,

How are you? I must say, it was difficult to figure out how to get this letter to you, but with the help of Fala and some crows, it should arrive safely. You may not be able to respond since I'm on a ship, and unless I'm mistaken, no one on your end can talk to birds. Aye, we're still on Lisha's ship. Jordan and me have decided to join the crew. Lisha—that is, the captain (I should get used to calling her that)—is letting Jasmine and Oliver stay on, which surprised us until she explained what had happened. Jasmine I can see, maybe, especially because ~~Lisha,~~ the captain and her are so close, but if it were up to me, guilty or not, I would take the opportunity to sack Oliver. I know, you're probably thinking that's why Lisha's captain and not me. And you're probably right.

It's hard to believe how much has happened since we set off from Stonehaven. I don't have enough paper to tell all of it, but here's one thing that happened that I've been thinking about a lot. Me and Jordan were sitting around the deck at dinner. The sea was choppy that day, so Nat was looking greener than usual (we hadn't dropped him off yet). We made him look over the side to try and see his reflection, but of course that just made it worse. You should have seen his face! We laughed so hard, and you should've seen the look he gave us, he was so angry! We ran away 'cause we knew he couldn't chase after us, all groggy and seasick as he was. Someone must've stepped on Quito while we were running around. He fell backwards and let out such a howl. His face turned red, and he started shouting and cursing us out, and went on and on about how he'd always been useless and trying to prove himself, and how wonderful Mr. Loxlyheart was to take in a nothing like him. I was gonna say something, tell him to calm down, that we didn't mean anything, but Lisha got there first. She said, "I wouldn't have hired you if I thought you were a nothing. Mr. Loxlyheart's the one who believes that. If there's anyone you should be cursing, it's them what hired you and then abandoned you to their enemies. If the roles were reversed, do you really think Mr. Loxlyheart would be as good to you as we are? Do you think he'd give you a second chance? Face it: he's not coming back for you." Quito looked at her and then back at the others, tears welling up in his eyes. Lisha came over and knelt down. "Aye," she said, her voice firm. "I know it hurts. You trusted him. He protected you. And now he left you. But that doesn't have to be the end. He's led you to believe that you're powerless. But you're not. You know why Mr. Loxlyheart tried to control you? It's because he's afraid of you. Young, untrained minds, unfettered by the structure of society, independent, free ... he fears that. And so he tried to control you, make you think that you're powerless. But you're not. A leader is nothing without followers. Mr. Loxlyheart couldn't do anything without you. He depends on you. The moment you decide that you're worth something, that you don't have to listen to him, he's lost. He only affects you because you let him affect you. You can choose to not care what he thinks, to be yourself and find your own way. Now that Mr. Loxlyheart's gone, you have nothing to hold you back. You're not alone, Quito. You're free."

He looked up then, and his eyes were wide. Lisha kept looking at him. I don't think she even blinked. There was this strange change in his face—I don't know how to describe it.

"Free, a?" he said in that funny accent of his. "You're right, A am free, an A's not gonna take orders from no one. Mr. Loxly'eart's gone. But, you know what? Tha's all right. Right? Who needs 'im? Who needs 'im. I'll find my own way. I'm me own master now."

"Aye," said Lisha, "I think you are."

Quito ran off after that. He's refused to do any chores since then—his whole "not taking orders" thing.

He kinda took what the captain said to the extreme. When anyone tries to tell him that it wasn't want she meant, he just jeers at them. Oh, and the captain went and had a talk with Hilda, too. I don't know what she said, but Hilda's stopped glaring at us all the time. She's still a bad cook though. And she still acts cold and standoffish, but less malicious.

The captain considered keeping them on for a while, just they'd have to learn a few things, like maybe we could help them or something, but in the end she decided there was too much bitterness. Neither side was going to trust each other in a hurry. She's gonna make arrangements for them though, like find them jobs and things to do. They can't understand why she's helping them, and neither can most of the crew. I'm not sure I do either. Helping them after they betrayed us to people who wanted to kill us? I mean, I get the whole noble effort, the 'Oh, maybe we could change them,' but it's naïve, really. I mean, sure, some of the things the captain said really seemed to get through to Quito and Hilda, but just 'cause they're not our enemy anymore doesn't mean we're automatically friends. Quito and Hilda are still damaged from what they went through. I get that the captain wants to help them, but there's only so much she can do. You can't change someone who doesn't want to be changed. They've got to sort out the rest of their baggage on their own.

I hope I can see you soon,
Your friend,
    Lali.

There you have it. Mind you, the story was not about just one of us. Not Jasper, not Lisha, and certainly not me, Kit Taylor. Although this is the end of this part of the story, it is the beginning of another.

We never did find out what Xylon was so mad about—what the "other" way to destroy the Ultimate Power was. And we never learned what happened to Minuette, or to Mr. Loxlyheart. All I can guess is that he's still out there somewhere. But without the Power, he's no threat to us.

What will we do next? Who can say? Maybe the rest of us will join up with Lisha and sail around the world. Here, though, I must say farewell, until we meet again.

The End

?

Dear Jasper,

It has been a while since I last saw you, ma chérie. Too long. I have missed you so much and hope you will come to visit. ~~Your "goodbye" was so rushed I wanted to~~ I did not quite know where you would be, so I addressed this to the toyshop. ~~If this does not reach you, well. . .~~ I am really lonely here. It is so isolated. But I cannot come back. ~~I cannot bear to see~~ How have you been? Well, I hope? I wish you would come visit me. ~~But I know you~~

I would like you to come visit me, but I cannot tell you where I am. ~~because~~ I hope to see you, ~~even though I~~

Fidélement,
I love you,
    Minuette.

Dear Jasper,

I cannot bear it if you stay away any longer. I have to see you. Without you, it feels like half of myself is missing. Please come to see me. I love you. So much. I love everything about you. You make me feel good about myself, like I have a purpose. I have never felt this way before, and I never will again ~~now that you are.~~ I hate not seeing you. I need you. You must come back. ~~But you cannot. You cannot come back, not ever again. I will never get to see you again. Never. But I have to believe I will or I will not survive.~~ I know you ~~would have~~ wanted me to be happy, but, oh, I do not even know what that is anymore. I cannot keep denying it, but I have to. You would have wanted me to be happy, but I just cannot without you. I love you. I am so in love with you. It is the only thing that keeps me alive, that keeps me up. It is why I get up in the mornings and force myself to eat. It is me. It is all I am and all that will remain of me. Jasper, I love you, ma chérie.

Minuette.

Jasper,

Jasper, there is something I need to say, to do. My heart is like a ruined castle—desolate, yet once so grand. My emotions swirl like the storm clouds above, and my heart pounds like the waves crashing against the rocks.

If this were an epic poem, my tears would flood the earth and my heart's cry would charm the birds from the sky. If this were a fairy tale, I would swim under the waves until I became a mermaid. But there is only me. So I lie on the beach and I count the stars laid out on the infinite black page of the sky, feeling our story would be told in them if only I could understand. The end of all things is written up there. But I do not need to stars to tell me the end. I know it. This is the end.

Music is all; there is music in the ocean and in the human heart. When I was with you, life was music, too. A song written just for us. But music can be sad as well, and our song has turned bitter long since past. But I do not hide from the pain—I welcome it. Anything I feel shows me that I am still breathing. Your one last wish was that I should go on and be happy. Your one last wish, and I cannot fulfill it. I live on—mais oui, I must. I am bound to that, but never again can I feel pure, unadulterated happiness. All of my songs have a melancholy melody, every smile a tear.

This is the last letter I shall write you. Ç'est finis. I have to find something else. Some other way to fulfill my promise. This is not working anymore. I had hoped never to have to say goodbye to you again. But I will always have you. Every beat of my heart is a love note. Our two golden hearts lie side by side, resting forever in the sun like dried flowers.

I cannot keep pretending you are out there, living somewhere beyond the reach of these eyes, across the ocean of my tears, and past the horizon that I can never cross. You know the star that burns so brightly the light obliterates its own source? I must become like that star. I cannot keep pretending. The eddies and vicissitudes of time will carry my soul to eternity, and I shall go to death when the times comes with your name on my lips and the laughter of a child in my heart. For that is what we were, two children.

With l'amour eternal,
    Your Minuette.

About the Author

Mira Singer has been making up stories for as long as she can remember and will more than likely continue to do so through the unforseeable future.